Meet Meg, Bella and Celina—
three loving sisters, desperate to escape the
iron rule of their fanatical rector father…

One by one they flee the vicarage—
only to discover that the real world holds its
own surprises for the now disgraced Shelley
sisters! How will they get themselves out of
the scandalous situations
they find themselves in?

Can betrayed widow **Meg**
learn to love again?

Will pregnant and abandoned **Bella**
find the man to turn her blush of shame
to the flush of pleasure?

And how will virginal courtesan-in-training
Lina discover the meaning of true passion?

Find out in…

The Transformation of the Shelley Sisters

*Three sisters, three escapades,
three very different destinies!*

Louise Allen has been immersing herself in history, real and fictional, for as long as she can remember, and finds landscapes and places evoke powerful images of the past. Louise lives in Bedfordshire, and works as a property manager, but spends as much time as possible with her husband at the cottage they are renovating on the north Norfolk coast, or travelling abroad. Venice, Burgundy and the Greek islands are favourite atmospheric destinations. Please visit Louise's website—www.louiseallenregency.co.uk—for the latest news!

Novels by the same author:

INNOCENT COURTESAN TO ADVENTURER'S BRIDE

Louise Allen

First published in Great Britain 2010
by Mills & Boon, an imprint of Harlequin (UK) Limited,
Large Print edition 2011
Eton House, 18-24 Paradise Road, Richmond, Surrey TW9 1SR

© Melanie Hilton 2010

ISBN: 978 0 263 21854

Harlequin (UK) policy is to use papers that are natural, renewable and recyclable products and made from wood grown in sustainable forests. The logging and manufacturing process conform to the legal environmental regulations of the country of origin.

Printed and bound in Great Britain
by CPI Antony Rowe, Chippenham, Wiltshire

Prologue

London—March 4th, 1815

'You, my dear Miss Celina Shelley, are most definitely an asset of the business.' Mr Gordon Makepeace folded his hands on the desk blotter in front of him and smiled.

Lina had never seen a crocodile in the flesh, but she could imagine one very clearly now. 'I believe you mean that I am an asset *to* the business, Mr Makepeace. That is, I hope that by keeping the accounts and managing the housekeeping here at The Blue Door I am repaying some of my debt to my Aunt Clara for taking me in.' She looked at the closed door that communicated with her aunt's rooms. 'I really should go and see how she does. I was on my way to her when you arrived.'

'I do not think so.' The smile had vanished. 'We

don't want you catching whatever it is she has, do we?'

'My aunt has a chronic disease of the stomach. That is hardly contagious.' Lina stood up and went to the connecting door. It was locked.

'Sit down, Miss Shelley.' The vague feeling of discomfort that had been almost unnoticed under the greater anxiety about her aunt became a chill shiver of alarm.

Twenty months ago Lina had run away from her miserable home life in a Suffolk vicarage to find refuge with her aunt. She had known of her only from one letter written to her mother years before and it had been a severe shock to discover that Aunt Clara, far from being the respectable spinster of her imaginings, was Madam Deverill, owner of one of London's most exclusive brothels.

But Lina had burned her boats now; there could be no going back to the wretched safety of the vicarage, back to one of the only two people who loved her, the sister she had run away and left. Her father would never allow her over the threshold and the scandal of where she had been would tarnish her elder sister.

Lina had fled impulsively, snatching at the tenuous lifeline of that hidden letter. She had been so utterly miserable, she had felt so trapped, that escape was all she could think of, especially after Meg, her other beloved sister, had left. Now her conscience nagged her with the knowledge that she should not have left Bella alone.

Her elegantly alluring aunt accepted her without a murmur, gave her a room on the private floor at the top of the house with windows that looked out to the roofs of St James's Palace, and proceeded to treat her as a daughter. How could she go back? Aunt Clara asked her. Her father would bar the door to her. Bella was the sensible, stoical sister, her aunt said. If she wanted to leave, too, she would. But Lina's conscience still troubled her.

Gordon Makepeace had been a silent partner in the business ever since a crisis with a difficult landlord some years ago had plunged Clara into near-bankruptcy. His money had saved the business and now it flourished again, she explained to Lina when her niece insisted on taking over what work she could that did not involve her directly with the purpose of the establishment. Now, every month, Lina counted out the guineas that represented Makepeace's share of the profits.

He had been a shadowy figure up to now, but this last bout of sickness had left Madam Deverill too ill to leave her bed and he had simply walked in and taken over. 'Why are you keeping me from my aunt?' Lina demanded. 'You have no right—'

'I have a considerable sum invested here; as Madam is not fit to run the business at present, I have been looking at the books.' He waved a hand at the stack of ledgers. 'I can see that opportunities are being missed, avenues of income are not being explored. I intend to take things in hand. There will be changes.' It was a threat, not a suggestion.

'What changes?' Lina asked. Aunt Clara would be better soon, surely? She could not intend that this man should make decisions.

'There are services that are not offered. Highly profitable services.' He raised an eyebrow as though daring her to speculate. But Lina had listened while her aunt had explained the business to her in terms that even the most innocent daughter of the vicarage could grasp. The Blue Door sold sex. Luxurious, indulgent sex accompanied by excellent food, good wine and choice entertainment.

'But I will not have virgins here,' Madam had said. 'Or children, or girls doing things they aren't willing to. My girls get a fair wage and I make sure they keep healthy.' And the fierce light in her eyes as she spoke had told Lina that these were more than merely house rules. Once, long ago, she realised, someone had forced her aunt to do things against her will and that had left deep scars.

Later she had discovered, to her stunned surprise, that her mother and her aunt had both been courtesans in their youth. At first she was too bewildered for questions, then, still almost unable to believe it, she had dared to ask.

'We fell in love with brothers,' Clara had said with a bitter twist to her smile. 'And they seduced us and abandoned us here in St James's, where we had innocently followed them. We were young and lost and heartbroken and it did not take long for us to be found by a brothel keeper.

'We grew up fast,' she added, seeming to look back down the years. 'We saved, we found wealthy "friends" and I started my own house that grew eventually into The Blue Door. Your mama, bless her, never became accustomed—she took over the housekeeping and the books, just as you have.'

There was so much to come to terms with there. Lina asked only one question. 'But however did Mama meet Papa?' For surely the fiercely moral Reverend Shelley had never been inside a brothel in his life, except perhaps to harangue the occupants on their evil ways and the certainty that Hell's fires awaited them?

'She met him in Green Park. Annabelle always

dressed well, like a lady. He tripped over and sprained his ankle, she stopped to offer him assistance—it was love at first sight. Then he was not the Puritan prig he grew into,' Clara said with a sniff. 'That came later. She never told him what she was, of course. He believed her when she said I was a widow and she was my companion. They married, he took her off into the wilds of Suffolk, they had three daughters and he became, year by year, more rigid, more sanctimonious. And she fell out of love and into a sort of dull misery with him.

'I do wonder,' her aunt had said thoughtfully, 'if your father found out, or came to suspect, something about your mother's past. We will never know now, although her letters tell of him becoming more and more suspicious and unreasonable. She met Richard Lovat and they eloped. She wrote to me, confident that your father would let you all come to her—you were only girls, after all. But he refused. Annabelle was beside herself—Lovat took her abroad, but she died in Italy two years later. I do not think she ever forgave herself for leaving you.'

Now Lina felt her vision blur and she wrenched her attention back to the man on the other side of the desk. She had left Bella as her mother had left her daughters. Well, she was paying for her heed-less, selfish, panic now, it seemed. 'What do you mean to do?' she asked, trying not to show how she felt. Like all bullies he would feed on her fear.

'Realise some assets, for a start. You, to begin with.'

'Me?' She swallowed.

'You *are* a virgin, are you not, Miss Shelley? A most valuable asset—a pretty, well-bred young lady.'

'No!' She stood up so abruptly that the chair fell over with a thud.

'But yes. Or I will demand the return of all my investment, and to meet that your aunt will have to sell the entire establishment, for I am certain she does not have the ready cash.

'I will buy her share, of course, and then the pampered little trollops who work here will service *all* the clients—in every way the clients want. I'll have none of this picking-and-choosing nonsense. Some flagellation rooms, a Roman orgy every week, an auction of virgins—those will get us off to a good start. I've got the ideas and very profitable they are, too.'

Lina edged around to the far side of the chair. Her heart was thumping, her mouth was dry. Perhaps Aunt Clara's illness was contagious after all. She must be in a fever, dreaming this. 'You...you would auction me off to the highest bidder?'

'Oh, no, not an auction. I have an offer for you already from Sir Humphrey Tolhurst.'

'The magistrate?' But Sir Humphrey was fifty if he was a day. And pompous and only came to play cards and ogle the posture girls. She had seen him from the screened gallery that her aunt used to watch the activities in the salon.

'That's the man. I pointed you out to him in the street and he was very taken with you. He would not want to be involved in anything like an auction, of course; he values his privacy too much for that. I was able to set a very good price in consideration of that accommodation.' Makepeace chuckled. 'A very good price indeed.'

'And then what?' Lina asked, surprised to hear herself sounding defiant. She had never before turned and faced danger, or her father's bullying anger. She had always been the timorous sister, the nervous one who ran if she could not hide. But it seemed that, if pushed to extremes, she could try to fight.

'You can only sell my virginity once.' Legitimately, that was. The girls had told her all about the ways to feign a maidenhead, as they had so much else that should have shocked her to the core. But their

open, cheerful acceptance of the commerce between men and women, in all its weird and puzzling manifestations, had left her much wiser—in
theory—and reluctant to judge them.

'True,' he said. 'But it will give me a tidy sum to
invest in the equipment this establishment is lacking. Flagellation is all the rage.'

'Mother Moll's is the specialist in that,' Lina retorted, parroting the girls' gossip. 'There is too
much competition for another flogging school so
close.'

'Oh, no. Not for the *gentlemen* who require chas-
tising. This would be for those who wish to admin-
ister the punishment.'

'But the girls—'

'Will do as they are told or be out in the
gutter.'

Lina clenched her teeth to stop them chattering.
One of them, Katy, had shown her the scars she had
received after a vicious flogging at another brothel.
She had been imprisoned there until she'd managed
to escape by climbing down the drainpipe.

'I will leave,' she said, trying her best to sound
confident. 'I will go back to my father.'

'To the vicarage?' he enquired, startling her with
his knowledge. 'Oh, yes, I made it my business
to find out all about you, Miss Celina. Both your

sisters are gone now—did you know that? And your doting papa has struck your name from the family Bible and denies he ever had daughters, so my man tells me.'

Bella gone? But where? She had soon realised that her letters home were being destroyed, just as her father must have destroyed those from her sister Meg after she eloped. But she had always thought that Bella was safe at home. Sensible Bella, housekeeping for their tyrant of a father… Please God that wherever she was, she was safe and happy as Meg must be with James, the young officer she had run away with six years before.

She realised Makepeace was still speaking. 'You'll do as you're told, my girl, or your ailing auntie loses this house and her precious girls start earning their living like the common whores that they are.'

'When?' Lina whispered. There was the sound of doors slamming all around her, but they were in her head. If she had only herself to worry about she would run, even though she had nowhere to go. Anything, even going back to Suffolk and begging forgiveness on her knees, would be better than this. But that would leave Aunt Clara and the girls at the mercy of this scheming reptile. She could see no way out, none at all.

'Tomorrow. They will send a carriage at seven in the evening. And you be nice to Sir Humphrey or I know who will be the first one to try out the new flogging horse.'

Lina edged towards the door, unwilling to turn her back on him. The handle turned and she was out. But not alone. A big bruiser, a man she had never seen before, stood in front of her aunt's door.

Lina turned and walked away on unsteady legs to the room shared by Katy and Miriam. They were sprawled on the bed, laughing and playing with Miriam's collection of paste jewellery. As Lina walked in they looked up, their smiles of welcome freezing as they saw her face.

'What is it, Lina love?' Katy slid off the bed, her dyed red curls bouncing.

'Mr Makepeace has sold me to Sir Humphrey Tolhurst.' Lina heard her own voice, so flat and expressionless that she could hardly recognise it. She swallowed hard. If she gave way now she would collapse into hysterics, she was sure. 'Tell me what to do so it will be over quickly. Please, tell me.'

Chapter One

Dreycott Park, the north Norfolk coast—
April 24th, 1815

'He's coming!' Johnny, the boot boy, came tumbling through the front door, shirt half-untucked, red in the face with running from his post in the gazebo on top of Flagstaff Hill. He had been up there every day since the message had arrived that the late Lord Dreycott's heir was on his way from London.

Lina gave up all pretence of sewing and came out into the hall. Trimble the butler was snapping his fingers, sending footmen scurrying to assemble the rest of the staff.

She had not been able to settle to anything in the four days since Lord Dreycott's funeral. When she had fled from Sir Humphrey Tolhurst's house, terrified, desperate and wanted by the law, her aunt

had sent her to an old friend's rural retreat—to
safety, so Clara had believed. But now her elderly
protector was gone.

Lina smoothed down the skirts of her black afternoon dress and tried for composure. This was
the end of her sanctuary, a brief seven weeks since
she had fled from London, a price on her head
for a theft she had not committed. The heir was
coming to claim what was his and, no doubt, to
eject hangers-on from his new house—and then
what would become of her?

'Where are the carriages? How many?' the butler
demanded.

'No carriages, Mr Trimble, sir. Just two riders
and a pack horse. I saw them coming through the
Cromer road gate. They're walking, sir, the animals
looked tired. They'll be a while yet.'

'Even so, hurry.'

Hurry. Pack, take this money and hurry. The
elegant square entrance hall blurred and faded and
became a bedchamber. Aunt Clara, white-lipped,
her face drawn after a week of racking sickness,
dragged herself up against the pillows as Lina
sobbed out her story.

'He did not touch you?' she had whispered urgently
and they both glanced at the door. Makepeace's

bully boy might be back at any moment. 'I swear Makepeace will suffer for this.'

'No. Tolhurst did not touch me.' The relief of that was still overwhelming, the only good thing in the entire nightmare. 'He made me undress while he watched. Then he took his clothes off.' It took a moment to push her mind past the image of indulged middle-aged flab, mottled skin, the terrifying *thing* that thrust out from below the swell of Tolhurst's belly. 'And he began to reach for me… And then he gasped, and his eyes bulged and his face went red and he fell down. So I rang for help and pulled on my clothes and—'

'He was dead? You are certain?'

'Oh, yes.' Lina hadn't been able to bring herself to touch him, but she could tell. The bulging blue eyes had seemed fixed on her, still avid with lust even as they began to glaze over. She had stared in horror as her fingers fumbled with ribbons and garters. 'They all came in then—the valet, the butler, the younger son, Reginald Tolhurst. Mr Tolhurst knelt down and tried to find a pulse—then he sent the valet for the doctor and told the butler to lock me in the library. He said his father's sapphire ring was missing.'

'The Tolhurst Sapphire? My God.' Her aunt

had stared at her. 'Wasn't he wearing it when you—?'

'I don't know!' Lina's voice quavered upwards and she caught her herself before it became a shriek. 'I wasn't looking at his rings.

'I heard them talking outside. They said the ring was not in the room, not in the safe nor the jewel box. The butler said Sir Humphrey had been wearing it when I arrived. Mr Tolhurst sent a footman to Bow Street, to the magistrates.' She was gabbling with anxiety, but she could not seem to steady herself.

'He said I would be taken up for theft, that I must have thrown it out of the window to an accomplice. He said I would hang like the thieving whore I was.' She closed her eyes and fought for calm. Her aunt was ill, she must remember that. But she had nowhere else to go, no one else to help her. 'I climbed out of the library window and ran,' she finished. 'I didn't know what else to do.'

'You must go out of London until the truth can be discovered,' Clara said with decision, suddenly sounding more like her old self. 'I'll send you to Simon Ashley—Lord Dreycott—in Norfolk, he will take you in.'

'If I go to the magistrates with a lawyer,' Lina

said, 'they'll believe me then, surely? If I run away—'

'You live in a brothel. No one will believe you are innocent, and once they have you, there will be no attempt to establish the truth,' her aunt said with all the bitterness bred of years of dealings with the law. 'The Tolhurst Sapphire is famous and worth thousands. Did you read about that maidservant who was hanged a fortnight ago for stealing a silver teaspoon? It was found a few days after the execution where her mistress had lost it—down the side of the sofa. If they didn't believe her, a girl with a good character, they are not going to believe you. Help me get up.'

'But, Aunt—'

'Hurry, Lina.' Clara threw back the bedclothes and walked unsteadily to her desk. 'Put on your plain bombazine walking dress. Pack what you need in bags you can carry. *Hurry.*'

'There is no time to lose,' Trimble urged.

Lina blinked. This was the present and she had to focus on the present danger, not the past. The staff lined up, tugged cuffs and aprons under the butler's critical eye. Mrs Bishop, the cook, headed the row of maids; the footmen and the boot boy aligned themselves on the other side next to Trimble. It was

not a large indoor staff—ten in all—but a reclusive
and eccentric ninety-year-old baron had needed no
more. Where should she, the cuckoo in the nest,
stand?

'Miss Haddon?' Trimble gestured her to the front.
It was uncomfortable using a false name, but her
real one was too dangerous. Makepeace had considered that Celina Shelley sounded suitable for
a courtesan, so the law had known her real name
from the beginning.

Trimble seemed tense. Lina smiled at him in an
effort to reassure both of them. In the days since
her improbable protector had slipped away in his
sleep, eased on his last journey by copious glasses
of best cognac, an injudicious indulgence in lobster
and too many cheroots, the staff had looked to her
as the temporary head of the household.

She was, they accepted, Lord Dreycott's house
guest, a distant acquaintance in need of a roof over
her head because of the indisposition of an aunt.
Her eyes filled with tears at the memory of his
kindness, masked behind a pretence of cantankerous bad humour. He had read Aunt Clara's scribbled note, asked a few sharp questions, then rang
for Trimble and informed him that Miss Haddon
was staying for the foreseeable future.

Lord Dreycott had waved her out of his crowded,

book-strewn library with an impatient gesture, but she had seen how his other hand caressed the note, the twisted, brown-spotted fingers gentle on the thick paper. He was doing this for Clara, for some memory of a past relationship, she realised, and Lina had not taken any notice of his gruffness after that.

Now she took her place and waited, her face schooled into a calm expressionless mask as she had learned to do for years in the face of Papa's furies over some minor sin or another. Her fingers trembled slightly, making a tiny rustling noise against the crisp black silk, and she pressed the tips together to still them. Somehow she had to persuade this man to let her stay here without telling him why.

At last, the sound of hooves on the carriage drive. Paul, the second footman, swayed back on his heels to keep an unobtrusive watch out of the narrow slit of glass beside the front door then, as the sound of male voices penetrated the thick panels, he swung it open with a flourish. The new Lord Dreycott had arrived.

'My lord.' Trimble stepped through on to the arcaded entrance and bowed. 'Welcome to Dreycott Park.'

Staring past the butler's narrow shoulders, Lina

could see only glimpses of the horses—a curving dappled grey rump and a long white tail, the arch of a black neck, the bulk of oilskin-wrapped cases piled on a pack saddle. Then the grey shifted and she saw its rider fleetingly. A dust-coloured coat draped over the horse's rump; long soft boots without spurs sagged softly at the ankles; hair the colour of polished mahogany showed over-long beneath a wide-brimmed hat. He swung down out of the saddle and, even with the narrow view between butler and pillar, she saw the ease and suppleness of a fit man.

As he turned she dropped her gaze and Trimble backed into the hall to allow his new master entrance. Lina focused on where Lord Dreycott's mouth would be. That felt a safe place to look. It was becoming easier now, but ever since that night she had to make herself meet a man's eyes directly.

The male servants were deferential, trained never to stare, and she felt comfortable with them. Old Lord Dreycott's rheumy, long-sighted gaze had held no terrors for her, but when any other man met her eyes for more than a moment she felt the panic building, her heart pattered in alarm and her hands clenched with the need to control her urge to run. She must overcome it, she knew, especially with the new baron, lest he guessed she had something to hide.

The swirling skirts of his riding coat filled the doorway and the booted feet stopped just inside, set apart with a confident stance that seemed to come naturally, rather than as a deliberate statement of ownership. Lina found herself staring, not at his mouth as she had expected, but at the carelessly tied neckcloth at his throat. This was a tall man. Her eyes shifted cautiously up to his jaw, darkened with several days' stubble. When he pulled off the heavy leather gauntlets and slapped them against his coat it became apparent that it was dust-coloured because it was covered in dust.

'My lord.' Trimble coughed slightly as he took gloves and hat. 'On behalf of the staff, may I offer our condolences at the loss of your great-uncle? I am Trimble, my lord.'

'But I remember you,' Lord Dreycott said with a wide smile of recognition, his teeth very white in his tanned face. 'It is good to see you again, Trimble. Many years, is it not?'

'It is indeed, my lord. And this…' he turned as he spoke '…is Miss Haddon, his late lordship's guest.'

Lina dropped into a curtsy. 'My lord.'

'Miss Haddon. I was not aware that there were

any Haddons in the family.' His voice was deep and flexible with a faint touch of a foreign intonation and more than a hint of enquiry.

'I am not a relative, my lord.' The stubble on his chin was darker than his hair, except for a thin slash of silver that must trace a scar that had just missed his mouth. *Be persuasive and open*, an inner voice urged. *He must believe that you will be no trouble to him and might be useful.* 'Lord Dreycott was an old friend of the aunt with whom I used to live. When I had nowhere to go he was kind enough to take me in. I have been acting as housekeeper and companion for the past seven weeks, my lord.'

'I see. I am sorry to put you to inconvenience so soon after the funeral, Miss Haddon. The date of my arrival in the country was uncertain, but fortunately I called on my agent at once. He had received the news, but it was, I regret to say, the day of the service. We simply rode on.'

'All the way from London, my lord?' That was more than one hundred and forty miles. She remembered the interminably long stagecoach only too vividly.

'Yes.' He seemed surprised at the question, as though it was normal for the aristocracy to take to the high roads on horseback rather than in a post-chaise or private carriage. 'The horses were fresh enough and they are used to long distances.'

There was a bustle outside as the grooms arrived and led the animals away, Lord Dreycott's man striding behind them. The baron half-turned to see them go and Lina risked a rapid upwards glance. Overlong hair, deeply tanned skin, and, from the sharp angle of his jaw, not a spare ounce of flesh on him. He was tall, but not bulky: a thoroughbred, not a Shire horse, she thought, the sudden whimsy breaking through her anxiety. He radiated a kind of relaxed natural energy as though something wild and free had been brought into the house. Lina felt oddly fidgety and unsettled as though that quality had reached her, too.

'You will wish to retire to your rooms, I have no doubt, my lord. Your, er…valet?' Trimble eased the dust-thick coat from his lordship's shoulders.

'Gregor is my travelling companion,' Lord Dreycott said and turned back. 'I assume one of the footmen can look after my clothes.'

Lina contemplated his boots. It should have been a safe place to look if it were not for the fact that the swirling pattern of stitching that spiralled round them took the eye upwards, leading inexorably to legs that were long and well muscled. The boots did not look like English work.

Where had Lord Dreycott been? She tried to recall what his great-uncle had said about his heir. *A traveller, like I used to be. Only one of the family with any backbone*, the old man had grunted. *Only one with an original thought in his head. Scandalous rogue, of course. Shocking!* He had chuckled indulgently. *Never see the boy. He writes, but he's the decency not to come sniffing round for his inheritance.*

But this was not a boy. This was a man. Her stomach clenched as he moved to stand in front of her. Lina forced herself to look into his face for a second and wondered how gullible he was likely to be. Green eyes, cool and watchful in contrast to the easy smile he wore. Not blue eyes, not bulging, not filled with the need to use and take. The fear subsided to wary tension. But his scrutiny of her face was not indifferent, either, it was searching and intelligent and masculine and she glanced away to focus on his left ear before he could read the emotion in her own eyes. No, not gullible at all.

'I hope the rooms we have made up will be acceptable, my lord,' Lina managed, doing her best to sound like a housekeeper. That seemed the safest role for now. 'We… I cleared as much as possible into the baroness's suite, but the room is still very cluttered. The late Lord Dreycott's idea of comfort was a trifle, um, eccentric.'

She had tried to tidy up after the funeral, but soon abandoned the attempt to create anything like a conventional bedchamber. There were piles of books on every surface, rolls of maps, a stuffed bear, a human skull and pots of every kind. Papers spilled from files and from boxes that she felt they should not touch until the heir and his solicitor could inspect them; half-unpacked cases of antiquities and the desiccated remains of an enthusiasm for chemical experiments, perhaps five years old, cluttered every flat surface and half the floor.

The adjoining chambers, last occupied by the late Lady Dreycott until her death forty years past, now held motheaten examples of the taxidermist's art, vases with erotic scenes and dangerous-looking bottles of chemicals.

'My idea of comfort is also eccentric. I can sleep on a plank, Miss Haddon, and frequently have,' the amused voice drawled. 'You will join me for dinner this evening?'

'My lord, I am the housekeeper. It is hardly suitable—'

'You were my great-uncle's guest, were you not, Miss Haddon? And now you are mine. That appears to make it eminently suitable.' He was quite clearly not used to being gainsaid.

'Thank you, my lord.' What else was there to say? *And now you are mine.* Was it her imagination that shaded that statement with a possessive edge? She needed him, needed his tolerance, his acceptance of her presence in the house until she heard from Aunt Clara that it was safe to return. And there had been no word, even though the announcement of Lord Dreycott's death must have been in all the London news sheets days before. She dare not write herself; if Makepeace intercepted the letter, he would know where she was from the post-office stamps.

Soon she must establish herself as something more than a housekeeper, to be dismissed or kept at his whim, Lina realised. But as what? Somehow she must make the new Lord Dreycott decide to continue to shelter her as though he had an obligation to his great-uncle's guest, and this invitation to dine was a step along that path.

Her conscience pricked her; he would be harbouring a fugitive from the law, however unwittingly. The old baron had at least a sentimental attachment to her aunt to motivate him to offer his protection—and he had known the truth. This man had no reason to allow her so much as a bed in the hayloft and every incentive to call the local magistrate if he discovered who she was.

But the alternatives were to give herself up to imprisonment, trial and probable hanging or to flee into the unknown with no way of her aunt contacting her and only a few guineas to live on. Set against those choices a troubled conscience seemed a small price to pay for tenuous safety.

Quinn studied the young woman's averted face with a stirring of interest. What was his great-uncle doing housing this little nun? Her hair was scraped back into a tight knot at her nape and her body was shrouded in dull black from throat to toes. Old Simon was not known for his acts of charity; he had a well-earned reputation for scandal and he had kept a string of expensive birds of paradise well into his seventies. Was this girl his daughter, the product of his last fling before he returned to scholarly isolation in the country?

Surely not. No Ashley had anything but the arrogant nose that he saw in the glass whenever he bothered to look in one. No child of Simon's would have a straight little nose like this young woman's. The firm chin might be his, but not the blue eyes and blonde hair. This was not Simon's natural daughter. 'I look forward to dinner, Miss Haddon,' he said.

In answer she dropped a bob of a curtsy, her eyes fixed firmly on his collarbone. It was a perfectly ordinary collarbone as far as he was concerned, certainly not one to attract such careful study. 'At what hour would you care to dine, my lord?'

'Seven, if that is convenient, Miss Haddon.' Something rustled seductively as she moved and he frowned. He had just spent a year in the Near East, a region where silk was a commodity that all understood. That had been the whisper of expensive fine fabric and, now that he looked at the drab black gown with its dove-grey collar and cuffs, he saw the unmistakable gleam of pure silk. The modest gown was cut with elegance and made out of cloth more suited to a ballroom than a country-house hallway.

Quinn sharpened his focus on the smooth sweep of hair the colour of honey in the sun, the long lashes veiling the startling blue eyes. She moved again and a complex hint of spice and oranges flirted with his senses, subtle yet insistent. No nun, this, and no conventional housekeeper either. She was nervous of him, fearful almost. He could read her wariness as easily as he could that of a half-broken filly. It was puzzling—and arousing.

'My lord?' Trimble stood waiting for him. Quinn turned on his heel and strode across the polished marble to the staircase. At the foot of the stairs he turned and looked back. Miss Haddon was walking through an open doorway and he realised that the gown was not the dull garment he had thought it, not when its wearer was in motion. She swayed as she walked, her movements as subtle as her scent, and the silken skirts clung for a tantalising moment to the curve of her hip, the dip of her waist. This enforced return to England was going to be more interesting than he had expected, Quinn decided as he took the stairs two at a time in the wake of the butler.

Chapter Two

'That heathen servant has been in here, sniffing around.' Mrs Bishop, the cook, pounced on Lina the moment she appeared in the kitchen at half past six to make sure everything was going smoothly.

'I am sure he is not a heathen,' Lina soothed. 'Gregor sounds like an Eastern European name to me. Perhaps he is of the Orthodox faith, but a Christian nevertheless.'

Mrs Bishop had perforce been acting as house-keeper for eighteen months, ever since the last one had been driven out by the late Lord Dreycott's robust language, and she had welcomed Lina with open arms. Now she settled down to unload her worries.

'I can hardly understand a word he says,' she complained, not at all mollified. 'Accent that thick you could cut it with a knife.' As she had a north Norfolk accent that had taken Lina a week to comprehend, some mutual misunderstanding with the newcomer was only to be expected.

'Perhaps he just wanted some supper,' Lina suggested. 'Where has Trimble lodged him? I do not think he is a servant, precisely. Lord Dreycott called him a travelling companion.'

'Well, Mr Trimble's given him a room in the attic, but he looked at it a bit sideways, so Michael says.' Cook's nephew was first footman and an unfailing source of backstairs information on everything.

'It is the best he's going to get at the moment if he does not want to live in a lumber room,' Lina said. 'It is uncluttered, which is more than can be said for the family and guest chambers in this house. Was hot water sent up?'

'Hot water!' Cook went red in the face and banged down her ladle. 'Don't talk to me about hot water, Miss Lina. They've drained the copper! His lordship saw that sarco-whatsit in my late lord's chamber and said it would do as a bath and had the whole thing filled up with hot water, would you believe? And they both got in it, so Michael says—after they'd stripped off, mother naked, and got under the pump in the stable yard!'

'That is outside of enough!' Lina stared at the other woman. 'What if one of the maids had seen them? Or you or I?' The thought of Lord

Dreycott, stripped naked and dripping with water, was outrageous. Yes, that was the word. She was… shocked.

'All the footmen were up and down stairs with water cans for an age. They told Trimble to keep the female staff out of the way and then traipsed through the house dripping and got into the sarco-whatsit.'

'Sarcophagus,' Lina murmured. Trust his late lordship to keep a vast marble coffin in his bed-chamber. It was a miracle he had not insisted on being buried in it. 'Both of them together?' It was certainly big enough to bathe two large men in.

'Yes. Funny way to go on if you ask me,' Cook said darkly. 'You don't think he's one of them, you know—*mollies*—do you?'

'No,' Lina said, the memory of those green eyes running over her all too clear for comfort. 'Whatever else the new Lord Dreycott might be, I do not think he is attracted to men.' Cook still looked disapproving. Lina had been startled herself when the girls had explained that particular varia-tion in sexual preference to her, but on reflection it seemed no stranger than many of the things that the customers at The Blue Door asked of the girls.

'They travel together all the time, no doubt they are simply used to sharing bathing facilities,' she suggested. 'And I think they have been in the East, so perhaps bathing is different there.'

'Fine behaviour for Lord Dreycott, I must say. Foreign.' Cook returned to garnishing a dish of whitebait with a sniff that dismissed everything from beyond her home parish as outlandish and uncivilised.

'I am sure he will become a conventional member of the aristocracy soon enough,' Lina said. And after all, if the staff could learn to adapt to the old baron's eccentricities, this one could hardly be worse. Although, dripping through the house stark naked... No, she was not even going to think about it.

Those long, muscled legs, those shoulders... No. It was surprising to discover that however dreadful the experience with Sir Humphrey had been, and however alarming it still was when a man stared at her, her response when confronted by a young, handsome and intelligent man was attraction and curiosity. There had not been many men like that in her life, which no doubt explained it.

'He wants to know if we've got an ice house.' Michael appeared in the kitchen, clutching an armful of bottles wrapped in straw. 'I told him, of course we've got an ice house. Wants this putting in it and leaving.' He held up one bottle. 'And this one is for before dinner. They both look like water to me.'

'I am certain we will soon adapt to his lordship's little ways,' Lina said. Men in her, albeit limited, experience, were demanding creatures, but most of them were at least predictable once one had sorted out their preferences.

The sound of the dinner gong reverberated through the house and set Lina's heart rate accelerating with it. 'I had better go up.'

The clock struck seven. Lina gave Cook a reassuring smile—although which of them actually needed the reassurance was moot—and hurried up the backstairs. Trimble held the dining room door open for her. 'His lordship has just come down, Miss Celina.' He permitted himself an infinitesimal lifting of his eyebrows.

It did not take more than a moment to see why. Lord Dreycott was studying the portrait of his great-uncle over the fireplace, his hands on his hips, his head tipped back. It was as though the two men confronted each other, the impression made more vivid because the portrait must have been painted when Simon Ashley was about the same age as his great-nephew.

The figure in the painting wore a powdered wig and a full-skirted suit of spectacular figured silk in powder blue. Ruffles and lace foamed under his chin, rings flashed on his fingers. But all the ruffles and silk in the world could not disguise the arrogant masculinity of the stance or the intelligence in the piercing green eyes that stared down at the room. Lina had looked at it many times over the past weeks and wondered what that dashing rake had been like before extreme old age had dimmed everything but his spirit.

Now she could see, for his heir's resemblance to the young Simon was startling and, in his own way, he was dressed in as spectacular a fashion. Full black trousers were tucked into soft crimson suede boots, and a knee-length over-tunic of dark green figured silk was open over a white lawn shirt with an embroidered, slashed neck. His thick tawny hair was tied back at his nape and his pose made that determined chin and the long muscles and tendons in his neck even more obvious.

Lina could have sworn she made no sound, but she had only a moment to recover from the shock before Lord Dreycott turned. She dropped her eyes immediately, startled by a movement in the shadows at the back of the room. The man Gregor had also turned to look at her, his face impassive. He was dressed like the baron, except that he was all in plain dark blue save for his white shirt, and his hair was cropped short.

'Miss Haddon.' Lord Dreycott came forwards. 'You will forgive my costume; I have no European clothing suitable for evening wear as yet.'

'Of course, my lord.' Who could object to sitting down to dinner with an exotic creature from the *Arabian Nights* or *Childe Harold*? She felt like a drab little peahen against his peacock magnificence.

'Will you sit here?' He pulled out the chair to the right of the head of the table, then took his own, which Gregor held. The man stepped back, folded his arms and gazed impassively over their heads as the footmen began to serve soup.

'I have explained to Gregor that as it is highly unlikely that you intend to poison my food there is no need for him to taste it first,' Lord Dreycott remarked.

'Indeed, my lord?' Lina said, so taken aback that she spoke without thinking, 'As none of us knows you yet, we would have no reason to, would we?' He raised his eyebrows at her forthright tone and she realised what she had said. 'Forgive me, but do you have many attempts made upon your life?'

'Enough to make me wary,' he said. 'It is hard to

get out of the habit of precautions. Gregor, as you see, will watch my back whatever the setting.'

Lina choked back a laugh, the picture of the silent Gregor padding after Lord Dreycott at some society function tickling her imagination. The old baron had been outrageous, but he had never provoked her into almost giving way to giggles with her mouth full of soup. She could barely even recall the last time she had felt amused.

'Must you call me *my lord*, Miss Haddon? I keep wondering to whom you are speaking.'

'I am sure you will soon become accustomed to the title, and there is nothing else I may properly call you, my lord.' Lina took a bread roll and tried not to stare at the richly embroidered shirt cuff so close to her left hand. Certainly she did not want to contemplate the tanned hand with a heavy gold ring on one long finger.

'We could dispense with propriety,' he suggested. 'My name is Jonathan Quinn Ashley. No one calls me Jonathan and I suppose you will not accept Quinn as *proper*.' She heard the amusement in his voice at the word. She doubted he often gave much thought to propriety. 'You must call me Ashley, which is my surname. What is your given name?'

'Celina, my…Ashley. But really, I cannot, it would be most unsuitable in my position.'

'What position? You are a guest. And who are we going to scandalise?' Quinn Ashley enquired. 'Gregor is unshockable, I assure you. And after years in my great-uncle's service I imagine Trimble and the staff are hardened to far worse behaviour than a little informality. Is that not so, Trimble?' He pitched his voice to the butler, who was standing by the sideboard, supervising.

'Indeed, my lord. My lips are, however, sealed on the subject.'

'Very proper. Now, Celina, are we to dispense with the bowing and scraping?'

She looked up through her lashes and found he was watching her steadily. He did not appear to be flirting; his manner was friendly and neither encroaching nor suggestive. Her severe hairstyle and modest evening gown must be working, she decided. She doubtless looked the perfect plain housekeeper and was not in the slightest danger of any attempts at gallantry on his part.

'If that is what you wish, Ashley.' He nodded, satisfied, and went back to his soup. Lina took advantage of his focus on his food to study the strong profile. He looked intelligent and sensitive, she decided. How sad if he was the fifth son and all his brothers had predeceased him, as they must for him to inherit. 'Did you have many older siblings?' she enquired sympathetically.

He caught her meaning immediately. 'No, no brothers or sisters. Quinn is for my mother's maiden name, not short for Quintus.' They sat back while the soup plates were cleared and the fish brought in. The steady green eyes came back to her face and she dropped her gaze immediately. Sensitive and intelligent, certainly, but also disturbing. When she caught that look she felt very aware that she was female. 'Have you brothers and sisters?'

'I had two sisters, Margaret and Arabella,' Lina admitted. 'But Meg left the country with her husband, who is a soldier in the Peninsula, and I do not know where Bella is now.'

'So you are quite alone? What about this aunt?' He did not appear shocked by her absence of family. Of course, an interrogation about her antecedents was only to be expected.

'She fell ill and can no longer give me a home.' Ashley poured white wine into her glass as the whitebait were served and she took a sip, surprised to find it tasting quite light and flowery in her mouth. It was positively refreshing and she took another swallow. She was unused to wine, but one glass could not be harmful, surely?

'I see.' For a moment she wondered if he was going to ask what she intended doing once he employed a proper housekeeper, a question to which the only answer was *I have not the slightest idea*, but Ashley simply nodded and reapplied himself to his food, which was disappearing at a considerable rate.

'More fish, my lord?' Michael proffered the salver.

'Thank you. Forgive my appetite, Celina, we did not stop for more than bread and ale since London.'

She could not help glancing at the impassive man standing behind him.

'We can try,' Quinn Ashley said, apparently reading her mind. 'Gregor.'

He growled something in a language Lina could not understand and Ashley said, 'English, please, Gregor.'

'Lord?'

'Eat.'

'No, lord.' It was said with neither insolence nor defiance. 'Later.'

Quinn shrugged. 'Stubborn devil.'

'Yes, lord.'

'If the housekeeper can sit down to dinner with you, I do not see why your companion may not,'

Lina said. The silent man made her uneasy, but she hated the thought that he was hungry, and if he would not leave the baron to eat in the kitchen, then there seemed only one solution. 'Michael, please lay a place for Mr Gregor.'

It was Lord Dreycott, not she, who should say who ate at his table, but the new baron was so unconventional that the words were out of her mouth before she could bite them back.

'You hear, Gregor?' He did not seem offended that she was giving orders. 'The lady wishes you to dine with us. Will you insult her by refusing?'

The man muttered something in his own language that made Ashley laugh and took the seat opposite her. 'Lady.'

Michael began to serve the lamb cutlets. She only hoped they had enough to go round, now that a second large hungry male had been added to the table. Trimble slipped out, doubtless to warn Cook.

'I must send for my uncle's lawyer tomorrow. I assume the will has not been read?' Ashley moved away her half-empty wine glass and filled another with red wine.

'No. Mr Havers said they must first locate you. He seemed to think this would take some time. Your great-uncle certainly said it would.' *He's off somewhere in Persia, lucky devil*, were the old man's actual words. *Seducing his way through harems and getting into fights, I have no doubt.* Presumably the fights came as a result of making an attempt on a harem and its occupants. Images of silks and sherbet and tinkling fountains came to mind. Dare she ask him about them?

No. This man was just as steeped in sin as the clients at The Blue Door, Lina reminded herself. *And probably considerably more sophisticated and devious*, she added. She should be on her guard, she thought; not all wolves had bulging blue eyes and unpleasant manners. Lina took a sustaining mouthful of red wine. It slipped down, warm and soothing.

'My uncle had sent for me and I came as soon as the letter reached us. A message to go to Mr Havers first thing, Trimble, asking him to call at his earliest convenience.' Ashley returned to his cutlets. Across the table Gregor had silently demolished the remains of the fish and was now eating meat with the air of a man who expected there to be wolfhounds to throw the bones to. A footman came in and added a dish of stewed beef to the table.

'He sent for you? But he died in his sleep, and despite his age, it was unexpected.' The doctor had

actually muttered that he'd expected the aged rep-
robate to live to be a hundred.

'He wrote a year ago to say I must return to
pick up the pieces, as he put it. The letter took ten
months to find me and then I had to travel back
here. The old devil had his timing almost right, in
the end.' He paused and picked up his wine glass,
looking into the claret as though it was a seer's
scrying glass. 'I would have liked to have met him
once more, I owe him a lot, but neither of us would
have wanted me kicking my heels around the place
for long.'

'But it is so beautiful here,' Lina protested. She
had fallen in love with the wild grey sea just over
the wooded hill that sheltered the house; the steep
walks up through the woods on the opposite side
of the valley or through the park; the wide expanse
of sky that seemed to reach for ever.

'Beautiful? I hope that there are many of your
opinion, for I intend to sell it as soon as possible.'

'Sell it? But you cannot—oh, I beg your pardon.'
She cut her gaze away as Ashley lifted his head to
look at her. 'It is none of my business.' She had not
meant to speak so passionately or draw attention
to herself like that. Her nerves must be all over the
place. Lina took another mouthful of wine and felt
a little better.

'You seem very attached to the place,' he remarked.

He thought her anguish was for the estate, of course, not for her own position. Lina had thought that it would be several months at least before affairs were settled, time for her to find some way out of this impasse, or for her aunt to send news that the real culprit had been apprehended. But now, if Quinn Ashley meant to close up the house and sell at once, she could be without a home within a few weeks.

'I think it lovely,' she said colourlessly.

'And you are wondering what will become of you,' he said, his voice dry. He had not been deceived about her reaction for a moment. 'My great-uncle has left provision for all the staff, he wrote that he had discussed it with them. I am sure he will also have thought of you, Celina.'

She could only smile and nod. *Of course he has not! He did not know I existed when he wrote to you and, even if he did, I have no call upon him, none whatsoever.* But she had to hide her alarm somehow—if he saw how desperate she was he would become suspicious.

'I will take care of you, Celina,' Ashley said, the deep voice giving the statement the weight of an oath, the faint foreign accent adding a suggestiveness that had her looking up warily, then away as she found he was studying her in return. It was only that hint of an accent that made her uneasy, surely? He was an English gentleman, after all, and she was a guest under his roof.

She should protest that he was too kind, demur at accepting assistance from a complete stranger, but she bit back all the polite responses. What she should do, she decided rather hazily, was to charm him. Why had she not thought of that before? Lina took another mouthful of wine. It was quite delicious and really rather relaxing. Things seemed so much clearer now.

Attempting to charm the baron was dipping her toe into dangerous waters, though—how far was just enough to make him feel chivalrous and responsible, but not amorous towards her?

One stormy winter evening when business had been slack, Katy and Miriam, the closest to her in age and her particular friends amongst The Blue Door's courtesans, had amused themselves by trying to teach her how to flirt with a man.

'Don't think we can't act like ladies if we have to,' Katy had said. 'It isn't all wiggling your bottom and hanging your boobies out, you know. Lots of gentlemen like to pretend they aren't paying for it, that they're just getting very lucky indeed with some well-bred young lady. So Madam drilled us all in genteel flirting. You can't stay here for ever, can you? You need to find yourself a gentleman and learn how to wind him around your little finger in ever such a *nice way.*' *Just as Mama did,* Lina had thought with a pang of alarm. Was that what she must do to secure her future?

The girls had gone off into peals of laughter, then sobered up enough to spend the evening teaching Lina how to use her eyes, her fan, her voice, to entrap a gentleman.

She had never had reason to use that lesson, but she could try out some of the hints now. The sideways look from under the lashes was supposed to be enchanting. She tried it. 'Thank you, I am sure you will look after me.' Gregor made a noise deep in his chest, a laugh perhaps. She felt herself blush and looked down at her plate.

'Count upon it,' Ashley said, his voice deepening in a way that had shivers running down her spine, then, in an altogether different voice, 'Is that by any chance a trifle?'

'It is,' Lina said, ready to jump to Mrs Bishop's defence. 'I imagine she has added it to the desserts when she realised that there are three of us at table.' It was not the most sophisticated of confections and, from the way the custard on the top undulated, hinting at lumps lurking below, the poor woman must have been desperate for something to send up. The plates for the earlier courses had all returned downstairs scraped clean, even the beef casserole, which had probably been the footmen's dinner, had vanished.

'I haven't eaten one of these for years,' Ashley observed, helping himself and Gregor lavishly.

Lina took a rather more dainty almond cream and consumed it in tiny spoonfuls, wishing she had not challenged her nervous stomach with anything sweet. She smiled and nodded and laughed at any minor witticism they made and made play with her lashes until finally the men, having eaten the trifle, lumps and all, and a frangipane tart, appeared sated.

'I will leave you gentlemen to your cheese and port,' she said, getting up. The room seemed to shift a little. 'I trust you have a comfortable night. I will see you in the morning.' She met Ashley's eye, then wished she had not. Somehow the atmosphere had become close, intense, loaded with an emotion she did not understand. All she wanted was the sanctuary of her own room and the privacy to worry about whether she had the skills to manipulate a man like Quinn Ashley.

Chapter Three

'What do you make of the little nun?' Quinn lounged on his great canopied bed and watched Gregor checking doors, windows and hangings in his usual obsessive search for assassins and escape routes. 'Do stop that, Gregor. If there's a fire, I will climb out of the window. I do not expect any other danger in this house except from the hazards created by my late uncle's collection. And when we get to London it is likely to be pistols at dawn, not knives at midnight.'

'Nun?' The other man turned back from the wardrobe he was investigating. He spoke English with a heavy accent, but no reluctance, nor was there any sign of subservience in his manner now. It amused Quinn to observe his friend changing roles as the fancy took him or circumstances demanded. Gregor was enjoying teasing the servants and he was baffled by Quinn's indifference to his new title. 'That is no nun.'

'No?' Quinn sketched the scraped-back hair, gestured down his body as though to show the plain black gown, then mimed a wimple over his head. 'What is she, then, because I am damned if I can tell?'

'Trouble,' Gregor grunted. Satisfied with his search, he settled into a huge carved chair. 'A virgin. They are trouble always.'

'You think she's an innocent?' Quinn stirred himself enough to lever his long body up on his elbows and peer down the length of it to look at the other man. He was not so sure. Those sidelong looks from under the heavy lashes, the pretty shows of deference combined with a slight pout—those were not the little tricks of an innocent.

'She looks at you as though she has no idea what to do with you, but she would be quite interested to find out, if only she dared,' the big Russian said.

Quinn snorted and flopped back on the pillows. 'Jupiter and Mars, but I am tired. She is worried I am going to throw her out, that is all. And she is not used to the likes of us, my friend. I should not have fed her wine.'

'You do not want her? I would like her.'

'Offer her your protection, then.' Quinn closed his eyes and told himself that it was too late, and he was too tired, to go downstairs and start rummaging in the library. Those books would still be there to-morrow. As for women, the blonde intrigued him, stirred certain fundamental male responses, but she would still be there tomorrow as well. Women usually were, and this one was not going anywhere.

Now was a good time to enjoy being clean, fed, relaxed. It was a couple of weeks since he had last had a woman, but deferred pleasures were usually sweeter for the contemplation. Like revenge. The urge for that was stronger here, in his great-uncle's house.

London would give him both.

'She is frightened of me, although she tried to hide it,' Gregor's deep voice observed, cutting through his attempts to doze. 'Her eyes, they have fear in them when they look at me. I like my women willing.'

'And she is not afraid of me?'

'She is *aware* of you. And what is the word, almost the same?'

'Wary?'

'*Da.* Wary. Puzzled. You are not what she expects a nobleman to be like. And, of course, you are prettier than me, so she looks more at you.'

Quinn reached out a hand, took hold of a pillow and slung it in Gregor's direction. It was hurled back with considerable accuracy. 'Go to bed and stop thinking about women,' he said, catching it. 'Have they given you a decent room?'

'A servant's room, in the attics. It will do.'

'You are certain?' Quinn opened one eye and contemplated the motheaten bed canopy above his head. 'I can ring and have you moved to a luxurious apartment like this one. It would only take an hour or two to clear a path to the bed.'

'Tomorrow, perhaps. We have worried them enough today,' Gregor said as he got up and stretched hugely. 'They do not know what to make of us, they are fearful—or the little nun is fearful—and we shocked them with our bath.'

'I am not going to splash about in two inches of scummy water in a tin bucket,' Quinn said. 'We made certain the women were out of the way, didn't we?'

'The women are sad that they did not see us and the men are jealous because we are so magnificently made,' the Russian said with a wicked chuckle. 'Like stallions. Good night, lord.' He closed the door behind him just as the second pillow hit it.

Quinn lay still for a moment, then heaved himself up with a grunt, stripped off his clothing, tossed it on to a chair, blew out the candles beside the bed and fell back naked on to the covers in one continuous movement.

England. England after ten years, and now the dishonourable Mr Ashley was the fourth Baron Dreycott of Cleybourne in the county of Norfolk. A title he did not want, an estate he did not care about and, no doubt, a list of debts that would make no impression on his personal fortune. But all the hazards and discomforts of two months of travelling, all the squalor of a Channel crossing in the teeth of a late gale, all the grime and chaos of London, were worth it for the treasures in this house. And there was the added savour of the stir he would cause when he set about establishing himself in London.

Revenge. Quinn savoured the thought. Lies, arrogance, cowardice; three things he detested, three sins he intended to punish. It had not mattered so much for himself; he had been away and out of it. But Simon had suffered for his defence of his great-nephew and that was a score to be settled.

But he had waited ten years for vengeance; dreams of that could wait. As he dragged a sheet over himself and let sleep take him, he recalled the other thing he appeared to have inherited along with the title and the estate and the books. The wary little nun was an intriguing puzzle, because whatever else she was, she was not a housekeeper, he would bet his matched Manton duelling pistols on it. No, perhaps not those, he might need them.

Lina was doing her very best impression of a housekeeper the next morning, complete with a large apron that she wore like armour against the two disturbing male intruders.

She avoided them at breakfast, then almost bumped into Lord Dreycott in the hallway as they emerged from the small dining room. 'My... Ashley. Good morning.' In the cold light of day she regretted agreeing to use his name and worried about how her untried attempts at cautious flirtation had been received. Even one glass of wine, she concluded as she reviewed the previous evening in the cold light of day, was apparently enough to overset her judgement. Two had been foolish in the extreme. 'A message has been sent to Mr Havers. I would expect he will be here by ten.'

'So soon at short notice? What if he had something already in his diary?'

'You are the most important thing, hereabouts,' Lina said. It was the simple truth. 'If he had appointments, he will have cancelled them. Mr Armstrong from the local branch of your uncle's London bank, Dr Massingbird his physician and the Reverend Perrin will be close on his heels.'

'You sent for them also?' Ashley paused by the study door, obviously surprised by this initiative.

'There was no need to tell anyone,' she explained. 'The local grapevine will have already passed on the news last night. The local gentry will leave it until tomorrow when they know your men of business will have all been to see you, then we may expect a great many callers. His late lordship did not welcome visitors, so they will all be agog to introduce themselves.' Ashley shook his head, so she added, 'Cook is already baking biscuits and we have ample supplies of tea and coffee left over from the funeral.'

'I am not a betting man,' Ashley observed, 'but I will wager you a guinea against that ridiculous apron of yours that I will receive no social calls.'

'But why not?' Lina ignored the remark about her apron. She thought it gave her authority and an air of sobriety that had been sadly missing last night.

'Because, my dear Miss Haddon, I am not received in polite society.'

'But Lord Dreycott said that you have hardly been in the country for years,' she protested. 'None of them knows you.'

'However, they will all have heard about me. And some of them will remember me. It was not simply my uncle's reclusive nature that explained the lack of calls—we are tarred with the same brush. We will have a large number of biscuits to eat up, I assure you.' His face showed nothing but faintly amused acceptance of this state of affairs.

'Of course they will call. They have no reason not to—whatever have you done that they should react so?'

'Being the man who debauched, impregnated and abandoned the Earl of Sheringham's eldest daughter, is, you must agree, Miss Haddon, adequate cause for social ostracism in an area where Sheringham is the largest landowner,' Ashley said. 'The earl carries much weight, hereabouts. His son, Viscount Langdown, carries as much, and a horse-whip.' Lina stared at him open mouthed and he smiled, went into the study and closed the door behind him.

She watched the panels, half-expecting Ashley to reappear and tell her that it had been a joke in poor taste, but the door remained closed. Behind her there was a discreet cough.

'Trimble?' Lina turned to the butler. 'Surely his lordship is…surely that cannot be correct?'

The butler looked uneasy. 'Perhaps I had better tell you about it, Miss Haddon.' He held open the door to the salon. 'We will not be disturbed in here.'

She followed him and closed the door. 'He says he expects to be shunned by the neighbourhood,' she said, her voice low as she joined Trimble in the furthest corner of the room. 'He said he did something quite dreadful.'

'Yes, indeed, refusing to marry his pregnant fiancée is not the action of a gentleman and must bring opprobrium upon any man,' the butler said, his voice flat.

'He really did such a thing? When?' Lina stared in horror at the butler, but her mind was full of the picture of Quinn Ashley as she had just seen him. In his deplorably casual version of an English country-gentleman's riding attire, with his frank speech and his amused smile, it was hard to visualise the new Lord Dreycott as the heartless seducer he freely admitted to being. But of course, to have insinuated himself into the bed of an earl's daughter, he would hardly look like a ruthless rake.

'Let us sit down, Trimble,' she said. This was shocking news to absorb standing up. She had already spent one night under the same roof as a dangerous libertine, it seemed. Her mouth felt dry. *Seduced, impregnated, abandoned...*

'The long-established staff here know the story,'

the butler said, perching uncomfortably on the edge of a chair. 'His late lordship told us the truth of the matter. It seemed that Mr Ashley, as he then was, abandoned his pregnant fiancée ten years ago. Given that her brother was publicly threatening him with a horsewhip followed by castration, it seemed to his great-uncle that the prudent course of action was to send him off abroad with some haste. Once there, it seems, he decided he liked the life of a traveller and has seldom returned.'

Lina swallowed. She had no horsewhip-wielding brother to protect her. She had no one except a man whose promise to take care of her now seemed a cruel jest.

'But he was not the father of her child,' Trimble added with haste, no doubt reading her expression with some accuracy. 'Please be assured I would not have allowed you to remain in the house if that were so, Miss Haddon.'

'Why did she not marry the man responsible, then?' she managed, relief making her feel faintly queasy.

'Mr Ashley in those days was a charming, but somewhat unworldly, perhaps even innocent, young man,' Trimble continued, not answering the question directly. 'A studious, rather quiet gentleman, just down from university, his head full of books and dreams of exploration, as I recall him. I was only the first footman in those days, you understand. But, as his late lordship said, why would a beautiful, highly eligible young woman throw herself at the rather dull heir to a minor barony?'

'Because she needed a gullible husband as fast as possible?' Lina hazarded, distracted momentarily by the thought that Quinn Ashley could ever have been described as *rather dull*.

'Exactly, Miss Haddon. Her parents, when they became aware of her condition, set her to entrap him and, I fear, he was all too willing to fall for her charms and into love. The flaw in their scheme was that they had picked on a romantic, idealistic young man who, when confronted by a passionate young lady positively begging to demonstrate her affection for him by the sacrifice of her virtue, struck a noble attitude—as he told his uncle afterwards—and refused to dishonour his bride-to-be.'

'And then he realised what was happening?'

'Not, so he said, until she ripped all her clothes off and became hysterical. Her father, when subterfuge was obviously impossible, offered Mr Ashley a very substantial dowry to wed her. He refused, broke off the engagement—and so they laid the child at his door and characterised him as a heartless seducer of virtue.'

'But why?' Lina thought for a moment. 'Was the true father utterly impossible? Married, perhaps?'

'They were unable to establish which of her father's grooms it was, I regret to say.' Lina felt her jaw drop. 'She would still be in terrible disgrace when her condition became known, but the heir to a barony was a better father for her bastard than a choice of three stable hands.'

'The poor baby,' Lina murmured. 'What became of it?'

'I have no idea,' Trimble said, his austere face hardening. 'She, I believe, was married off with a very large dowry to an obscure Irish peer who needed the money.'

'But Mr Ashley took the blame and did not reveal the worst of her shame,' Lina said. 'And that ruined his reputation.'

'Exactly. He challenged Lord Langdown, who refused to meet him, threatening the whip instead. His late lordship attempted to intervene and was caught up in the scandal, his own name blackened by association. So you see, Miss Haddon, why we cannot expect callers from local society.'

'They would have forgotten by now, surely?' She did not like to think of Ashley ostracised for an injustice done to him ten years ago when his only

sin had been to refuse to make an honourable sacrifice of himself. How could he have married the
girl? There could have been no trust, no respect,
in that marriage.

But he was a gentleman and a gentleman must not
break off an engagement. Could he not have found
some way out of the trap without abandoning her
so brutally? Doubt began to gnaw at her strangely
instinctive support for him. No, she decided after a
moment's thought, against a powerful earl Ashley
would have had no leverage at all unless he had
been prepared to tell the truth about his fiancée.

'It might have been forgotten, if it were not for
the fact that, once abroad, Mr Ashley rapidly set
about losing what innocence was left to him, along
with any shreds of his reputation,' Trimble said in a
voice scrupulously free from any expression. 'The
learned journals were only too happy to publish
his writings from exotic parts of the world—but
his late lordship used to read me stories from the
scandal sheets with great glee. Not all Mr Ashley's
explorations were of a scholarly nature.'

'What sort of stories?' Lina asked, not wanting to know and yet drawn with the same terrible
curiosity that made a carriage crash impossible to
ignore. Harems again?

'I could not possibly recount them to an unmarried

lady,' the butler said. 'Suffice it to say that they make Lord Byron's exploits seem tame.'

'So he is not so safe, after all?' She was fearful, and she knew that she should be, but a shameful inner excitement was fluttering inside her, too. *Fool*, she admonished herself. *Just because he is not a fat lecher with bulging eyes it does not mean that he could not accomplish your ruin just as effectively and twice as ruthlessly.*

'I have every confidence that, in his own home and where an unmarried lady under his protection is concerned, we need have no fears about his lordship's honourable behaviour,' Trimble pronounced. Was he certain, or was he, a loyal family servant, unable to believe the worst of his new master?

At least I need have no fear for my reputation, *being under his protection, for the world already believes me to be a whore and a jewel thief,* Lina thought bitterly. It had taken a while, in the friendly comfort of The Blue Door, for the truth to dawn on her, but by taking refuge in a brothel, she had as comprehensively ruined herself as her mother had—and without having committed any indiscretion in the first place. *But what of my virtue?* Should she lock her door at night?

'Thank you for confiding in me, Trimble,' she said with what she thought was passable composure.

The doorbell rang. 'That will be Mr Havers, I have no doubt.' She had no intention of being seen by the lawyer, a man who might be expected to receive the London newspapers daily and who doubtless studied the reports of crimes with professional interest. A description of the fugitive Celina Shelley would have been in all of them, she was sure.

The butler went out, leaving her shaken and prey to some disturbing imaginings. It was one thing to find herself in a house with a man who looked like the hero of a lurid novel, quite another to discover that he had the reputation to match and was probably as much villain as hero. Last night she must have been mad to exchange banter with him, to try out her inexpert flirtation technique. It was like a mouse laying a crumb of cheese between the cat's paws and expecting it not to take mouse and cheese both in one mouthful. How he must have laughed at her behind that polite mask.

Trimble appeared in the doorway. 'His lordship has requested that the household assemble immediately in the dining room to hear the will read, Miss Haddon.'

'He cannot mean me.' Lina stayed where she was. 'I have no possible interest in the document. It is none of my business.'

'He said everyone, Miss Haddon.'

'Very well.' Perhaps she could slip in at the back and sit behind Peter, the largest of the footmen. Provided she could feel safe and unseen, then it would be interesting to hear Lord Dreycott's no doubt eccentric dispositions, she reflected, as she followed the butler's black-clad back, slipping into the dining room behind him. Yes, there was a seat, shielded by the footmen and the epergne on the end of the sideboard.

Lina settled herself where she could just catch a glimpse of Lord Dreycott, Gregor standing impassively behind his chair. He was drumming his fingers very slowly on the table in front of him and looking across at the portrait of his great-uncle. Lina realised that the faint smile on his lips echoed the painted mouth exactly. It was a very expressive mouth, she thought, wondering if Ashley could school it into immobility when he was playing cards. Unbidden, her imagination presented her with the image of those lips on her fingers, her wrist.

She clasped her hands together so tightly her nails bit into her palms. She must not think of...

'If everyone is here,' said a brisk masculine voice, 'then I will read the last will and testament of Simon Augustus Tremayne Ashley, third Baron Dreycott. To Henry Trimble, in recognition of many long years of loyal and invaluable service, the lifetime occupancy of Covert Cottage, a pension of seventy pounds a year, whichever items of clothing of mine he cares to take, unlimited fuel and game from the estate, the services of the garden staff for the maintenance of his grounds and the stuffed bear which he has always admired.'

Lina could see the back of Trimble's neck growing red, whether from emotion or the thought of the stuffed bear—she imagined that was a joke between his old master and himself—she was not certain.

'To Mary Eliza Bishop, in recognition...'

And so it went on, legacies both generous and eccentric to all the indoor and outdoor staff, even the boot boy. A donation to the church, *To replace the cracked tenor bell, which has for so long rendered my Sunday mornings hideous.* One hundred pounds to the charity for the widows of fishermen lost along this stretch of coast. Some books to fellow scholars and finally, *All that remaining of my possessions and estate not elsewhere disposed of in this document, to my great-nephew and heir Jonathan Quinn Ashley.*

'There is, however, a codicil dated five weeks ago.' The lawyer cleared his throat. *'To the lady currently a guest in my house; residence at Dreycott*

Park, with all her expenses met, for the period of six months from the date of my death and, at that date, the sum of one thousand pounds absolutely, in memory of the great affection I bear to her aunt.

'And I further instruct that my great-nephew Jonathan Quinn Ashley shall only inherit my books, maps, papers, parchments and documents provided that he retains full ownership of Dreycott Hall for a period of not less than six months or until he completes the editing and publication of my memoirs which I leave unfinished, whichever is the later. Should this condition not be met then all those papers, books, etc. etc. will pass to the Ashmolean Library, Oxford, absolutely.

'That concludes the will.' There was a crackling of thick paper as Mr Havers folded the document.

Chapter Four

Lina stared up at the enigmatically smiling portrait, stunned. Sanctuary and money beyond her wildest dreams, enough for an independent start whenever she chose to take it, the last generous gift from an old man who had the imagination and compassion to reach out to a total stranger and the generosity to commemorate an old friendship—or an old love. *'Thank you,'* she whispered.

'Can this be broken?' Quinn Ashley's voice was utterly devoid of any amusement now. 'I have no intention of retaining this house and estate any longer than it takes me to pack up the books and papers and place it on the market.'

'No, my lord, it cannot be broken,' the lawyer said with the firmness of a man who had confronted many an angry heir in the course of his career. 'The late Lord Dreycott consulted me most carefully to ensure that was the case, as he anticipated your objections. I should further point out that, as the lady has the option to remain here for six months, you will be unable to place this estate on the market until she chooses to leave, whatever your wishes to the contrary.

'Now, if I might ask for the use of a room to interview each of the beneficiaries, I can settle most of the practical issues during the course of the day, my lord.'

'Use the study,' Ashley said. 'I will discuss this further with you there now, if you would be so good.' Despite the distance between them Lina could see that he had his face completely under control, but he could not keep the anger out of his eyes. He met her scrutiny and she felt as though she had just turned the key to imprison a tiger in a cage. The horizontal bars of the chair-back dug into her spine as she pressed herself against them in instinctive retreat.

Then self-preservation took over from her worries about what Lord Dreycott might think of her now. She had to face the lawyer and he would want her name. Her heart pounding, Lina got up, ducked through the service door at the back of the dining room and hurried to the stairs.

'What the hell was the old devil thinking of?' Quinn demanded as the study door closed behind them.

'Ensuring that his memoirs are published, my lord,' Mr Havers said. 'I believe your great-uncle felt they might be overlooked for some years if you were at liberty to fit them in with your doubtless demanding programme of travels and your own writing.' He shuffled the papers into various piles on the long table against the wall, obviously indifferent to the fact that his news had set Quinn's plans for half the year on their head.

'And what is this nonsense with the girl? Is she the reason the estate cannot be sold for six months?' Quinn asked. 'Is she his natural daughter? She has no look of him.'

'I think it unlikely. I believe this is a quite genuine gesture in memory of his past attachment to her aunt. What is the young lady's name? Lord Dreycott was curiously reluctant to give it to me.'

'Haddon.'

Havers made a note. 'I am sorry, my lord. But I am afraid you are encumbered with this estate, and Miss Haddon, for the term of six months at a minimum, or you forfeit the library.'

Quinn placed his hands flat on the desk and leaned on them, staring down at the worn red morocco leather surface. He had intended selling up the estate, moving everything he wanted to retain to his town house and settling down to establish himself in London. There was pleasurable anticipation in combining a sensible business move with the prospect of a long-awaited revenge on polite society.

He had perfectly respectable reasons to transfer his centre of operations from Constantinople to London—respectable motives to do with trade and scholarship. Now he would have to divide his attention between this easterly parish on the shore, his uncle's memoirs and his real focus in London.

It was infuriating, but he knew when to yield to superior force. Great-Uncle Simon's tactics were, as always, masterly. There was no benefit exhausting himself and his temper in an attempt to get around the will; he was stuck with Dreycott Park until the autumn. And he was stuck with the responsibility for a nervous, flirtatious and puzzling young woman as well. He supposed he could just leave her here to keep the place in order for six months.

'I'll leave you to it,' Quinn said once he had his frustration under control. An outburst of temper would do no good. 'Feel free to use the desk, Havers. Who do you want first?'

'Miss Haddon, I think. Thank you, my lord.'

Celina was sitting on one of the hard chairs in the empty hall, her hands in her lap, her back straight. The apron had gone and she had enveloped her

— not needed

blonde hair in a thick black snood. She looked even more like an occupant of a nunnery than before.

She stood up when she saw him, her expression wary. *As well it might be*, he thought. *What am I going to do with you?* The option of simply leaving her here to run the house lost savour. His body stirred; it knew exactly what it wanted to do.

'Havers will see you first, Celina.'

'I am very sorry, my lord,' she said as though he had not spoken.

'For what?' He was in no mood to be conciliatory.

'For the fact that you cannot carry out your intentions, for the burden of my presence and for the diminution of your inheritance by the legacy to me.'

That sounded like a prepared speech. 'The money is in no way an issue, Celina. It was my uncle's to do with as he pleased and your presence in the household is no burden. If I appear less than pleased with my uncle's dispositions, it is because of the disruption to my plans.' *And the unaccustomed experience of having my own will thwarted, if truth be told*, he added mentally.

It was salutary, after years of doing what he wanted, when he wanted, how he wanted, to find himself constrained in this way just when he had resolved on a course of action. It was almost as though the old devil had second-guessed him and set out to throw a barrier in his path. Old Simon had been too cynical, and too unconventional, to worry about his own reputation and he would not have wanted Quinn thinking to avenge the slight on his good name.

'Thank you. It is generous of you to reassure me,' she said, her voice colourless. 'It will be uncomfortable for you here, if your neighbours will not call.' She was flushed now, her eyes, as usual, cast down. 'Trimble told me about the scandal. It is very shocking that a young man could be treated in such a way.'

'You believe me the innocent party, then?' Quinn found himself irritated that her answer mattered.

'Of course.' She sounded almost sure, he thought grimly. Not certain, though. How very wise of her. 'Trimble would not lie about something like that.' *But she thinks I might?* 'It was very honourable of you not to reveal the true parentage of her child.'

He shrugged. It had been romantic wrongheadedness and a wounded heart more than any loftier motive, he suspected, looking back now at his young self. 'That must have been a source of pride to you,' she added, laying one hand on his sleeve as though trying to offer comfort.

'I was a romantic young idiot,' Quinn said. The shuttered gaze lifted a fraction and he knew she was watching him sidelong from beneath her lids. 'That did not last long. Do not delude yourself that I am some sort of saint, Celina. The high-flown moral stance persisted just as long as it took me to discover the delights of the flesh well away from English double standards.'

Her pale hand was still on his forearm. He looked down at her bent head, the sweep of dark lashes against her cheek, the faint quiver of her fingers, the tender skin below her ear. The scent she wore, subtle and sophisticated and unexpected, teased his nostrils and his pulse kicked in recognition of her unconscious allure.

Or was it unconscious? he wondered. She had the grooming, the elegance, the little mannerisms of a woman used to pleasing men for a living. And yet, there was the apprehension in her eyes when she did permit them to meet his fleetingly, her lack of sophistication with wine, her retreats into shy propriety. A mystery, and Quinn enjoyed a mystery. And one involving contact with a pretty woman was even more enticing. He had six months to tease the truth out of her. As he thought it, he realised that he was not going to just take himself off to London and abandon her here. He wanted her.

He lifted her hand from his arm and raised it to his lips, just touching the tips of her fingers, letting his breath caress her. She stiffened and gave a little gasp, but he kept his attention on the pampered hand, the carefully manicured and buffed nails, the faint smell of expensive hand lotion. Celina cared for her skin like a courtesan, not a housekeeper.

'Why are you telling me this?' she asked abruptly. But she did not pull her hand away.

'You will hear some torrid tales from our respectable neighbours, I have no doubt. I thought it better that I warn you.'

'I see,' Celina said. 'I do trust you, Ashley.'

That was like a jab in the stomach. He did not intend for her to trust him, he wanted to tease and intrigue her for sport, but if she truly trusted him then he should honour that. And perhaps he would—she was under his roof, under his protection. She might even be the innocent virgin she would have him believe.

'I did not say you should trust me,' he said, wanting to unsettle her, to pay her back for unsettling him. Her head came up and those wide blue eyes looked into his as though she was inspecting the inside of his soul—always assuming she could find it. 'I simply wanted to set the record straight over that piece of history.'

'Of course.' The intense scrutiny dropped. 'As always, it is for the woman to take care and it is upon the woman that the shame devolves if she is not vigilant enough of her honour. Excuse me, my lord. Mr Havers will be waiting.'

The brush of her silk skirts across his legs as she turned had Quinn gritting his teeth as a sudden stab of lust took him unawares. He pulled open the front door and strode off to the stables, more angry with himself for even troubling about Celina than he was at her plain speaking.

Lina had been watching his profile: the flexible mouth, the strong, straight nose that was almost too long, the thin scar that was visible now the stubble was gone, the hooded green eyes, the elegant whorl of one ear. He had seemed relaxed, as though he was telling her the plot of some novel, not his own story of disillusion, disgrace and sin. She did not believe in his detachment. Quinn Ashley was an excellent actor, but he had to be deeply frustrated by what had just happened—any man would be.

Then he had kissed her fingertips and the scent of him, sandalwood and angry, tense male, had filled her nostrils and she had been unable to snatch her hand away. A more experienced woman would have known how to extricate herself, but she had been left there, gauche and enraptured. When Quinn turned back to face her and she saw the look in his eyes she could see he was not relaxed. Not at all.

I did not say you should trust me. The smile had reached his eyes with those words. A smile and something else, something assessing and male and dangerous. In letting him take her hand, in confessing her trust, she had yielded to him and that had stirred some animal instinct in him.

Idiot, she scolded herself as she tapped on the study door and let herself in. He attracted and fascinated her and that was lethally dangerous. One brush of his lips on her hand and she was disorientated, disconcerted and breathless. It was worse than the wine.

'Miss Haddon.' The lawyer rose to his feet. 'Please, be seated. This should not take long.'

Lina sat down and folded her hands in her lap, trying her best to look like a meek young lady and not a fugitive courtesan. With her hair invisible, her eyebrows and lashes, which were naturally darker, gave the impression that she was a brunette. Surely there would be nothing to spark Mr Havers's suspicions, even if he had read her description in the newspapers?

'Now, if I may have your first names.'

'Lina,' she said, watching him write *Lina Haddon* in careful script across a document.

'And which bank would you wish the money deposited in, Miss Haddon?'

'I do not have a bank account.' Was it against the law to open one in a false name? Perhaps she would need papers to prove who she was. But surely in six months her name would be cleared. Or she would be hanged.

Lina repressed the shudder. 'I must organise something. Might I have an advance of cash?' It would need to be enough to make good her escape if they found her, but not so much that Mr Havers would think it strange. 'Twenty-five pounds would be excellent.'

'I am afraid that the money only becomes available at the end of six months, Miss Haddon.' He made another note. 'But all your costs will be met and that would include a reasonable clothing allowance and pin money.'

'*Oh.*' But she could not leave and find herself a new hiding place without cash in her hand. If she had a thousand pounds, she could hire an investigator, an agent to contact her aunt, a lawyer, flee abroad if necessary; but now, with no money, she must stay here or her aunt would not know where to find her.

And she needed to help Aunt Clara fight Makepeace, she could not just run away and abandon her. 'Of course. I did not quite understand.' She would have to stay here under the protection of a man who might turn out to be no protection at all, but thoroughly dangerous himself. 'Thank you, Mr Havers.'

'Thank *you*, Miss Haddon. Would you be so good as to ask Trimble to come in next?'

Lina delivered the message, then found herself staring rather blankly at the front door, at a loss what to do next. Cook would prepare luncheon and needed no further instruction, the house was as orderly as any that closely resembled a chaotic museum could be, and the thought of hemming yet another worn sheet was intolerable.

On impulse she ran upstairs, changed into stout shoes, found her cloak and told Michael, 'If anyone wants me, I have gone for a walk up to Flagstaff Hill.'

'His lordship says we're to have a guest bedchamber made up for Mr Gregor,' the footman said. 'I'm confused about him, I must confess, Miss Haddon. I thought he was a servant to start with, but he sits down to dinner like a gentleman.'

'I think he likes to tease us,' Lina said, 'to

confound our expectations. Give him the red bedchamber.'

'But that's—'

'The one where we put all the worst examples of the taxidermist's art, including the crocodile. Exactly. It is about time that Mr Gregor realises he is not the only person in this household with a sense of humour.'

It seemed a very long time since she had laughed out loud, not since before Simon Ashley had been found cold in his bed. He had kept her in a ripple of amusement with his dry wit and scurrilous anecdotes, the wicked old man.

She was still smiling when she passed the archway into the stable yard and glanced through it at the sound of voices. Gregor was holding the head of the grey horse she had glimpsed when the men had arrived and Quinn Ashley was walking round it, running his hands down its legs, lifting each hoof in turn. Lina knew nothing about horses, but she knew beauty when she saw it and this animal with its slightly dished face, big dark eyes, long white tail and mane and air of disciplined power was beautiful.

Ashley and Gregor must be checking the animals after their long ride, she supposed, seeing an equally handsome black tied up at the rear of the courtyard with a sturdy bay beside it. She drew back against the arch and watched. The men were talking easily together, dropping a word here and there, hardly troubling to complete their sentences. Lina could remember when it had been like that with her sisters, Bella and Meg. They had been so close that one or two words, a phrase or a smile was enough to share thoughts and feelings.

Where are you? she asked in a silent plea for an answer that never came. *Be safe, please be safe and happy.* If she ever got out of this mess, she would devote her legacy to finding her sisters, she swore, hurrying away from the arch and the sight of the men and their easy, unthinking friendship.

She ran, paused only to open the simple iron gate into the park, then slowed as she followed the overgrown track that climbed up the side of the ridge that separated the park from the sea, sheltering the house within its wooded slopes.

Once carriages would have carried houseguests along this route up to the gazebo on the top where they could survey the sweep of coastline in one direction or the fine parkland in the other. But it had been many years since old Lord Dreycott had entertained houseguests who enjoyed picnics and flirtations in the coppices and the track had dwindled almost to a footpath.

Lina climbed on, only half-aware of the alarmed call of jackdaws and crows, the flash of colour as a jay flew across the path. If—no, *when*—she was cleared of this charge of theft, then what should she do? Aunt Clara had been so good to her it seemed like treachery to think of leaving The Blue Door, but she could hardly spend the rest of her life in a brothel.

Perhaps Clara imagined she would take over and run it one day. Lina could not suppress a wry smile at the thought of a virgin as abbess of a select nunnery. She had heard many of the names for houses of ill repute—school of Venus, vaulting school, smuggling ken, house of civil reception—but *nunnery* was the one that had startled her the most. As well as being an ironic name, it seemed that nuns were a popular male fantasy and The Blue Door had enough habits hanging in its bizarre wardrobe room to equip a small convent.

But she must acknowledge the fact that, however much she loved her aunt and liked the girls, that could never be her life, only a temporary sanctuary, one that could ruin her permanently by association.

Panting slightly, she reached the top of the hill. Set on stout wooden pillars right in front of her was the gazebo, built to add another twenty feet to the vantage point for anyone with enough breath still to climb. Lina lifted her skirts in one hand, took a firm grip on the rickety handrail with the other and mounted the steps.

At the top she went to the seaward side and leaned her elbows on the rail. The wind was fresh up here, bringing the scent of the ocean with it, and she pulled off her snood and hairpins, shaking her hair free so it blew out behind her in the breeze.

No, she could not live in a brothel for ever, nor run one, not with her lack of experience. And she had no intention of acquiring the practical knowledge, not after that hideous experience with Sir Humphrey Tolhurst. The thought of a man paying to touch her, of having to feign pleasure at the act, do whatever he wanted when she did not like or desire him, made her feel sick.

Now, if she could only come out of hiding, she had the resources to find herself a little cottage somewhere while she searched for her sisters. But she would not forget her aunt or the girls at The Blue Door, or look down on them for making the choices that they had. They had been forced into it, just as she had, but unlike her, or even Mama, they would find no escape. She would—

'Why, I have found the little nun at last and she has cast off her wimple.' He moves like a cat, Lina thought, spinning round on the platform to confront Quinn Ashley as he reached the top of the steps.

Then what he had said penetrated. 'How dare you! How dare you call me a nun!' But she had stood still while this man had kissed her fingertips, stood still and quivered with terrified pleasure. The thought of her own perverse weakness only fuelled her anger. Her loose hair settled round her shoulders in a cloud, partly obscuring her sight, and she pushed it back. 'You...libertine, you...'

He took two strides across the platform and caught her wrists in his hands before she could strike him. 'Do you seek to insult me, Celina? You will have to do rather better than that. I will willingly admit to *libertine*. *Rake* as well, for I can see that word forming on those very pretty lips of yours. Come then, let me give you stimulus for your vocabulary.' And he pulled her to him, bent his head and kissed her.

Chapter Five

Celina had never been kissed on the mouth by a man before. Sir Humphrey had been too eager for her to disrobe to worry about preliminaries so she had nothing to compare this kiss with, no expectations of what it would be like. She tried to stay composed, in control, ready to pull free the moment Ashley relaxed his hold, but the shameful reality was that her brain forgot how to work and her limbs how to struggle, the moment his lips pressed against hers.

Whatever she had expected from a kiss, it had not been this totally enveloping sensual experience. Ashley's warm lips moving over hers were disturbing enough in the intimacy of the gesture, but she could taste him as well and she felt the brush of his tongue against the seam of her lips and guessed he wanted her to open her mouth. Stubbornly she managed to keep it closed, even while she inhaled the scent of him mingling with the fresh smells of the spring woodland all around them and the tang of the sea breeze. His body was hot and hard and so much stronger than hers that even struggling seemed pointless. Or was it that his strength was arousing and, shamefully, she did not want to struggle?

Ashley released his hold on her wrists and put one hand in the middle of her back, the other hand raking deep into her loose hair. He growled, a husky sound of appreciation, as he shifted his stance to turn and get his back against the rail and Celina found herself pressed intimately close as his tongue began its assault on her closed lips once again.

She felt so strange. She ached and yearned and trembled and the inner voice that cried *Stop!* was drowned in the roaring of her blood and the hammering of her pulse. Lina parted her lips, felt the thrust of Quinn's tongue. Heat flooded through her at the intimacy of the intrusion and for a moment she could not react. Her body, though, knew what to do; her own tongue moved, tangled with his, the taste of him filled her senses.

He was aroused; she felt him hard and urgent pressing against her. A flutter of alarm brushed against her mind and was drowned in the torrent of new sensation. Ashley's hands moved, one sliding down, urging her against him, the other slipping between their close-pressed bodies to cup her breast.

Long, knowing fingers found the edge of her bodice, slid beneath it to find the tight-puckered nipple. A stab of fire lanced from his fingertips to her belly, terrifying in its effect.

She was aware, hazily, that in a moment she would be beyond rational thought, utterly at the mercy of her own untutored sensuality and Ashley's skilful seduction. *We were so innocent...* Her aunt's words seemed to ring in her ears. *Innocent, seduced, ruined.*

No, stop this. Now. He thinks I have yielded, she thought, then closed her teeth hard, released them as she felt his recoil, pushed out of his arms and was away down the steps, heedless of the slippery surface and the ancient rail.

She was almost at the bottom when she lost her footing and pitched down the final six steps, bumping painfully on the sharp wooden edges to land in an undignified, bruised heap on the ground. It hurt enough to bring tears to her eyes, but she was not going to dissolve into sobs in front of him, she thought fiercely, drawing in gasps of breath while she tried to work out if anything was broken.

Ashley came down the stairs after her with even

more reckless haste, two at a time, and vaulted over her huddled body at the bottom, kicking up the deep leaf mould as he landed. 'Hell, woman, of all the stupid things to do! These stairs are lethal. Don't move.' He knelt beside her. 'Don't move *anything*. Where does it hurt?'

'I have been up and down those steps a dozen times,' Lina retorted, indignation taking her mind off her bruises, and almost off the clamouring demands of her body. He was so close. 'They are only dangerous if one is running away from a libertine! This is all your fault.'

'There was no need to run—a simple *no* would have sufficed. Does that hurt?' He took hold of her right ankle, his big hand gentle as it encircled the slender bones.

'Yes,' she snapped. 'Everything hurts. And take your hands off my…my nether limb. You would not take any notice of *no*, I have no doubt of that! A sledgehammer would be required to discourage you.'

He sat back on his heels and grinned, her anger seeming to wash right over his head. To her relief he did not seem inclined to take advantage of the fact she was sprawled on the ground in front of him, her petticoats up to her knees and her ankle still in his grasp. A minute ago she had been melting in his arms... She twitched her skirts down as he said, 'It is a very charming *nether limb*, but I really do need to check.'

He appeared to have absolutely no shame for what he had just done as he undid her laces and eased off the boot, then the other one. 'Now, can you wriggle your toes? Good. Circle your ankle. Now your hands—fingers, wrists. There, nothing broken.' He slipped her boots back on and laced them, then got to his feet and held out his hands. 'Up you come. What was that?' he asked, his arm coming round her when she gave a yelp of pain.

'My ribs are bruised. I bounced on those steps all the way down,' Celina said resentfully. 'And my bu... My pos... I landed with a thud.'

'I see. I had better carry you back.' Ashley stooped and swept her up before she could protest. 'And do not struggle or I might drop you and then you would land on your bu... On whatever unmentionable part it was you have just bruised so painfully.'

Lina found herself settled against his chest with nothing to do with her right arm but wrap it around his neck. In sensation novels the heroine, when swept into the hero's masterful arms, was prey to a multitude of sensations, most of them described as fluttering, swooning or joyful.

This did not happen when one was bruised, embarrassed and angry and the man doing the masterful sweeping up was not the clean-cut hero rushing to the heroine's rescue, but quite obviously the villain of the piece, with libertine tendencies lurking behind a thin veneer of humour and charm.

'This is entirely your responsibility, my lord,' she snapped, so close to his ear that he flinched. There was a mark in the lobe—it was pierced for an earring, she realised, shocked. At least he had the decency not to sport it in English society. As a first experience of a kiss, a first romantic encounter, this was not at all what she had dreamed of. It had been anything but tender; in fact, it had been shamefully disturbing and almost violently arousing.

'How so? I did not tell you to throw yourself down those stairs.'

'I was escaping from your assault.'

'You assaulted me,' he protested. 'You bit me.'

'You kissed me first.'

'I was *trying* to kiss you,' Ashley corrected. 'And it was very pleasant—up to a point.' He was grinning, the wretch. 'And you tried to hit me.'

'And that did not tell you anything about my wishes in the matter?' Lina demanded. *I should be alarmed. I could have been ravished just now.*

Or would even the most hardened rake attempt seduction on top of a windswept look-out deep in the woods? It had seemed like seduction just now. It had seemed like madness.

'I was coming to the conclusion that we were not entirely of one mind—and then you opened those very lovely lips and I was lost. For a few seconds I was completely off guard.'

It was difficult not to smile back. But of course, this sort of disarming behaviour was probably standard tactics for a predatory rake. 'Lord Dreycott,' Lina said with all the severity of which she was capable—which, to be frank, she knew was not much, 'you should not have tried to kiss me in the first place.'

If he only looked like Sir Humphrey Tolhurst or one of the other habitués of The Blue Door, then she would be terrified of him. Because this man was handsome and charming and made her laugh, and left her feeling as though her bones were melting along with her will-power, he was more dangerous than they were, not less. The devil, as Papa was fond of saying, wore a pretty face when he was tempting the unwary sinner.

'I know. But you were so utterly irresistible. I was intrigued enough by the nun, but when she was sud-

denly a furious Valkyrie, eyes flashing, that mane
of blonde hair flying in the breeze, I was lost.'

'What is a Valkyrie?' Lina asked, suspicious
that it was another cant term for a loose woman.
Ashley began to make his way down the steep path,
his muscles moving in intriguing and disturbing
ways.

'A Norse female horsewoman who carries the
dead warriors back to Valhalla, the home of the
gods, from the battlefield. But never mind Norse
legend—why were you so furious when I called
you a nun?'

'Because…' Lina found explaining was beyond
her. 'Why did you?'

'The plain gowns, the prim necklines, the scraped-
back hair, the downcast eyes.' He turned his head
a little to see her face. His own was amused, but
she could read the speculation in his eyes. 'A perfect little nun. I assume it was your idea to make
yourself look older than you are and more suitable
as a housekeeper.'

'Oh.' So, he had seen right through that! 'I did
think it was more appropriate. And after your great-
uncle died and we were in mourning, black was
the only proper colour.' She had thrown gowns
into her portmanteaux almost at random when she
had fled. One had fortunately been black, another

a soft blue grey and the third plain white, so with dye, the coloured trimmings removed and the necklines raised with the judicious use of ribbons and muslin, she had sufficient sombre gowns to be respectable.

'Great-Uncle Simon would not want mourning,' Ashley said with decision. His foot slipped, but with a twist he had his balance back, despite the burden in his arms. He was strong, Lina realised, strong and fit and hard. She closed her eyes for a moment and let her head rest on his shoulder before she had the will-power to lift it again. 'In fact, I think I will forbid it to the entire household. No, you may get out your pretty gowns again.'

'I have just dyed them all black,' Lina said, pulling herself together and opening her eyes again. It was not true, she had three more gowns untouched, but she was not producing those, all chosen with the help of Aunt Clara. Quinn Ashley would like them far too well, she was sure.

'Buy some more,' he said carelessly. 'You can afford to now.'

'Yes, I suppose I can. Mr Havers told me I may have pin money. But in any case, I am the housekeeper.'

'Do I need a housekeeper?' he asked. 'Can you

not just act as the mistress of the house and order
the servants to do what is necessary?'

Mistress of the house? There were so many layers
of innuendo and meaning in that phrase that Lina
could feel herself blushing. 'Please, my lord, put
me down?' Lina asked as they reached the edge
of the wood and level ground. 'I would be most
embarrassed if the staff saw me like this.' He set
her on her feet at once. It jarred her bruises, but
she bit back the exclamation of discomfort in case
he scooped her up once more. 'If I had no work to
do, then I would feel I was being a parasite, living
off your charity.'

He was still holding her, one big hand cupping
each elbow, standing far too close. His breathing,
she realised with a thrill of awareness, was very
slightly uneven. The effort of carrying her? She
doubted it, he was very fit. No, he was still aroused
by their encounter.

'You will be living off Simon's legacy. I am dis-
missing you as housekeeper, but you may retain
your post as companion, if you like.' He began to
stroll back towards the house and Lina, trying not
to hobble, walked beside him.

'To whom?'

'To me when I am here. I will be lonely with
none of the local gentry prepared to receive me.'

He made no attempt to try to sound either lonely or pathetic.

'But Gregor is here.'

'He is going back to London once we have sorted some of the books and papers. He will open up the town houses, hire servants, talk to our business agents.'

'I thought you never came to England,' Lina queried. 'How do you—?'

'That does not prevent me investing or buying property in this country. I have agents and lawyers and customers here. I shall send the library from here to my house in Mayfair once I secure it.' She glanced up at his face to find it suddenly serious, introspective. 'I expect to spend more time in London in future—at the libraries, the British Museum, the learned societies.'

'But are you not a traveller?'

'I am also a writer. It is time I wrote more, spoke more at the societies, or I will end up like my great-uncle, having to coerce someone into finishing my work after my death.'

'You are a scholar, in effect,' Lina said. She was surprised, she realised; despite what Trimble had said, she had not taken his scholarship seriously. 'But I thought you a—'

'Libertine? I am an adventurer, I admit. I am also

a traveller and a trader. How very inconsiderate of me to wear so many labels. But we are all multi-faceted, are we not? You seem meek and mild and modest and yet you spit like a hellcat when roused. And you kiss—' They had reached the stable yard again and he stopped, just past the archway. 'And you did not answer my question. Why so furious at being called a nun?'

'Because—' She could feel herself blushing again. 'Because of the cant use of nunnery and nun,' she blurted out and, despite her aching bruises, almost ran from him round the corner and through the service entrance to the house.

'Cant?' Quinn stared after Celina. Admittedly he had been out of the country for a long time, but when he was last here the only cant meaning for nunnery was brothel. He had been away from England far too long, that was certain, if young ladies understood the meaning of argot like that. He turned on his heel and went back into the yard where Gregor was lounging on a mounting block in conversation with the head groom.

'Good day, your lordship.' The man—Jenks, he remembered—touched his forelock. 'I was just telling this gentleman about his late lordship's hunters. Sad day when he decided to sell them, that was.

You've a fine pair of riding horses, my lord. Arab blood, I can see.'

'Yes, out of an English hunter mare for size by an Arab stallion for endurance. They are brothers. Tell me, Jenks, I have been coming to the conclusion that I have been away from England so long I am forgetting the language—what cant uses for nun or nunnery are there?'

The man looked incredulous, then grinned. 'Well, my lord, only meaning I know is for an academy, if you know what I mean, and its young ladies. A cony warren, my lord.'

'A brothel, in effect? Yes, that was my understanding also.' So that explained the fury, but it did not explain why a respectable young lady would know what it meant. Gregor was obviously keeping a straight face at the cost of painful self-control. 'Thank you, Jenks. I have indeed been away too long.'

'And you can stop looking like that,' he said to Gregor once they were out of earshot of the groom. 'I was perfectly aware of *that* meaning, I was simply wondering if there was another I did not know.'

'It is a good word for a brothel,' Gregor said, seriously. 'Your English is amusing, I find. Perhaps I will seek one out when I am in London and perform my devotions with the pretty nuns. A pity you are in disgrace, my friend, or you could give me introductions and I could chase the society ladies as well.'

'It will take a little while. I can secure invitations around the edges of society to begin with,' Quinn said. 'And then I move in.' He had given this some thought during the long journey back to England.

There had been time to plot his reinstatement into the *ton*, time to think about how uncomfortable he could make those who had tricked and condemned him and whose scheming had left his great-uncle to a lonely old age for the sin of defending him. He had not realised until that last letter just how isolated the old man had become, and guilt at his own absence did nothing to lessen his anger.

'We could have some fun amongst the less respectable, more dashing, ladies.'

'Almack's?' Gregor asked hopefully. 'I have heard of Almack's. Many pretty virgins. Rich ones, also.'

'Almack's would not let either of us through the doors,' Quinn assured him. 'But I would pay a good sum to see you there, a big bad wolf amidst the lambs.' No, they would not admit either of them... yet. But the new Lord Dreycott with his reputation as a traveller and scholar could insinuate himself into the world of the men of learning, many of whom were influential members of society. If he played his cards right, he could be accepted back almost before those who recalled the old scandal were aware of his presence. Then he must rely on his wits and his money to stay within the charmed inner circle while having his pleasure with its womenfolk and his revenge on its men.

It would be amusing. The prodigal returns, far from penitent and reformed, but possessing now all the wickedness he was unjustly expelled for in the first place.

He had not lied to Celina; he did intend to spend more time in London in scholarly pursuits, in writing, in the libraries, at lectures, about his business interests. But he had no intention of skulking around pretending to be shamed by a ten-year-old scandal. He was not at all embarrassed, merely coldly determined to enjoy every facet of London life, and that included, when he was in the mood, the world of the *ton*.

And this time, if any wives or daughters of the aristocracy threw themselves at his head, he would have not the slightest scruple about taking everything that they offered. A momentary stab of self-disgust caught him off balance. Once he had been the perfect young English gentleman:

gallant, virtuous, scrupulous. *Fool*, he thought. *Look where that got you.* Innocence once lost was lost for ever—he was what he had become, the product of hard choices and sharp disillusion.

But meanwhile he had no intention of trying to ingratiate himself with minor Norfolk society. He had Great-Uncle Simon's memoirs to complete, the library and papers to sort out and the intriguing and mysterious Miss Haddon to... To what? Quinn asked himself as he went upstairs to wash before a belated luncheon. That all depended what she really was. Innocent or something else?

That kiss on the lookout platform high in the trees had been pleasurable, but its ending had not just been frustrating and painful, it had also been confusing. He ran his tongue between his lips as he made himself think of it analytically, conscious that the memory of Celina's hot mouth, her soft body, the vicious little nip of her teeth, was as arousing as it was unsatisfying.

She had not reacted like a shocked and sheltered virgin, he concluded, ignoring the heaviness in his groin as he washed in cold water. She had resisted for a moment, but he thought that was surprise and anger. There had been an awareness there, a flare of passion and a calculating cunning to feign surrender so she could lure him in, bite and escape.

She had been angry with him, unmistakably, but she had also let him carry her, had talked to him calmly and with interest.

Last night she had seemed to get tipsy and to flirt—was that a ploy, or innocence out of its depth?

No, the mystery of Celina Haddon was most definitely still as intriguing as ever. Quinn raked his hands through his hair, caught sight of himself in the mirror and grinned. It seemed that it would be necessary to kiss Miss Haddon again if he wanted to find out more.

'You look very pleased with yourself,' Gregor remarked, emerging from a door a little further along the corridor as Quinn shut his own behind him. 'Have you seen the room your little virgin has put me in now?'

'She is not my little anything, at the moment,' Quinn said, as he looked past the Russian into the room behind. 'Hades, is that a museum?' The bed was stranded in the midst of a veritable zoo of immobile creatures of every variety of feather, fur and scales.

'I think so.' Gregor kicked a stuffed alligator with one booted foot. 'She has a sense of humour, Miss Celina.'

'She is punishing you for teasing the household,' Quinn observed. 'Choose another room.'

'And have her think she has frightened me with her creatures?' The other man grinned. 'No, I will thank her lavishly. Perhaps she would like to be entertained in here. She might find it…exciting.'

'Hands off.' Quinn spoke mildly, but Gregor made the fencer's signal of surrender.

'I would not dream of poaching in my lord's hunting grounds.'

'Any more of that *my lord* nonsense and I'll crack your thick skull,' Quinn retorted as they made for the head of the stairs. 'And I am not hunting.'

Liar, he thought as they made their way into the dining room to find Celina seated at the table, her hair twisted up into a simple knot at the back of her head. A few tendrils escaped and curled at her temples and nape. The colour was high in her cheeks and she met his eyes with wary defiance in her own. *Oh, yes, I am hunting and she knows it. But what is my quarry? A little doe or a cunning feline? That is the question.*

Chapter Six

As Lina had predicted, the lawyer was followed next day by first Dr Massingbird, the physician, then Mr Armstrong from the bank and finally the Reverend Perrin, looking, as Michael the footman observed after he had shown him to the study, as though he had sat on a poker.

None of them had required a summons. Doctor Massingbird seemed more than happy to call upon a gentleman who offered him a most excellent Amontillado and could compare notes on the Iberian Peninsula where he had once been an army doctor, but Mr Armstrong had the air of a man who knew he must do his duty by his bank and the vicar looked ready to perform an exorcism when he was shown in.

Quinn had not been exaggerating his reputation in the neighbourhood, she realised. She also realised she was thinking of him not as Lord Dreycott, nor even Ashley, but most improperly simply as *Quinn*. She had been kissed by the man, she told herself, and that certainly argued a degree of intimate acquaintance that explained it, even if it did not excuse it.

She kept finding excuses to pass through the hall and keep an eye on the study door, waiting with bated breath for either the vicar to stalk out of the presence of sin in high dudgeon, as her father most certainly would, or for Quinn to explode with anger after receiving a lecture on his dissolute ways.

Neither occurred.

She was arranging flowers in a vase on the hall table when the vicar finally emerged, looking slightly less rigid than when he had arrived. 'Mr Perrin.' She dropped a neat curtsy, her hands full of evergreen stems.

'Miss Haddon. I trust we will see you in church on Sunday as usual?'

'Certainly, sir.' She had attended every Sunday since her arrival, the rhythms of a country Sunday curiously soothing, even though she had been so unhappy in her own village and old Lord Dreycott had flatly refused to accompany her.

The vicar smiled at her and nodded approvingly. 'Excellent. Miss Haddon, do you have a respectable female to bear you company now circumstances here have changed?'

'Mrs Bishop, sir.'

'Hmm. A good woman, but I would wish you had a *lady* in residence.'

'Thank you for your concern, but I feel quite... comfortable with the present circumstances, sir.'

That was hardly true, but advertising for some respectable companion was too fraught with dangers to be contemplated. 'Should I need the benefit of female guidance, I am sure I might call upon Miss Perrin's advice.' The vicar's sister, small, timid, with a perpetually red nose and the air of anxious piety, would hardly be much protection against a hardened rake, but the thought seemed to please the vicar.

'Of course you may, Miss Haddon. Perhaps you would care to join the Ladies' Hassock Sewing Circle?'

'I would love to; however, my needlepoint is sadly clumsy.' It was excellent, in fact, but Lina had sewn far too many hassocks for her father's church in Martinsdene to want to start again now.

Trimble produced the vicar's wide-brimmed hat, his gloves and cane and ushered him out of the door, leaving Lina to reflect that they had now received all the calls they were likely to.

'Would the Ladies' Hassock Sewing Circle not be amusing?' The study door swung open to reveal Quinn lounging against the jamb.

'You were listening at the keyhole,' Lina said severely, disguising the fact that her hands had become suddenly shaky by jamming foliage into the back of the vase.

'Of course. Think of the gossip you would pick up at the sewing circle.'

'I never want to sew another hassock as long as I live,' she said vehemently, then could have kicked herself as speculation came into the green eyes. 'My aunt is very devout,' she explained, crossing her fingers in the folds of her skirt before sweeping the plant trimmings into her trug and adjusting the vase.

'There is no need to hurry off, Celina. I am unlikely to ravish you on the hard hall floor.'

'Or anywhere, my lord, so long as I have a weapon in my hand,' she retorted, adding the trimming knife to the trug.

'Am I not forgiven?' Quinn had not seen fit to have his hair cut, nor to adopt a more formal style of dress in anticipation of his callers. Lina wondered whether he was aware of how well the buckskin breeches and high boots, the white of his unstarched linen and the relaxed fit of the tailcoat over broad shoulders, suited him. Probably very aware, she concluded, just as he knew how spectacular he looked in his Oriental evening clothes. But it was not vanity, she suspected, but quite deliberate manipulation of those around him.

Today he wanted to make the point that he was a country gentleman at ease in his home and, while courteous to his visitors, not in any way concerned to impress them. *Take me as you find me*, he seemed to be saying. *I am Dreycott now.*

'Are you asking my pardon, my lord? If you are sorry, then of course I forgive you.'

'But I am not sorry,' Quinn said softly. 'Only that it was a less-than-satisfactory experience for both of us.'

'If you are not repentant, then you cannot hope for forgiveness.' *Now I sound like Papa!*

'I am reproved, Celina.' The green eyes mocked her, putting the lie to his words. 'And how are your bruises today? And the part you sat upon so hard?'

'My bruises are multi-coloured and I am somewhat stiff, my lord.' Lina put her arm through the handle of the trug. 'If you will excuse me, I have the vases to do in the dining room.'

'Why have I become *my lord* again?' Quinn

asked. He straightened up and stood, with one hand on the door jamb, looking at her steadily.

Lina hoped she was not blushing. 'I find it hard to speak to you in any other way after yesterday.'

'So your tongue becomes formal, to act as a barrier,' he said. 'And how do you think of me, I wonder?' Now she *was* blushing and he had seen it and that wicked smile was creasing the corners of his eyes and twitching at his mouth. 'As Quinn now, perhaps?'

The lessons in flirtation came to her aid. Lina lowered her lashes, fluttered her free hand and said demurely, 'I could not possible say...my lord.'

As she hoped, he thought she was laughing at him and not being serious. The grin became a smile and he shook his head at her. 'The vicar thinks you should have a chaperon. He obviously considers this a house of sin.'

'He enquired if I had one and I told him that Mrs Bishop was quite sufficient, as you will know as you were listening at the door. And the *house* is not sinful, my lord.' With that she stepped into the dining room and shut the door behind her. Would he come in? No, she heard booted steps on the marble heading for the front door.

Lina stood and stared at the empty vase set ready for her flowers. She was enjoying her encounters with Quinn, she realised. She liked his frankness, his teasing, the lack of hypocrisy and cant, even as she was wary of him and frightened of her own reaction to his dangerous charm. The *frisson* of sensual awareness that quivered through her at the thought or sight of him was predictable, she told herself. She was so inexperienced with the opposite sex that any handsome man paying her that sort of attention would produce the same effect.

Quinn was, she could see clearly, the first adult male she had ever been so close to other than her father, and he happened to be an attractive, virile, intelligent, charming, unscrupulous male into the bargain. If temptation was made flesh it would probably be called Quinn Ashley.

It was very fortunate that she had observed the consequences for a woman who fell into sin at first hand. Most of the girls working at The Blue Door had started their journey to the brothel with seduction at the hands of a sweetheart—just as Mama had. A briar thorn stuck in her thumb and she sucked it, wincing at the metallic taste of blood. Papa would turn that into a sermon—the apparently innocent loveliness of the flower hiding pain and danger. But she did not need a preacher to warn her that she was flirting with peril.

Celina began to work on the arrangement,

straightening her bruised back as though to stiffen her resolve. Quinn Ashley was too much temptation even for an experienced society lady, let alone her. She must avoid him whenever possible.

Lina succeeded in staying out of Quinn's way most effectively. She appeared at luncheon and dinner, made unexceptional conversation, refused to notice double-edged or teasing remarks and took her walks when she was certain that he and Gregor were shut up in the library.

Long trestle tables had been set up where the men were laying out and sorting papers as they retrieved them from all over the house. It seemed strange that the wicked Lord Dreycott could so immerse himself in scholarly pursuits. He ought to spend his time with his horses, his guns, his brandy and his cards, she thought resentfully, then she could categorise him very neatly.

For four days after that encounter in the gazebo life at Dreycott Park fell into a routine so disciplined and predictable that Lina felt sometimes that she had dreamed the demanding pressure of Quinn's lips on hers, the strength of his arms, the heat of his mouth. She was living, it seemed, with a gentleman scholar and his assistant.

In the morning after breakfast, during which a

large amount of post appeared, he and Gregor rode out or walked or exercised. They went into the long barn with rapiers and, according to Jenks, practised swordsmanship exhaustively. They wrestled and fought, attracting an audience of all the male staff, which drove the women of the household to exasperated nagging when none of the heavy work was done.

Then the copper was emptied to fill the marble bath and following luncheon they disappeared into the library. After dinner Quinn went to the study to read through his uncle's work on the memoirs and make notes on how to complete them while Gregor continued to search through cupboards and shelves for paperwork. When they had the papers sorted, Quinn explained, they would begin on the books, creating a brief catalogue as they boxed them up.

The fifth day was Sunday. Lina put on her usual costume for attending church since she had arrived at Dreycott Park, the once-white gown that had been dyed to a soft grey, tied with a deep amethyst ribbon under the bosom. With white cuffs and narrow white lace at the neckline it looked sombre yet attractive, she thought, as she pinned up her hair into a complex plaited twist that her aunt had taught her. Simple pearl stud earrings, her gold cross, plain black-kid ankle boots and a bonnet trimmed with more of the amethyst ribbon completed the ensemble.

She picked up her prayer book and went down to breakfast. It was proper to join the men in the small dining room, she decided, instead of taking her tea and toast in the kitchen as usual.

They stood up as she came in. 'Good morning. It is a lovely day, is it not?' Then she saw that they were both clad in immaculate and conventional tailcoats, pantaloons and Hessian boots—and that they were both staring at her.

'Celina, good morning. We are all dressed for church, I see.'

So that was what they were staring at. This was the first time she had worn her Sunday best. 'You are coming to church, too?' It had never occurred to her that they might; Gregor because she assumed he was not of the Protestant faith, Quinn because she found it hard to visualise him sitting attentively through a sermon with the eyes of the entire parish on him, speculating about his past and present sins.

'We make a point of attending the religious rites of whatever community we find ourselves in,' Quinn said. 'Unless, of course, non-believers are unwelcome, which they are in some parts of the world. Religious observance is usually of great significance to a tribe,' he added as though they were discussing diet or clothes.

'You are not a believer, then?' Lina asked, taken aback at the concept of the parishioners as a tribe to be studied. She did not think she had ever met someone of an atheistical persuasion before.

'I am a sceptic. Certainly my great-uncle's spirit has not visited to inform me that we were both wrong and I should repent immediately.'

It was a shocking thing to say, but the image he conjured up of old Simon's spectre appearing in the bedchamber with dire warnings about repentance while Quinn sat bolt upright in bed in alarm almost made her laugh out loud. Lina fought to keep a straight face. 'It is a charming church and Mr Perrin delivers an interesting sermon.' Despite his dry appearance, the vicar had a mild sense of humour and a genuine concern for his flock which she admired.

'Is there a box pew for the Park?'

'No. We—I mean *you*—have a pew set aside, but all of them are rather charming medieval benches with carved ends, not enclosed ones.' *And the congregation will have an uninterrupted view of their shocking new lord of the manor*, she thought, wondering if that had prompted his question. He did not appear alarmed at the prospect.

Trimble came in with a newspaper on a salver. 'A newspaper at last, my lord. Friday's *Morning Chronicle* has only just arrived from London. What has happened to *The Times* I regret I cannot say— some inefficiency at the receiving office, I have no doubt. I will enquire. I trust those two papers will be suitable?'

'Eminently, thank you, Trimble.'

Lina stared at the folded paper beside Quinn's plate. If it had been *The Times* she would not have worried: sensational crimes several weeks old would not feature there. But the *Chronicle* always ran crime stories, and followed them up whenever a titillating snippet came out; there was a chance that something about the fugitive Celina Shelley would be in there.

Quinn showed no inclination to look at the paper yet and Gregor scarcely glanced at it. 'I wonder… might I see the paper for a moment? I…there is an advertisement I would like to find if it is in that issue.'

'Of course.' Quinn handed it across and went back to his gammon and eggs.

The front page was all advertisements as usual. She made a show of skimming past notices about artificial teeth, anatomical stays, the Benevolent Society of St Patrick's annual general meeting, Essence of Coltsfoot for coughs and several notices of lotteries. The inside two pages were without notices, but a glance showed her it was all international and court news. The back page, however, was full of snippets. Fire at Kentish Town…protest against threshing machines…bizarre accident to a pedestrian in Newcastle…the Tolhurst Sapphire.

There was only an inch, but to Lina's eyes it seemed to be printed in red ink. *Sir George Tolhurst, lately succeeded as baronet after the tragic death of his father, Sir Humphrey Tolhurst, has offered a reward of one hundred guineas for information leading to the capture of Miss Celina Shelley, a young woman of dubious character, who removed the famous Tolhurst Sapphire from the finger of the expiring baronet after inveigling herself into his Duke Street house. Miss Shelley, a well-favoured and genteel-seeming young female, is of middling stature with long straight yellow hair and blue eyes.*

She laid the *Chronicle* down beside her plate, the blood loud in her ears as she fought down the panicky instinct to grab the paper and flee.

'More coffee?' She picked up the pot, newly re-filled by Michael, and moved it towards Quinn's cup. 'Oh! Ouch!' She jerked, the coffee splashed out and on to the folded paper. 'I am sorry.' Quinn reached out and took the pot from her hands. 'It was so heavy and my arm is still sore from falling the other day. Oh, dear, your newspaper!' Lina took her napkin and dabbed fiercely at the coffee stain, the soft newsprint disintegrating under the assault. 'Now I've made it worse!'

'Allow me, Miss Haddon.' Trimble removed the paper and held it up. 'It will dry by the range, my lord. There is now a hole, but it can be made readable, at least.'

'Have you scalded yourself?' Quinn sounded more concerned about her welfare than the state of his newspaper. He certainly did not seem suspicious. But why should he be? It was only her own awareness of danger that made the item seem to leap from the paper at her. 'No? But those bruises are still bad? Gregor, you must lend Celina your pot of bear fat. A sovereign remedy, I understand.'

'Thank you, but arnica is perfectly adequate.' She smiled at Gregor, not wanting to offend, although she suspected he had probably killed the animal in question himself with his bare hands. The restrained elegance of formal morning wear made him look, if anything, larger and more forbidding than usual. 'We should be going soon,' she added with a glance at the clock. 'The carriage will be at the door.'

Jenks had sent round the barouche with the top down so they could enjoy the sunny weather. With the betraying newspaper announcement safely illegible her mood lifted and Lina wished she had a parasol to twirl. Instead, she allowed herself to be handed into the forward-facing seat opposite the two men and prepared to enjoy the treat of a drive through the park to Upper Cleybourne church.

The bells were ringing, the cracked tenor that had so annoyed Simon spoiling the joyous peel. 'Listen,' she said, 'that's the bell the legacy will replace.' They came out of the gates and pulled up on the little green outside the church. It was already thronged with parishioners chatting in the sunshine and heads turned as the Dreycott barouche came to a halt.

Lina descended, preoccupied with sorting out reticule and prayer book and smoothing down her skirts. Then the change in the sound penetrated and she looked up. All around the little groups were falling silent as they stared and the faces that watched them were set and unwelcoming.

So, the gossip mills have been working to grind out all the old history and they've made up their minds, have they? she thought. There were people with whom she had thought herself on cordial terms, with whom she expected to exchange smiles and greetings and village news, who were staring now. They froze her with the same disapproval they directed at the men—it was much worse than she had feared.

We'll see about that, Lina thought. Inside she quailed—disapproval had always shrivelled her soul—but now she lifted her chin, set her shoulders back and made herself walk up to Mr and Mrs Willets and their family.

Mrs Willets had been amiable when Lina stepped off the stagecoach in Sheringham, tired and confused. Lina had fallen into conversation with the Willets's new governess, who was being met by Mrs Willets in their carriage, and, after a whispered word from Miss Greggs, the matron had been happy to take up Lord Dreycott's guest. Now the squire managed an uneasy smile of greeting, his wife looked daggers and their daughters edged behind their father.

'Good morning,' Lina said brightly. 'Have you met Lord Dreycott yet? He is most anxious that his late uncle's legacy to restore the cracked bell is dealt with urgently. Won't it be a joy to have a musical peal?'

'Er, no.' Mr Willets looked harassed. 'I mean,

yes, it will. Good morning, my lord.' He bowed and Quinn inclined his head in response.

'Mr Willets. Madam. May I introduce Mr Vasiliev?'

Gregor bowed, Mrs Willets glared at Lina, the girls giggled. Lina gritted her teeth into a smile and swept on to the next group with much the same result: wary politeness from the men, thinly veiled hostility from the women and no attempt to introduce daughters.

By the time she reached the church door she was seething and her nervousness had become lost in her anger for Quinn. How could they be so rude and unwelcoming to a man they had never met, just on the basis of ancient gossip?

Perhaps he hasn't noticed, she thought. *Perhaps he thinks this is just typical English village society.* Then as she reached the porch she turned and saw Quinn's face. He was smiling, but his eyes were like chips of green ice.

Chapter Seven

Well, no-one has actually spat on my boots yet, Quinn conceded as he walked up the path in Celina's wake. It was like following a small, very fierce frigate, wheeling to turn its guns on any enemy shipping it passed. He was touched by her anger on his behalf but he had expected, and to an extent merited, this reception. *She* did not deserve to be treated like this by those sanctimonious prigs who had shunned his uncle. He certainly did not want to have her fall out with her acquaintance over him and he was not happy about it.

He caught up with her in the porch and bent to murmur in her ear, 'Not so fierce!'

'I had not expected them to be like this,' she whispered back. 'I am so sorry. They are decent people—I thought.' She was not normally so confrontational, he sensed. If asked, he would have said her instinct was to avoid trouble, not face it. It was touching that she was so strong in his defence, like a kitten defending a mastiff, tiny claws out, tail bristling.

'And they think I am *not* decent. Most perceptive of them,' he said and was taken aback by the look of reproof she flashed him.

'Do not say that! They must respect you, even if they do not like you. You have responsibilities here—these are your people now.'

'Not for long,' he retorted. 'I'll be as pleased to get rid of them as they will be to get shot of me.' He showed his teeth in what should have been a smile and the verger who was hastening forward to escort them to their pew flinched visibly.

'Good morning, Mr Bavin,' Lina said. She stepped towards the man and Quinn saw him relax. 'How is the rheumatism this morning? You look very sprightly, if I may say so.'

She is good with people, Quinn thought as the verger positively beamed.

'Much better, thanks to the tincture you sent down, Miss Haddon. Done me the world of good, it has.' He preceded them down the aisle and stood to one side while they filed into the front right-hand pew. Quinn could feel the tingle in the back of his neck that told him he was being watched as the congregation came in behind them. Let them stare if it amused them.

Celina was on her knees, head bent, hands folded. He watched her from the corner of his eye; so, she had taken on the duties of the lady of the house, looking after the local sick. Her aunt had been pious, she said. Was that where she had acquired her instinct for parish works?

He sat back in the hard pew, Gregor silent beside him, and thought about the incident at breakfast with the newspaper and the coffee. An accident? But Celina was not clumsy; he watched her more closely than he hoped she realised and she moved with a natural grace. Nor had she been favouring that arm and he did not believe it hurt her so much she could not control a coffee pot.

The organ wheezed into life and the congregation rose, searching their books for the first hymn. Quinn had no intention of singing, but he realised Celina was fumbling with her hymnal. Her hands were unsteady. *Damn it*, he thought, it was nerves about coming to church that had made her shaky at breakfast and now, with her fears about their reception confirmed, she was trembling.

Quinn reached out, removed the hymn book from her unresisting fingers, glanced up at the board hanging on the pillar and turned to the right number. 'There you are.'

She shot him a grateful smile and began to sing in a clear contralto while Quinn tried to recall the last time he had stood in an English church finding hymns for a lady. It must have been that Sunday when Angela Hunton, the Earl of Sheringham's eldest daughter, the young lady with whom he had believed himself deeply in love, proposed that they anticipate the marriage bed by making love in the summer house.

It was probably the first—and last—time that innocence and romantic idealism had saved his skin. If he had not refused, shocked to the core at the very suggestion that he sully the purity of the lady he worshipped, then he would now be married to a promiscuous little liar and bringing up another man's child.

Beside him Gregor, having heard the first verse through, was joining in with the singing, his rumbling bass putting up a good fight with the organ. Celina glanced across in surprise, caught Quinn's eye and bit her lip to suppress a smile. He smiled back and bent to pick up her prayer book to find the place in that for her.

That kiss in the gazebo had been a mistake in timing, if nothing else, he concluded. An armful of

Miss Haddon had been delightful and the taste of those lips gave him moments of pleasurable recollection even days later, but he had handled it badly. He had not understood her, and, he was all too aware, he still did not.

In his experience women fell into four categories, so far as carnal pleasure went: the professionals; married women and widows who were more than willing to be persuaded to share their beds; respectable married women and widows who needed more subtle persuasion; servants and innocent young ladies who were most certainly neither fair game nor satisfying flirts.

The hymn ended and they sat. Celina took the prayer book from him with a murmured, 'Thank you.' Their fingers tangled for a moment and Quinn made no effort to remove his hand, enjoying the feeling of Celina's slim fingers enmeshed with his. She retrieved hand and prayer book and faced the front, her cheeks pink. She had stopped shaking, he noticed.

Which of his categories did Celina Haddon fit into? Was she a fallen woman making a very good attempt at an appearance of virtue? A married woman or widow—virtuous or otherwise—in hiding for some reason? He found he was suspicious of this aunt who was so vaguely unable to look after her. Or perhaps she was exactly what she purported to be, a respectable innocent. But if an innocent, she was certainly an unusual one who knew slang terms for brothels, who melted into his arms, who had so many of the little tricks of an accomplished flirt.

The Reverend Perrin's sermon was, as Celina had promised, intelligent and even mildly witty in a dry kind of way. But their reception as they emerged into the sunlight again was not noticeably improved by the congregation's spiritual experience. Shoulders were turned, people they had not met on their way in walked away as though to ensure they did not have to speak.

Gregor, as he always did when he thought Quinn was threatened in some way, moved in very close behind them, making Celina glance over her shoulder. If you were not used to him, it must be like being followed by a large bear, Quinn thought. He was even growling, although Quinn doubted he realised it.

'It is all right, Gregor,' he said. 'The peasants are not about to rise up and attempt to slaughter us with pitchforks and pruning knives.'

The Russian said something and Celina whispered, 'What was that?'

'An unrepeatable slur on the parentage of everyone

here, involving an unnatural act and a donkey.' He watched to see if he had shocked her, but she only bit her lip again and ducked her head to hide the smile.

'That was dreadful,' Celina declared once the carriage was moving again. 'You would think that on a Sunday at least basic good manners would prevail!'

'The Earl of Sheringham is a notable local aristocrat,' Quinn said mildly. 'They would take his side.' Ten years ago social ostracism, the unfairness of the accusations, the shame of his inability to force a duel, had burned into his soul like acid. Now he had become the man they had accused him of being and he had the strength and the will to face down his accusers and make them eat their lies. But it made him angry that Celina was upset. He should not have attended church, he thought, then she would not have been exposed to that.

The fact that he cared about her feelings struck him as novel. What did it matter if this woman with her secrets, this intruder into his life, had her feathers ruffled? A week ago he would have shrugged and forgotten it. But Celina—

'Gregor, why do you guard Lord Dreycott's back so closely?' she asked, cutting across his thoughts.

'And when you came to the Park, you checked all the locks, the windows. Trimble told me.'

No! He did not want to talk about that. Or to think about it. Quinn's elbow in his ribs came too late to stop Gregor. 'Quinn saved my life when he bought me,' he said simply. 'Now I guard his.'

'Bought you?' Lina stared at Gregor, aghast. 'You mean you are a *slave*? But that is dreadful—and illegal! How could you?' she demanded, turning on Quinn. 'That is barbaric!'

'I could have left him to die, I suppose,' Quinn drawled. 'Would that have shocked you less? Gregor was a Christian slave of the Ottomans, captured in battle. He does not take well to…orders.' To her amazement the Russian grinned at Quinn. 'So they beat him almost to the point of death, which was the only way to subdue him, and then sold him. I saw him and bought him.' He shrugged as though he was speaking of taking on a new farm worker at a hiring fair.

'Me and a girl who had been hurt. And he freed me,' said Gregor. 'So I pay him by looking after his life that he is so careless of, seeing that he will not take my money now I have it.'

'You were very cheap,' Quinn said, sounding bored. 'It would be an insult to ask for repayment.

And you have saved my life half-a-dozen times over.'

'And you mine. I am still in debt.'

It was one of the mysterious manifestations of male honour, Lina realised. They were as close as brothers, closer perhaps, and yet they had to feign indifference to those feelings, keep count of who had saved whose life.

She felt a little ill, looking at the rock-solid bulk of Gregor. What had they done to reduce him to near death? And what sort of man bought such pitiful wreckage and nursed it back to life? *A good man*, she thought. *But he would not thank me for saying so. And a man who saves another man's life may still be a danger to women. But what did he do with the woman who was hurt? The one neither of them seem to want to speak of.*

'Well, it is a relief to hear that we are not breaking the law by harbouring a slave,' Lina said prosaically. 'What happened to the woman?'

'She is free now,' Quinn said flatly, then showed no inclination to continue.

Lina could not think of a single coherent thing to say on the subject of Gregor's story, not without becoming embarrassingly emotional. 'I hope you will not mind a very simple luncheon. The late Lord Dreycott always gave the servants the day off from after breakfast until dinner time on Sundays, so there is just a cold buffet laid out.'

'No, I do not mind.' The carriage pulled up in front of the house and Gregor jumped down as Quinn answered. 'Would you take a turn around the garden with me?'

The small jerk of the head directed at the other man was not lost on Lina. So, what did Lord Dreycott wish to talk to her alone about?

'Of course, my lord,' she said, still preoccupied with the parishioners' hostility and Gregor's dreadful story. She followed him through the little gate and into the pleasure grounds. 'The gardens have been very neglected.' They stood and look at the roughly scythed grass and unpruned shrubs. 'His lordship was not much interested, I am afraid.'

'Do you know anything about gardening?' Quinn asked, taking her elbow in a light grip and steering her towards a dilapidated summer house. 'I suppose I should get this put into order before I sell it, but although I can recite you reams of Persian poetry on the subject of gardens, that is of no practical use when confronted with the wind-blown north Norfolk coast. I doubt we could ever recline under a palm tree here while I peeled you grapes.'

He brushed off the seat inside the summer house and gestured to her to sit.

'Gardening? No, not really.' Lina tried to dismiss the picture Quinn had conjured up; it was too close to her fantasies about harems. Would he like her in fluttering, diaphanous silks? 'But I can talk to the gardener, if you like, and see what can be done to make it look more cared for. There is just the one man, you see.'

'Tell him to hire some help,' Quinn said. He sat down, careless of his beautiful tailcoat on the lichen-covered seat. 'Celina, thank you.'

'Whatever for? It is no trouble to speak to the man. It will be quite interesting, in fact. I told you, I would like to be useful.'

'That is not what I meant.' He leaned forwards, his forearms on his thighs, and stared down at his clasped hands. 'Thank you for coming so fiercely to my defence at the church. I am sorry if my presence embarrassed you with your friends.'

'They are not my friends.' *My friends are all in a London brothel, my beloved sisters are lost.* 'They are acquaintances, that is all. And I am ashamed for their behaviour.' He was very still, sitting so close beside her, and gradually the indignation subsided, leaving her with the realisation that she was alone in a secluded spot with the dangerous rake who had kissed her.

But now that she had begun to know Quinn

Ashley a little she could see that there was more to him than a shocking reputation that he seemed more than willing to live up to. It was confusing. If she did not like him, admire him for his restraint at the church and his rescue of Gregor, she could be afraid of him, which was obviously the safe thing to be. As it was, the best she could manage was to be wary.

She was still furious with herself for even letting him provoke her into revealing she knew the other, disreputable, meaning of *nun*. He had said nothing more about it, but, on the other hand, neither had he done anything more to alarm her. Perhaps her flight from the gazebo had convinced him that she was virtuous and he should not attempt kisses, or worse.

'You have left many friends behind?' Quinn asked, making her jump. He straightened up and looked at her, the speculation in his eyes holding more than a simple question. It was the expression of a man assessing a woman and she felt it like a touch on her skin. She reminded herself that many men had an unpleasant predilection for corrupting innocence, but she could not feel the shudder of fear she hoped for, the reaction that would protect her. She simply felt the instinctive attraction of female to male.

'A very few, close friends. We lived near each other. And my sisters, of course.' Her world had become bounded by the walls of The Blue Door and her memories and dreams of her sisters. Now she was a friendless, fugitive virgin and utterly in Lord Dreycott's power. Did he realise how vulnerable she was? Was he titillated by it? Perhaps he thought she was too innocent to see her own danger.

'You want to go back to them, I assume, when you have the money?' Quinn asked, reaching for her hand. Lina made herself relax and let him take it. If she began to struggle, she thought she would panic and that, perhaps, would excite him more. But all he did was turn it over so he could study her palm.

Flirt, a little, an inner voice said. *Be confident and light-hearted. Do not let him sense your anxiety or see how he affects you. If he is stimulated by stalking a virgin, confuse him.* 'Do you so wish to be rid of me, my lord?' she asked, pouting a little. His eyes fixed on her mouth and Lina ran her tongue nervously between her lips.

'Why, no, you are a charming addition to the household,' Quinn said, his attention once more on her palm. He traced the crease that curved around the base of her thumb and she quivered, fighting not to close her fingers around his, trapping them. 'Such a long life line. Look at all the adventures.' His fingertip touched here and there where other, shorter, lines braided into the main one.

'You read palms?' It was curiously difficult to speak normally with his shoulder touching hers and the heat of his hand cradling her fingers.

'A beautiful Romany taught me.' Quinn hesitated, then opened his left hand, palm up. 'You see the break in my life line? I am sure she would tell you that was where she knifed me in the back and left me for dead.'

'What happened?' Lina's hand closed around Quinn's in a startled grip.

'Gregor happened. We were in Constantinople and he had gone off for a few days trading to leave me to my new inamorata. He strolled back in to find me ruining a particularly fine kelim rug, stopped the bleeding and went to retrieve my gold.'

'And the Romany? What did he do to her?'

'I did not ask him,' Quinn said. 'It taught me never to trust a woman, even a naked one.'

'So where was the knife?' Lina asked, determined not to be shocked. And, truth be told, she was as riveted as she ever had been when reading a sensation novel. His grip had shifted to open her hand again and his long fingers moved gently over the back.

'In her hair.' Quinn's smile was rueful. 'Now, you could be hiding a pair of duelling pistols in that bonnet.'

'Perhaps I am.' She let the silence drift on for a moment, full of unspoken words. 'But I have no intention of removing it to show you, Quinn.'

His given name slipped out and Lina bit her lip as though to catch it, too late.

'You keep secrets, Celina,' he observed.

'As many as your Romany, I have no doubt, my lord. But none so lethal.' *Although I killed a man… or I was the instrument of his own lust killing him.* 'Will you read my fortune? For, if not, I must ask for my hand back so I may go and make sure that luncheon has been set out.' She was pleased with the light, amused tone of her voice.

'Let me see.' He lifted her hand to study it, the movement bringing them closer together. 'A strong life line. Here.' He touched a point and frowned. 'Perhaps a moment of risk.' His voice became puzzled for a moment. 'Soon, I think. You must take care—if you believe such things. Your head line is straight—you are honest and intelligent, but perhaps too controlled by emotion. Ah, yes, see your heart line?' He traced the line curving under her fingers. 'Loving, intense—that is what overrules your head sometimes. And combined with this...' he brushed his finger over the swell of flesh at the base of her thumb '...the Mount of Venus, I can tell you are passionate as well.'

Quinn lifted her hand to his lips and touched them to the soft mound, making her shiver.

'Why, thank you, my lord, it lacked only a camp fire and some silver to cross your palm with! I see you sometimes wear an earring, which would complete the illusion. There was just such a lurid fortune-telling in a Minerva Press novel I was reading only the other day.' He released her and she stood up.

'I was Quinn a moment ago,' he said, as he towered over her.

'And I was careless,' she murmured, glancing sideways under her lashes as she moved away. 'I will see you at luncheon. My lord.'

Chapter Eight

She's a married woman who has run away from her husband, Quinn decided on Tuesday morning as he stripped off his sweaty clothes. He and Gregor had been wrestling and using singlesticks and his muscles tingled with the exercise. He ducked under the big pump in the stable yard with a gasp as the cold water hit his heated skin. That was the only explanation that appeared to make sense of all the puzzles the woman presented, he argued to himself, scrubbing soap into his chest.

Celina was wary of men and yet she possessed a number of knowing little tricks and was comfortable with dinner-table conversation. She was assured with the servants and with their few callers, competent with the household management. A husband who had beaten her, perhaps? Or forced himself on her.

'Harder,' he ordered the groom who was bent

over the pump handle. The male staff were used to him and Gregor now, the audience for their morning training fights had shrunk and the work of the yard went on around them as if two large, naked, dripping men were a commonplace sight.

He frowned as Gregor turned and he saw the familiar pattern of white scars lacing his friend's back. Cruelty to anyone, whether it was a woman, a child or a beaten Russian slave, made him coldly angry.

He brought his mind back to the mystery of Celina. He had been suspicious about the aunt from the start—she did not exist, he was fairly certain. Somehow Celina had known Simon and the cantankerous old devil had given her sanctuary. It had probably appealed to him, hiding another man's wife. And it explained why she had not been referred to by name in the codicil to the will—to put a false name might invalidate it and a fugitive wife would certainly not be living under her real name.

'We're late,' the Russian said as the stable clock struck noon. 'The water will be getting cold.'

'Come on, then.' Quinn scooped up his clothes and padded off over the stone setts. The hot baths to be found throughout North Africa and the Middle East were a luxury he sorely missed, but a good soak in the great marble sarcophagus was a reasonable substitute after exercise.

The kitchen door was shut, in accordance with the routine that saved the blushes of the female staff, and he and Gregor climbed the service stairs to the first floor before opening the door on to the deserted bedroom corridor.

'I've got a theory,' he said, low voiced, as they strode along, leaving wet footmarks on the old chestnut boards. 'I have come to the conclusion that Cel—'

The door in front of them opened and she came out as he spoke, her head bent over the pile of folded linens in her hands. She walked straight into Quinn and all three of them stopped dead. The linens went everywhere, a fluttering snowstorm of chemises, petticoats and nightgowns. Quinn lost his grip on his own clothes and dropped them, aware that Gregor had strategically clasped a shirt to his midriff, preserving essential decency if not much else.

Empty handed, he and Celina stared at each other for a frozen moment. He realised that he was trying to lock eyes with her to stop her looking down but, by instinct it seemed, she dropped to her knees to scramble after her scattered underthings. Quinn dropped, too; it was the safest thing to do, given that his body was reacting enthusiastically to the mental images feminine underwear conjured up. He seized the nearest item of clothing and clapped it over his loins.

Celina bundled up the rest of her things, got to her feet and backed through the door she had come out of, eyes wide, cheeks pink. The door slammed in their faces as Gregor doubled up laughing.

Quinn looked down; his modesty was being inadequately sheltered behind a flimsy piece of frivolity with fine lace and silk ribbons. Glowering at his friend, he tapped on the door, opened it a crack and tossed the chemise through before closing it again. They retreated down the corridor and into Quinn's room.

Gregor mopped his streaming eyes. 'Blue ribbons are not flattering to you,' he choked.

'Celina was not shocked,' Quinn said, clambering into the cooling bath and sinking up to his chin. 'She was surprised to bump into us, she was flustered, but she was not shocked. Not as a sheltered virgin walking slap bang into two nude men ought to be.'

'You are right,' Gregor agreed, sobering up and climbing into the other end. 'You were saying just as the door opened—'

'I think she is a married woman who has run

away from her husband,' Quinn said. 'She does not react to men like an innocent, but neither does she behave like a wanton.'

'You will tell Havers?' The Russian scrubbed at his chin in contemplation.

'No.' Quinn submerged completely and resurfaced streaming water. 'By English law a married woman's money is her husband's. If she has run from some bastard who beats her, then the last person Simon would have wanted to give money to would be him.'

'What are you going to do with her, then?'

'I'm thinking on it.' But he already knew what he would do. He would offer Celina a *carte blanche* and make her his mistress. It would save him the bother of finding a *chère amie* in London. She'd agree to it, she'd be a fool not to; it was an attractive, convenient arrangement for both of them and when he left he would add to Simon's legacy, make sure she had enough to keep clear of her husband for ever. He just needed to find the right moment to put it to her.

Lina sat on the end of her bed and regarded her scattered laundry. *Well!* It was not as though she had never seen a naked man before—they could occasionally be found wandering the corridors of

The Blue Door, usually somewhat the worse for drink and pursued by one or more of the girls, giggling as they tried to shoo them back into the bedchamber.

But the effect of those two large men at close quarters was… She searched for a word. *Overwhelming.* They were both magnificent, although she found herself strangely unmoved by Gregor's solid bulk. She had seen him first, seen the white lacing of whip scars over his torso, and recoiled to find her eyes locked with Quinn's.

It had not been until she had ducked down to scoop up her underwear that she realised just why he was holding her gaze so intently—he had not wanted her looking down. She fanned herself with a folded corset. There was absolutely no escaping the fact that she wanted to touch Quinn, to run her hands over those sculpted muscles, the broad shoulders, the lean hips. What did his skin feel like? And the crisp dark hair? Stripped, he was so unlike Tolhurst that they might have been separate species.

Now she had another secret to hide from him, she realised. *Desire.* How would she have reacted if Makepeace had tried to sell her to Quinn? she wondered. But Quinn would have no need to buy virgins from a villain like Makepeace and he would not force a girl, either, she sincerely hoped. He did not need to. He would use seduction, deploy his charm and his body and his skill to lure a woman into his bed.

'Dangerous,' she said to herself as she began to gather up the scattered clothes. 'That is a primrose path to perdition if ever I saw one.' How easy it had been to be good when she had never been tempted to be sinful.

'It is a beautiful evening,' Quinn remarked as the dessert plates were cleared. Lina paused, her napkin in her hand. She had been about to rise and leave them to their port or the strange oily clear liquor that Michael fetched every evening from the ice house and which was never offered to her.

'The moon is full, the wind has dropped and I think I can hear nightingales. Would you like to walk in the garden, Celina?'

She glanced at Gregor. 'All of us?' By mutual, unspoken consent not a word had been exchanged about the contretemps outside her bedchamber and, after a somewhat stilted start to the meal, they had all relaxed into the normal polite exchange of conversation.

'No, not me,' the big Russian said. 'I go and pack now. I leave for London tomorrow.'

Oh. She knew he had been planning to, but the realisation that tomorrow she would be alone with Quinn was disturbing. 'I am not sure.' She did not trust Quinn not to tempt her, she did not trust herself to resist, and yet the thought of wandering in the moonlight with nightingales singing was powerfully romantic. Her life, Lina thought with a sudden flare of rebellion, had been very short of romance.

Quinn just smiled at her with his eyes, the first unguarded expression he had allowed to cross his features since his somewhat unsuccessful attempt to shield both their blushes with the aid of her camisole.

Temptation again. If she was careful, very careful, perhaps it would be safe to take that enchanted stroll. He would not force kisses on her, she was certain…*almost* certain—and she was on the alert. It was just a matter of will-power, Lina thought, feeling her resistance swirling away like water down a hole.

'It would be very pleasant,' she said, her voice sounding prim to her own ears. 'Just for a little while.'

Quinn draped her shawl around her shoulders, his fingers barely touching her, and opened the long window onto the terrace. The breeze was soft and held the scents of green leaves, not the sea. The liquid birdsong seemed to pour over her senses like warm oil as they stepped out.

'How lovely,' Lina murmured as Quinn drew her arm through his and strolled out on to the lawn. They walked in silence for a while. It was easy to be with him, she realised, jerking her head upright as it tilted treacherously sideways, drawn to his shoulder like iron to a magnet.

But even the beauty of the silvered moonlit scene was not able to soothe her worries for long. *Gregor is going to London. Would he hear something about the Tolhurst Sapphire? Would he read about the hunt for a blonde young woman called Celina? Why have I not heard anything from Aunt Clara?*

'What did he do to you?' Quinn asked, his tone matter of fact, as though he was discussing the temperature.

'Who?' Lina knew she had started in alarm.

'Your husband.'

'My—' *He thinks I am* married? 'My husband?'

'Yes. I assume that is who you are running away from.' Quinn drew her arm tighter through his. 'I could not understand you at first, you see, Celina. Not an innocent, certainly not a wanton. Then I realised, you must be married.'

'Oh.' Her brain struggled to make sense of the implications of that assumption. Then she rallied; this could be a way to disguise her real fears. She was certainly in hiding, so now she could cease to pretend about that. 'What makes you think I am running away from anyone?'

'Instinct. I have been in hiding, eluding capture, often enough to sense when someone else is.' He did not wait for a response from her, which was fortunate because Lina could think of nothing to say. 'Did he beat you? Or force you?' Quinn's voice was controlled, but she could hear the anger under it and her heart warmed.

'Forced me,' she said, clinging to as much of the truth as she could. 'He was twice my age and...' She could not control the shudder.

'So old Simon gave you refuge.'

'Yes. He knew my aunt, and she is unwell. I could not stay with her, so she wrote to him.'

'Haddon is not your real name?' She shook her head. 'What is?' She shook it again. 'You'll not trust me? No, I suppose not; that is asking a lot if you are frightened of the man. But I am hoping for a *little* trust, Celina.' They had reached the end of the lawn where a bench had been set under a sweeping oak tree. 'Will you sit a while?'

Mutely she let herself be led to the bench,

wondering where this was going. Quinn sat beside her and took her hand. 'I thought perhaps you might like to become my mistress.'

Distracted by talk of her problem, Lina had forgotten the immediate danger. 'No!' She stood up, dragging her hand free. She had expected Quinn to try subtle seduction; the blunt question was shocking. 'How dare you? Do you want to ruin me?' She took several agitated steps away and then swung round to face him as he rose to his feet. 'Foolish question! Yes, of course you do.'

'You ruined yourself most effectively when you ran away from your husband,' Quinn pointed out.

'It was not my fault,' Lina retorted.

Quinn shrugged. 'The world does not see it that way, I'm afraid.'

'And neither do you, I suppose.' Oh, yes, he was kind, when it suited him, but he was also quite ruthless. Cruelty and abuse made women like her vulnerable and Quinn Ashley had no scruples about exploiting that vulnerability, it seemed. She was quite sure he was generous to his mistresses, treated them well, in just the same way as he was good to his horses and would never beat or overface them. Not a cruel man, nor a vicious one. *Just a man,* she supposed with an inward sigh, shaken by how disappointed she felt in him.

'I take the world as I find it.' He leaned one shoulder against the support of the rose arbour, a safe yard or so away from her. In the moonlight, with the nightingales and his exotic Eastern clothing, he was a character from the *One Hundred and One Nights*. He had even put a diamond stud in his ear, a teasing reference to the fortune-telling incident, she supposed. A creature of mystery and romance and… *And smoke and mirrors*, Lina told herself. *He is not what he seems. I see the glamour, but there is shame and ruin behind it.*

'No, you do not,' she contradicted. 'You bend the world to suit yourself. You refused to bow to conventional expectations and marry Lord Sheringham's daughter; you create scandal and gossip wherever you go; you have no sense of responsibility to anything or anyone, except Gregor, as far as I can see.

'Men can carry on like that and are considered romantic and dashing. Women show even one-hundredth as much independence and we are condemned as shocking, loose, wanton.'

'I said the *world* considered you ruined,' Quinn pointed out, refusing in the most aggravating manner to show anger in response to her tirade.

'I did not say *I* thought you shocking or loose or wanton.'

'I would be after one night with you.' *I feel wanton, just thinking about it.* Her mouth felt dry and there was the strangest sensation low down inside, a sort of hot, fluttering feeling that was not quite apprehension, an ache down the inside of her thighs.

'I do hope so,' he said with a grin that was clear in the moonlight.

'Oh! You are impossible! I will not sleep with you.' *He is so certain he can have me just for the asking,* she thought, the strange feeling inside transmuting into anger. *I do not need him; no-one now can save me except myself.* Lina marched up until she was virtually standing on the toes of Quinn's soft boots. 'I am in trouble enough as it is without becoming your mistress.'

'We have not discussed terms yet,' he said, folding his arms and smiling down at her. Perhaps anger was the wrong tactic, for it seemed to stimulate him. Although most things appeared to do that. 'You may change your mind.'

'There is nothing to be discussed.'

'I would be generous.'

'If I had said *yes*, then we could discuss whether I would become a cheap whore or an expensive whore. As I am not about to become any kind of whore, the question is academic.'

'Don't use that word, Celina.' Quinn frowned at her. Ah, she had succeeded in ruffling his feathers, had she? Perhaps he was a little hypocritical after all. 'I asked you to be my mistress, not to share your favours around my male acquaintance.'

They were uncomfortably close, even though he remained still, arms folded. 'So a financial arrangement, being kept, does not make me a whore?'

Lina did not know where she found the nerve to stand up and argue back at him like this. It was as though it was too important to back away from, a point of principle to be fought over. It was a completely different situation, for this man was not uttering threats, but she felt the same courage seeping into her as she had when she had confronted Makepeace.

Somewhere along the road on her panicky flight from the vicarage she had acquired the steel to stand her ground and fight. Lina caught her breath; she was so used to being the timid sister, the nervous one who would not say boo to a goose, that the discovery that she had changed without noticing was as stunning as Quinn's immoral proposal.

'Marriage is a financial arrangement,' Quinn pointed out. Lina jerked her attention back to the man in front of her. 'Or did you marry your husband out of love? It does not sound like it.'

'I had no choice in what I did,' she said tightly. *But I had; I could have run away again. Yet I did not, I stayed and tried to do something for Aunt Clara and the girls. I am not a mouse any more...* 'I was forced into it by threats to other people. But marriage is—should be—permanent. It gives protection to children...'

She felt her voice trailing away as she thought of the sort of protection that her own mother's marriage had given her. 'What am I supposed to do when you go abroad again, or tire of me? Find another man, presumably.'

'You have an inheritance already. I will make sure that when we part you will never, unless you wish, have to give yourself to another man. I do not promise you luxury, Celina, but I will ensure you have independence, provided you are prudent.'

Why me? The question came into her head like a bucket of cold water thrown over her disordered thoughts. Here was this attractive, experienced man taking the trouble to make her a thoughtful offer that took account of her circumstances, an offer that made her, despite her fears and her scruples, feel flustered and flattered and tempted.

Because I am convenient, that is why, not because

I am special to him in any way. Quinn is tied by the need to deal with his uncle's legacy, with the memoirs. He doesn't have time to spend just now to find a congenial mistress, sort out arrangements. But here I am, just along the corridor, a woman of some experience, so he thinks, and one in a position of weakness he can exploit.

'Why me?' Lina asked, making her voice soft, hiding the anger that was not directed at him as much as it was at her own foolish fantasy that he was attracted to her.

The question threw him off balance, the first time she had seen Quinn Ashley at a loss. Women did not ask *why?* when a man like this picked them out; they were expected to smile gratefully and say *yes*. 'You are a very attractive woman,' he said after a moment. 'I like you, I thought you were…that you did not dislike me.'

'And I am so convenient,' Lina said, sliding the comment in with a smile.

'Yes—' Quinn must have seen the trap yawning at his feet for he sidestepped it with enviable ease '—if convenience is a factor in such things. Mutual attraction is, surely, what matters.'

'Then how fortunate that you are so attractive and charming and sophisticated and experienced, my lord,' Lina murmured. Quinn narrowed his eyes and unfolded his arms. Something in her tone was obviously not convincing him. 'However, I do not find that outweighs the fact that you find it acceptable to take advantage of my situation to gratify your own desires.'

'Damn it, Celina.' He straightened up, frowning, and reached for her.

'Call me a dreamer, my lord,' she said, sidestepping, 'but I really could not care less if a man has looks, charm and experience. Or money. All I want from a man is someone who holds me in affection, thinks of me as a person, not as a commodity.'

She remembered some of the girls at The Blue Door talking about their clients. *It isn't that he is unkind*, one said of a particular man, *but he doesn't think of* me *at all, just what I give him. He looks right through me.*

'You want me to say I love you? Is that what you want?' Quinn demanded. 'If lies smooth the path, then lies you can have, Celina. But I thought you more honest than that.'

'Now you are insulting my intelligence, and my emotions,' she said between stiff lips. 'Nothing you could say would make me believe that you loved me, and nothing you can do will bring me to your bed. Is that clear enough?'

'Are you not afraid I will seek out your husband

and hold that over your head?' he enquired. 'You seem to be attributing the worst of motives to me.'

'No, I do not,' Lina said. 'To behave like that would offend your sense of honour and you would not want to do anything to lower yourself in your own esteem, would you?'

She turned on her heel and walked away, heart pounding, hardly able to breathe with tension. Behind her the silence was more frightening than an explosion of wrath would have been.

Chapter Nine

Quinn stared after Celina's retreating form, incredulity and anger fighting for supremacy. Of all the infuriating, sanctimonious, unreasonable females it had been his misfortune to encounter, she was the worst. She wasn't repelled by him—she wasn't that good an actress. She was in a situation where he would have expected her to welcome any help she could get and instead she stuck her self-righteous little nose in the air and carried on as though he was some ancient lecher attempting to corrupt a virgin.

What were her alternatives? Creep back to her husband and hope to be forgiven? Well, no, not if the man was unkind to her. But she had made her bed and if she was not prepared to lie on it—or his—then her options were severely limited.

She had as good as told him she would only sleep with him if he professed an emotional attachment, then snubbed him when he refused to go along with such nonsense and, to cap it all, she sneered at his sense of honour.

What Mrs Celina Whatever deserves is for me to find out exactly who she is, Quinn thought, striking off across the lawn towards the stables. That would bring her to an understanding of just how lucky she was to have a generous offer made to her by a man of principle who was capable of protecting her.

No, it wouldn't, he told himself a minute later, kicking a dandy brush clear across the stable yard. *It would confirm all the things she thinks of me.*

He clicked his tongue and Falcon put his head over the half-door of his stall, whickering a greeting. 'Do you think I'm a bastard?' he asked the horse as a soft muzzle was thrust into his hand. 'A fat lot of use you are, you'll tell me anything for food, won't you?' Falcon snorted, tossing his head and rolling a dark eye. 'And if I tell him, Gregor will inform me I'm a fool and recommend the nearest whorehouse for the itch that needs scratching.'

'My lord?' It was Jenks, his shirt loose over his breeches, a shotgun in his hand. 'Sorry, my lord, didn't see it was you at first. That horse is a worry to me—he won't let me shut the door and make all secure.'

'I didn't mean to disturb you, Jenks. And I'm

sorry about Falcon. He isn't used to closed doors and not being able to run free.' *And neither am I. And I'm not used to having to consider anyone else, either. Damn it, the man's probably got to be up before sunrise.* 'If it is any consolation, he would probably half-kill anyone foolish enough to try to steal him.' He tugged the long forelock as the stallion butted against his arm. 'I'll take him out for an hour. Get back to your bed and don't wait up.'

Lina sat up in bed, her arms wrapped around her legs, her chin resting on top of her knees, and tried to sort out the thoughts and emotions that were assaulting her from all sides.

I want him and he's an arrogant, insensitive rake. I'm not a scared little mouse any more. I'm brave... I think. He doesn't care about me, only my body. Does that matter so much if I want him, too? But that makes me wanton. But why doesn't it make him wanton? I can fight now. I stood up to Quinn. If I say yes I would risk ending up with my whole life defined by the fact that I've lain with a man. But have I got to spend the rest of it without ever knowing what love is?

Perhaps I will go to the gallows without ever knowing. 'Oh, God, the gallows.' That was the reality she should be worrying about, not the question of the equality of men and women or whether be-coming one man's mistress would be something she would regret for the rest of her life. Her life might be very short indeed, with little room for regrets. In which case, why not make love with Quinn?

And assume you are never going to prove your in-nocence? Lina asked herself, flopping back against the pillows. *Just give up? Never.*

Legally, Quinn had to allow her to stay, so stay she would, whether he liked it or not. His lordship could take himself off to Norwich if he wanted to find a sophisticated brothel to deal with whatever urges her refusal was leaving unsatisfied.

She reached out to snuff the candle. The room was lit now only by the moonlight from outside. It cast the old furniture in silver and laid eerie shadows over the strange objects that littered the room. The soft breeze flapped a curtain and sent the elaborate rope trimmings swinging. *Gallows rope.* Lina shut her eyes and made herself think of Bella and Meg. If she tried hard enough she could conjure up a dream of them all together again, of laughter, of happy endings. She felt her lids begin to droop.

Quinn gripped the great carved newel post at the head of the stairs with one hand and hauled off his boots with the other. The uncarpeted corridor creaked like a Chinese emperor's nightingale floor and Gregor, every bit as alert for assassins as any emperor, had ears like a bat. He'd be out demanding to know what was going on when all Quinn wanted was to go to sleep.

He'd ridden hard and far, through the park, down to the coast road, out over the marshes to the sea. When it was daylight he'd bring Falcon down to the beach again to exercise him in the sea, but he wasn't risking a strange coast and unknown currents at night, however bright the moon.

Now Falcon was dozing in his stable, the fidgets worked out of him, and Quinn was pleasantly tired, shoulders aching a little from holding the stallion in check and rubbing him down. His mind, finally, was clear. So, Celina did not want him, not for money, anyway, and he was not prepared to pay with any emotional commitment. It was going to be sticky, the next few days, with her bristling like a porcupine every time she encountered him.

Quinn grunted under his breath. *Too bad.* He was going to have to embrace celibacy for a while—somehow he could not find it in himself to ride into Norwich in search of a woman—and she was going to have to live with him watching her for any signs of weakening.

He padded down the corridor, boots in one hand, past Gregor's room, grinned at the sound of snores rumbling inside, past Celina's chamber door. And froze.

There were no snores coming from inside, but there was a thud, a choking gasp, the sound of a struggle. Quinn put down his boots, drew the thin blade from the sheath inside the left one and cracked open the door.

The moonlight flooded across the bed and for a moment he could not make out what he was looking at. Then he saw it was Celina, tangled in the sheet, her hands clawing at her throat, her bare legs kicking. He strode to the bed and caught at her hands, realising as he did so that the sheet had wound itself around her throat, choking her.

'Easy, easy, let me.' He tossed the blade on to the bedside table and took hold of the sheet, trying to get past her frantic hands to find the corner. She was fighting desperately, her eyes screwed up, deep in her nightmare. Her fingernails tore bloody tracks down the back of his hands and forced a hiss of pain from him.

Quinn dragged at the linen, pulled it away from her windpipe, found the end and yanked it free. Celina fell back, gasping for breath, her hands locked around his wrists. 'No! You can't... I am innocent...innocent... No!'

'Celina.' He shook her, harder than he meant to, control hampered by her clinging hands. 'Wake up, you are having a nightmare.'

Her eyes opened, wide and dark in her pale face. Her mouth opened in a scream and, with his hands trapped, Quinn did the only thing he could think of to silence her. He kissed her.

Under him he felt Celina's body tense, arch up to throw him off; he felt the desperate heaving of her breast against his and then, suddenly, she went limp. Quinn lifted his head and stared down at the sprawled figure. The faint was no ruse, she was unconscious and the bed looked as though... as though he had ravished her on it.

Quinn fought back the feeling of nausea, got to his feet and struck a flame. When he had a pair of candles lit he assessed the damage. His hands, raked by her nails, were already stiffening and her nightgown was marked with his blood. When he lifted the candlestick he could see red grooves where the sheet had wound tight around her throat. The bedding was churned into chaos by her struggles and her legs were bare from mid-thigh down.

He could not call for a maid, not and hope to explain this, but he could not leave her, either. Quinn pulled off his neckcloth, ripped it into strips and bound his hands to keep the blood from staining anything else, then he lifted Celina's limp form off the bed and on to the *chaise*. He smoothed the night-gown down over her legs and found the blanket, tossed to the floor, and put it over her. Then he made the bed. There was no blood on that, thankfully.

There was nothing to be done about her marked throat and bloodstained nightgown. Quinn eased Celina up into his arms again and turned back to the bed before he realised he could not simply tuck her in and leave her to wake in the morning to find herself in that state. He was going to have to stay until she woke. As he lowered her towards the bed she stirred, murmured and her arms tight-ened around his neck.

Now what? He could hardly lie down with her; it would be enough to send her into hysterics, waking up to find him in her bed. She burrowed her head snugly into his shoulder and clung, limp and trust-ing and deep in an exhausted sleep. *Hell*. Quinn sat down on the *chaise*, leaned back, swung up his legs and settled Celina as best he could against himself. It was going to be a long night.

Quinn woke to the sound of a faint scratching. He reached out a hand for his knife, then found he was entangled with a body. *Celina?* The memory of the night before came back with horrible precision as the door opened and an arm appeared, the hand clutching his boots. They were lowered to the floor just inside. *Gregor.* He whistled softly and the Russian's head appeared, his expression comical as he took in bed and *chaise.* Then he frowned, his eyes focused on Quinn's bandaged hands.

Go away, Quinn mouthed.

The other man's eyebrows shot up, then he grinned. *Goodbye*, he mouthed back and the door closed as silently as it had opened.

Quinn let his head sink back against the curved rail of the *chaise* and stared up at the ceiling in the dawn light. Gregor was off to London now, thinking heavens knew what, but Celina would wake soon. She was already stirring, her lips moving against his throat where his shirt had come open when he took off his neckcloth.

He eased his cramped limbs as best he could, wincing as he flexed his hands. *Damn, but that hurt.* And he had to find an explanation for the injuries too. As he thought it, Celina woke, her first gentle movements stiffening into awareness as she found herself in his arms. Was she going to believe him?

* * *

Celina came out of a dream of being safe and protected. *Blissful*, she thought, as she dreamed of arms holding her against a large male body. Then she woke fully and found that there *was* a man and his arms were around her, holding her to his chest, and her hips were curved into a definitely male lap and this was not a dream. She tightened every muscle, tried to wrench free even as she opened her mouth to scream, and her voice croaked out of a throat that felt sore and bruised.

'Let me go!' She hit the man's chest with a clenched fist and he released her, one arm still steadying her as she lurched upright. 'Quinn,' she said flatly. 'I might have known. Can't you take *no* for an answer?'

'You had a nightmare,' he said, his face stark. There was no amusement in it, no lust, only tension and dark shadows under his eyes. 'The sheet was round your throat and you were choking, struggling—' He broke off to touch her neck lightly. 'There are marks.'

She looked down and saw her nightgown, streaked in blood. 'Oh, my God—'

'It is mine.' He held up his hands, the makeshift bandages stained, too. 'You fought me.'

He did not resist when she pushed herself away,

took the few steps to the edge of the bed and sank down on it. Her hands were stained, too, she saw, all around the nails. She had clawed at him. 'A dream?'

'You must have thought someone was trying to strangle you,' Quinn said, sitting with his elbows on his knees, his bandaged hands held away from contact with his body.

Lina put her hands to her throat. *No, not strangling, hanging.* She had dreamed she was in Newgate, in the condemned cell. They were leading her out, taking off the shackles, taking her to the scaffold, pushing her off into space to jerk and dangle...

'Celina!' He launched himself at her, caught her by the shoulders and held her as the room spun sickeningly.

'I'm sorry, I am all right.' He let her go, the absence of his strength a wrench. 'Yes, I remember. Did I call out?' She must have screamed if Quinn had heard her from his own room.

'I was coming back from a ride. I found I was not sleepy,' he said without emphasis, but she felt herself colouring. 'I heard noises from your room and thought someone was attacking you. But you were entangled in the sheet, clawing at your throat. I tried to free you. You—' He looked uncomfortable.

'You came round and then fainted. I tried to put you back to bed, but you clung on, so we ended up on the couch instead. I did not think you would want to wake in bed with me.'

In the fog of the fading nightmare she remembered another dream. It had slid into the first in the weird way dreams had: a man. Was it Tolhurst? Only this time he was holding her, kissing her, his weight was on her and she could not get free. And yet it was not all unpleasant. There was something sweet, something she could not quite grasp as the wisps of memory faded.

'Your hands,' Lina said, her voice rasping sore in her throat. 'Let me see.'

'No. it is all right.'

'It is *not* all right. I hurt you and you were trying to help me. And just now I leapt to conclusions, I assumed the worst.' Doggedly she got to her feet, walked to the washstand and poured from the jug into the wide basin. 'Cold water will be best. Come and put your hands in it, soak off those bandages.' When Quinn made no move to join her, she turned and looked at him. 'I am sorry.'

'Don't be.' He got to his feet and came across. 'And do not make me into some sort of scrupulous gentleman just because you passed the night safely in my arms. I prefer my women conscious.'

'Are you trying to shock me?' Lina asked, finding she could smile. 'Because after yesterday evening… Oh, my goodness, look at your hands! Quinn, I am so sorry. That is going to scar—and whatever will you say caused it? People will assume—'

'That I was attempting to ravish a woman?' He stared down into the water, picking the makeshift bandages loose. 'I went for a ride last night, found a fox in a snare, tried to free it and was savaged for my pains. Will that do?'

'Yes,' Lina agreed, rummaging in a drawer. 'That will be convincing. I have some salve and lint here. If you can dry your hands, I will dress them and then find an old soft sheet to tear up for bandages.' She threw on a wrapper, startled to find that she had been unselfconsciously talking to Quinn dressed in nothing but a flimsy nightgown, and went along the corridor to the linen cupboard. There was a pile of laundered sheets too thin for use, kept for bandages and patching.

When she got back with the softest, Quinn was drying his hands, dabbing at the raw tracks where her nails had scored across the tendons. 'Here. Sit down.' She smoothed salve on the lint, then took his right hand and pressed it gently over the wounds, then repeated it for the left.

It was an accident, she told herself, but it was

hard not to blame herself. It must be exquisitely sore and the scars would disfigure hands that were long and elegant, despite their strength. Lina bandaged as lightly as she could to keep the dressing in place. 'There, you should be able to hold reins or a pen and even get gloves on if you have some large ones.'

'And what about you?' Quinn reached out and tipped up her chin. 'You have some interesting marks and my imagination fails to come up with any innocent explanation for them other than the truth, which no one will believe.'

Lina moved away and picked up a hand mirror. Quinn's touch on her chin was strangely pleasant, although, she thought with a rueful grimace, his touch anywhere would be. Her neck looked exactly as though someone had tried to strangle her. 'I will develop a sore throat,' she said, 'and wrap it up in flannel. I don't think the marks themselves will show over the top of my higher-necked gowns and once the redness fades in a few days I can safely make a recovery and remove the wrapping.'

'Go back to bed,' Quinn said, as he picked up the basin of water. 'I'll pour this away and bring the bowl back. What about your nightgown?'

'Er...nose bleed,' Lina improvised, digging in a drawer for a strip of flannel and a fresh nightgown.

'We are obviously an accident-prone household. I do hope Gregor gets away safely.'

'He's gone,' Quinn said, negotiating opening the door, balancing the basin and picking up his boots with the grace of a juggler. 'I'll knock before I come back.'

Lina changed in haste, wrapped her neck in a length of red flannel that felt immensely comforting, and scrambled back into bed. How did Quinn know Gregor had left? Did that mean the Russian knew that Quinn had been in her room? The thought was not as worrying as it might have been, she realised. Between Quinn's propositions and her own thoroughly wanton fancies she was becoming immune to embarrassment. Or perhaps it was this strange new feeling of confidence; she had stopped worrying about things she could not change and which, set against the prospect of the scaffold, were of little importance.

The tap on the door was followed by a respectable wait before Quinn opened it to bring in the empty basin. 'I'd best hurry and get into my own bed before Peter appears with my morning tea,' he remarked. He paused in the doorway, his mouth twitching. 'You need a nightcap to finish off that picture,' he remarked. 'You look like Little Red Riding Hood's grandmother waiting for the wolf.'

Lina twitched her dowdy flannel wrap tighter around her neck. 'I am quite well aware of the risk from wolves, my lord.'

Quinn grinned. 'I had noticed that,' he remarked as he closed the door behind himself.

Chapter Ten

Lina expected the events of the previous evening and night to make things awkward between herself and Quinn once the intimacy of the bedchamber was behind them. But the need to play their parts in front of the staff only deepened the feeling of complicity between them.

She remembered to exclaim in concern at the sight of Quinn's bandaged hands at breakfast and to provoke him by making a great fuss over his humane efforts to free the fox. It was not difficult to speak with a catch in her voice, for her throat felt bruised both inside and out and the staff brought her honey to go in her tea and promises of the recipe for Trimble's late mother's infallible remedy for quinsy of the throat.

'I do not appear to be coming down with a cold,' she told Quinn, answering his convincing concern about whether she should be resting in her room.

She really should be treating him with cool reserve, but that was impossible when she was so grateful to him for rescuing her from her choking nightmare at the cost of painfully lacerated hands. And he had behaved impeccably afterwards, which confused her. If he could only be consistently wicked she would at least know where she was with him.

'I think I will take a walk into Upper Cleybourne and go to the shop,' she said. 'Perhaps the fresh air will help my throat.'

'Would you like me to accompany you?' Quinn asked as the footman left the room with a tray full of empty dishes. 'I can renew my attempts on your virtue in sunlight for variety.'

'You—' Lina put down the spoonful of warm milk toast with honey that she had been about to eat. 'Last night you behaved faultlessly. Now you say you still want to make me your mistress?'

'Of course.' Quinn watched her from under hooded lids, his eyes amused at her indignation. 'If I was simply in the grip of uncontrollable lust, then I would have tried to ravish you last night, which, you will agree, would not have been the action of a gentleman.' He paused as though expecting a response, but Lina did not rise to the bait. 'As it is, I am perfectly in control of myself and just as determined as I was last night to reach an agreement with you.' He paused, again waiting for her retort, but she simply glared at him. 'And it is not, my dear Celina, because you are *convenient*.'

'If you are not looking for convenience, my lord,' she said with a sweet smile as the footman came back with a fresh pot of coffee, 'then I suggest you ride into Norwich. I am sure there are places that can supply the commodity you seek in abundance.'

'Yes, but not the quality, I suspect,' Quinn replied.

There really was no response to that, not in front of the servants. What would Quinn say, she wondered, if he discovered that the experienced married woman he thought he was propositioning was actually a virgin with a completely theoretical knowledge of the arts of love?

There were the arts of love and the art of loving, Lina thought as she walked through the park an hour later, the red flannel replaced with a soft silk scarf. Quinn was doubtless well versed in the former, but he quite obviously had no intention, or desire, to look for love—and love was the only thing that made the risks of lovemaking worthwhile, she decided.

Without it the woman was vulnerable. She would

be left no longer marriageable, possibly with child and, if she had been so foolish as to fall in love with the man, emotionally shattered. Look at what had happened to Mama and Aunt Clara—ruined, deceived and abandoned. Their only recourse had been to selling themselves and they had not even been left with child. The simple fact of their lost virginities was sufficient.

Virtue, Lina told herself firmly, would have to be its own reward. Not, of course, that virtue would reward her now she had lived in a brothel. If that came out, she was as ruined as she would be if she had sold herself there.

The walk helped blow away the last wisps of the nightmare and she felt better by the time she reached Morston's Stores. They sold everything from boot laces to papers of pins, ink and sealing wax, sewing requisites and tobacco. They were also the receiving office for the mails and the depot for the London newspapers, she was reminded as she met Mrs Willets in the doorway, her daughters at her back. The squire's wife had a folded newspaper in her basket, the *Morning Chronicle* banner clear at the top.

'Miss Haddon.'

'Mrs Willets.' Lina smiled. Perhaps she could

mend bridges a little now it was obvious that Quinn's arrival had not resulted in scandalous behaviour to rock the neighbourhood.

'A word with you, if you please. Anna, June, carry on home without me.' Lina found herself marched around the corner of the shop and into the mouth of a sheltered alleyway. 'Miss Haddon, I must ask that you do not approach either my daughters or myself, now that you have seen fit to associate with the new Lord Dreycott.'

'Associate? Mrs Willets, his late lordship had taken me into his home. By remaining there, as I am entitled under the terms of his will, I am not *associating* with his great-nephew, if by that you mean engaging in immoral behaviour.'

'It most certainly is what I mean. You are residing in the same house as a notorious libertine and with no chaperon.' Mrs Willets was pink in the face, her voice strident with righteous indignation. 'How you had the effrontery to introduce him to the congregation last Sunday, I cannot imagine.'

'As I have an entirely clear conscience with respect to Lord Dreycott, and as he is now a notable member of local society, I saw it as my duty,' Lina retorted. Her conscience was clear—she had refused Quinn's advances and her inner desires were no business of anyone else.

'Your duty? Hah! Well, I see it as my duty to protect the respectable women and girls of this parish, Miss Haddon, and I can tell you that you are not welcome here, you Jezebel.'

'What will you do, Mrs Willets? Have me stoned in the village street? Your assumptions say more about your own mind and lack of charity than they do my morals. Good day to you.'

Lina drew her skirts to one side and swept past the affronted matron and into the shop. 'Good morning, Mr Lucas. Have you any broad blue satin ribbon?'

For a moment she thought he was going to refuse to serve her, then the shopkeeper pulled open a drawer and laid it on the counter. He might have turned his back on Lord Dreycott in the churchyard, but a substantial part of his income came from the Park and she suspected he was not going to risk losing it, even if the squire's wife disapproved.

Lina untied her bonnet and took it off so she could match the lining with the ribbons in the drawer and replace the frayed ones that trimmed it now. One looked perfect and she took it out and went to the door with it to hold it against the bonnet in the better light.

Mrs Willets glared at her from the other side of the street where she was talking to one of her bosom bows. Presumably taking one's bonnet off in public was a further sign of depravity. Chin up, she went and bought two yards of the blue satin and the sealing wax Trimble had asked for. Mr Lucas made up the parcel and she paid cash and went out with it, ignoring the staring women.

It took the gloss off the lovely morning, she thought as she walked back between the gate lodges and along the carriage road through the park. The thought of six months in hiding in a village where she was now shunned was not a pleasant one, although she supposed she could go to church and do her shopping in the nearby towns of Cromer or Holt.

If she could only find out what was happening in London. Was Aunt Clara better or worse? Had she found anyone to help clear Lina's name? Then the idea came to her. Mrs Golding, the cook at The Blue Door, lived out, at her daughter's house off the Strand. She could read, she was devoted to her employer and had always been friendly with Lina. A letter to her, enclosing one for Aunt Clara, could be delivered without anyone else being any the wiser.

Now she had the idea, she could not wait. Lina ran; her bonnet blew off and hung down her back and her hair began to come down, but she did not care. Breathless, she arrived at the front door just as it opened and Quinn came out.

She beamed at him and he smiled back, then took her round the waist with his bandaged hands and lifted her, laughing up at her flushed and excited face. 'Put me down,' she gasped, still laughing, but he merely turned on his heel so she was spun round in a circle, hair flying.

'You look as though you lost a farthing and found a guinea,' he teased, coming to a halt at last and lowering her until her feet touched the ground.

'I am going to write a letter.' Lina felt the laughter gradually ebb away to be replaced by a feeling she could not understand. She felt a little breathless, rather serious, almost apprehensive. And yet it was not an unpleasant sensation. Quinn must have seen something in her face, for he sobered, too, moving closer, his hands still at her waist, his gaze steady on her face.

Then he blinked and dipped his head to deliver a rapid kiss on her parted lips. 'What am I thinking of, standing looking at a beautiful woman and not trying to kiss her? I must be losing my touch.' But his tone was at odds with his serious face and the slight frown between the dark, straight brows. And then he released her and strode off towards the stables, leaving Lina on the steps, her fingertips pressed to her lips, her pulse racing.

There was no writing paper in her room, so she went to the study once she had restored her wind-swept appearance to normality and made sure her scarf hid the red marks on her neck. The door was not locked, so she assumed there would be nothing on view that Quinn wanted to keep private, but she was taken aback by the piles of papers on every surface.

It was all neatly ordered, docketed with coloured slips tucked in here and there, and she glanced at the piles, curious to see what it all was. Blue slips, she realised after a few minutes, related to old Simon's memoirs and a small stack of papers covered in a strong, neat black hand sat next to a far larger one, many of the pages yellowing and the handwriting thinner and more sprawling.

Other piles with green slips related to the estate and finally there was a smaller section with red labels. *Ottoman Court; trade and shipping; religious ritual; harems and the position of women*, Lina read as she walked along the trestles, peering at the work. Quinn Ashley was organised, knowl-edgeable and very hard working, she realised when she had walked right around the room.

She sat at the desk and drew a clean sheet of

paper towards her, but it was a moment before she dipped the pen in the inkwell. She had dismissed Quinn as a dilettante, a seeker after sensation and Eastern luxury, and he was nothing of the kind. He had been right when he had said that he had many facets and she wondered now if she understood him at all. Which was the true Quinn Ashley? The ruthless rake who happened also to be a scholar and a traveller, or the scholar who enjoyed the pleasures of the flesh and thought it hypocrisy to pretend that he did not?

And what does it matter to me? she thought, dipping the quill with sudden decision. *He is not so unprincipled that he will force me and if I become uncomfortable, why, then I will have to be firm with him and keep one of the maids with me at all times.*

She sealed her letters, one within the other, using the wafers from the box on the desk. Was that secure enough? There was wax and a heavy old seal, which, when she looked at it, did not resemble the Dreycott coat of arms. That would give no clue if the letter was intercepted. She melted two blobs of wax and pressed the seal into them, then went to ask Trimble to have one of the grooms bring a gig round. She would have him drive her into Holt, not Cromer, which was closer, and then she could post her letter at a safe distance. Soon, she prayed, she would have news.

Four days passed uneventfully. Without Gregor's assistance Quinn spent longer in the library and Lina, with his blessing, threw out all the most motheaten and disintegrating stuffed specimens. The chemicals were packed up and dispatched to the nearest pharmacist's shop for safe disposal after Quinn's cautious investigations had revealed arsenic, antimony and sinister purple compounds. They went to church on Sunday and were comprehensively cut.

Gregor wrote reporting that both houses were in good order, a section that Quinn read out at breakfast. He then read the rest of the letter to himself, grinning in a way that led Lina to the conclusion that Gregor had been exploring London's pleasures with enthusiasm.

There was no letter for Lina. Perhaps, she consoled herself, there was much to report and Aunt Clara was writing at length, but by the fifth day following the one when she had posted the letter, she was finding it hard to keep her spirits up, and Quinn noticed.

Teasing failed to raise a smile; she responded to outrageous flirting by snapping at him and she was so distracted that once or twice she was half-way downstairs before she remembered to run back and wrap a scarf around the fading marks on her neck.

'His lordship's compliments, and would you join him for tea in the study, Miss Haddon.' Lina looked up from her sewing to find Trimble in the doorway and managed a smile for the butler.

'Thank you, yes, I will.' That was new; perhaps he wanted help with the papers, she mused, folding the sheet and following Trimble out.

She poured tea, cut cake and produced at least three intelligent questions about the progress of the memoirs. She thought she was doing rather well until Quinn said, 'What is wrong? You were so happy a few days ago. Is it your sisters? Was the letter to them?'

'No.' Lina shook her head, touched that he had even remembered about Meg and Bella. 'Nothing to do with them. I am just rather low in my spirits, that is all.'

'I am sorry—' Quinn broke off at the sound of carriage wheels on the gravel outside. 'We have a visitor.' He went and opened the study door a crack. 'Let us see if we want to be At Home or not.'

Trimble could be heard greeting someone and from his voice it was not someone he knew. 'I will ascertain if his lordship is receiving. Who should I say is calling?'

There was a deep rumble, then, quite clearly, '…from Bow Street. My warrant…'

Lina dropped the cake slice with a clatter as she stumbled to her feet. Quinn swung round from the door, closed it and strode across the room to catch her arm. 'Do not faint on me! Are they here for you?'

She nodded, her mouth too dry to even whisper *yes*. There was nowhere to escape to, not with Quinn's hand hard on her forearm, the Runner on the doorstep.

'Behind that screen.' He jerked his head towards the back of the room and the battered old folding screen of tooled Toledo leather that he had pinned maps and lists to. As she stood there staring at him, he grabbed his cup, saucer and plate and shut them in a drawer, then moved to the small table she had been sitting at and sank into the deep armchair. *'Go.'*

'Thank you,' Lina whispered. 'Oh, *thank you.*'

He shook his head at her, his face grim. The door began to open and she ran.

'My lord, a person is here from Bow Street,' Trimble said as she huddled into the corner, her skirts drawn tight around her legs.

'Never tell me Gregor has got himself arrested?' Quinn said. His voice had the deep, amused drawl that, she was learning, could hide quite different emotions.

'I could not say, my lord.'

'Show him in, then.'

'My lord.' The voice was middle-aged, confident, with a pronounced London accent. Lina resisted the temptation to peer through the join in the screen.

'Have a seat.' Quinn's tone was affable but with an undertone that suggested that if this was a wild goose chase he would not appreciate being troubled. 'What can I do for you—' there was a rustle of papers '—Inchbold?'

'Is there a young female residing here, my lord?'

'Several. Six maids—house and kitchen, a brace of laundry maids—then there's the outside staff—a poultry girl, dairymaid—'

'I mean a female who can pass herself off as a lady,' Inchbold said. 'Mid-twenties, blonde hair, blue eyes. Pretty thing by all accounts—see, my lord, there's a sketch.'

'Why, certainly, there's a resemblance to the young lady who resides here with me, I suppose,' Quinn acknowledged readily, after a moment when he must have been studying the picture. Lina bit on her clenched fist to stifle her gasp of alarm. He was going to betray her. She was trapped in this tight corner… 'But why do you ask?'

'This female is wanted for a capital crime, my lord. The theft of the Tolhurst Sapphire from the just-dead body of Sir Humphrey himself. For all we know, she murdered him, too, although it looks like a seizure. The theft alone is a hanging matter, my lord.'

'Good God.' In the silence that followed Quinn's exclamation, Lina thought the men would hear her heart thudding. She clenched her fingers around the edge of the table she was pressed against in an effort not to slump to the floor in a faint. Through the buzzing in her ears she heard Quinn say, 'That is serious indeed. You may be assured of my total co-operation, Inchbold.'

Chapter Eleven

Quinn was going to betray her, give her up. She would not weep, she would not struggle, Lina resolved, an awful calm beginning to descend. If nothing else, she could behave with dignity and courage. If they thought her passive, there might be a ghost of a chance of escape later. But the pain of Quinn's reaction cut like a knife.

'This female's name?' Quinn asked.

'Celina Shelley, my lord.'

'Ah, it would seem we have a discrepancy. The young woman living here is Celina Haddon.'

'False name, my lord,' the Runner said confidently. 'You'll find they'll do that—change one name, but keep another. Classy bit of stuff, for all that she's a thief and a whore. Comes from one of the better houses of ill repute, place called The Blue Door near St James's Palace.'

There was a silence before Quinn said, 'When and where did the theft take place?'

'In London, my lord. Sir Humphrey's house in broad daylight, it was. March fifth of this year.'

'Unless you can explain to me how a woman might be in two places at once, with the English Channel intervening, then you have the wrong Celina, Inchbold. I'll agree they are both of the muslin company, but the cunning little madam in *my* keeping was warming my bed in Calais for most of the fourth of that month.'

'The information we have is that the young woman here arrived at Dreycott Park alone on the stage, my lord.'

'That's right.' Lina opened her eyes and found she could breathe again. Whatever Quinn was doing, he was not handing her over—at least, not yet. 'I had urgent business in Calais, but I knew my great-uncle was not in good health, so I sent her on ahead. The little wretch spent the money I gave her for a chaise on a new bonnet, hence the stage.'

'You sent your mistress to your great-uncle's home, my lord?'

'He was not well and I knew she would cheer him up,' Quinn said laconically. 'Unfortunately, I had no idea he was as ill as he was and in the event I did not arrive until almost seven weeks later, by which time he had died. I had to go back to Paris from Calais, which delayed me.'

'She's got papers to prove who she is, I suppose, my lord?' Inchbold asked.

'Shouldn't think so for a moment.' Quinn sounded as though he was shrugging. 'Women like that don't. No passport, that's for sure. I put her on a fishing boat belonging to some acquaintances of mine. Why? Are you doubting my word, Inchbold? Or do you think I can't recognise a woman I've been enjoying for weeks?' The amusement had gone from his voice now to be replaced by the cool anger of a gentleman whose statement was being questioned by a menial.

'No, no, of course not, my lord. If you say this female was with you—'

'I said she was travelling from France that day,' Quinn corrected sharply. 'It might *just* be possible she was involved if this event took place in the small hours of the next morning.'

'Quite, my lord.' The man was sounding rattled now. 'No, it was late afternoon. Can I speak to the young woman? For my superiors' satisfaction, you understand.'

'Of course. When she gets in. She's taken a fancy to long country walks for some reason. Come back after dinner, Inchbold, and you can talk all you like.'

'My lord.' From the sound of his voice the Runner was on his feet and making for the door. 'Thank you for your co-operation, my lord.'

There was the sound of the front door closing, of wheels on the drive. Lina stayed were she was, not at all certain her legs would hold her up. She heard Quinn pull the bell rope and a few moments later the door opened again.

'Trimble, get Jenks in here at the double. And, Trimble, no member of staff speaks to that Runner, or to any other stranger asking questions, on pain of instant dismissal. Is that clear?'

'My lord, I will see to it at once.'

Quinn came to stand by the screen. 'Stay where you are.' His voice was cold and Lina shivered and obeyed, listening to the sound of Quinn's booted feet pacing on the boards until there was a tap at the door.

'Ah, Jenks. That gig that has just left—I want you to follow it, see where it goes and if the driver is joined by anyone else. Don't let yourself be seen. When you are certain he's fixed wherever he ends up, come back to me.'

'My lord. Up to no good, is he? We'll see about that.'

'You can come out now,' Quinn said when the room was silent again. 'Stay at the back away from the window.'

'Thank you.' Lina got as far as one of the hard upright chairs and sat down, shaking. 'Thank you so much. I thought—'

'And I thought you were telling me the truth and in fact you are a demi-rep from a St James's brothel.' He looked furious as he stood in front of her, hands fisted on his hips. 'I have just given my word to an officer of the law that you are not here. Now, tell me the truth this time or I'll have him back here so fast you won't be able to say *hanging cleat.*'

'I did not steal the sapphire. I am not a prostitute.'

'And you don't know this brothel, The Blue Door, and you've never met this Tolhurst?'

'I live there.' Quinn's eyebrows rose. 'And I was in his bedchamber when he died. And I did not steal *anything.*'

'How did you get here?'

'My aunt owns The Blue Door. She is unwell and she sent me to Lord Dreycott because they knew each other, a long time ago. I told him the truth. Aunt was certain they would not believe me.

Quinn, if they still have not found who took the sapphire, they'll hang me.'

'And you saw fit to make me an accomplice after the fact,' he said grimly. 'Well, we had better make certain Inchbold believes me, hadn't we? Come upstairs.'

'Why?' Lina stayed where she was. This was a man she found she did not know at all: hard, angry, all humour and sympathy banished.

'So I can get some return for my lies before dinner?' She felt herself go pale. 'No, nothing so pleasurable. So we can put on a convincing performance when Inchbold gets back. I just hope you can act.'

'I've no idea. I'll try.' The look he gave her promised a multitude of consequences if she did not, and none of them were good. Shaking, Lina followed him from the study and upstairs.

Quinn halted at her bedchamber door. 'Show me your clothes.' Beyond questions, Lina opened the door and pulled wide wardrobe and drawers. 'Put this on,' Quinn said, picking up a deep blue silk gown, one of the few she had not dyed.

'I need a maid for the lacing.' Lina reached for the bell.

'Leave it. You'll make do with me. The less the staff are involved in this, the better, I don't want to risk their safety, too.' He took her shoulder, turned her round and began to unhook the back of the gown she was wearing.

'Quinn! You cannot undress me!'

'Why not? Or do you only feel comfortable when money has been exchanged?' he asked.

'I—no, that isn't it.' Lina clutched the bodice of the gown, unsettled more by his brisk handling than she might have been if his fingers had lingered on the bare skin as they brushed it. Quinn gestured impatiently and she let the gown drop, snatching up the other one and pulling it over her head under his cool green gaze.

He laced the new gown up just as impersonally, then turned her back to face him. 'That must go,' he said as he tugged out the infill of lace at the neckline. Lina gasped as she looked down to find her breasts half-exposed in the taut silken cups of the bodice. 'Better,' Quinn said. 'Have you paint for your face?'

'No, I told you—'

'Come to my room. That sketch is too damn good for my liking,' Quinn said, his hand hard on her arm as he marched her across the corridor. 'But it looks as you do now—big innocent blue eyes, hair up neat and tidy. What was the idea? Did he like pretending he was getting an innocent?'

'Yes, but—'

'Then we make sure you don't look like an innocent any more; we'll find the real Celina under the mask of virtue. Sit down.' He pushed her into an upright chair at the dressing table by the window and went to rummage in the dresser, coming out with a small box. He opened it and Lina saw the inside was fitted out with tiny pots, tubes, brushes and sponges.

'Macquillage?'

'From time to time we find ourselves in situations where looking like respectable Westerners is dangerous,' Quinn said, opening jars and lining a selection up on the table. 'Sit still.' He began dabbing and brushing, taking tiny amounts from different pots.

Lina sat like a dummy, obediently turning her head this way and that, opening and closing her eyes as she was told. She felt sick, she felt terrified, as bad as she had in the hours after Tolhurst's death. The danger was real now, not the faraway horror she had managed to turn it into. She could almost hear the creak of the gallows steps.

'Don't cry,' Quinn said sharply, a fine brush an inch from her left eye.

'I'm not,' Lina said, swallowing. He was so angry with her. Of course he was, he had every right.

What would they do to him if his deception was discovered?

'There,' he said at last, taking her by the shoulders and turning her to face the mirror.

Lina gasped. The woman who looked back was her, and yet not her. Subtle shading had narrowed her face, heightened her cheekbones. Her nose looked shorter, her eyes darker. 'I look older,' she said, momentarily distracted from her anxiety by the altered image.

'You look different enough, but not too different. It makes a misunderstanding possible,' Quinn said. Doing something seemed to have reduced his anger from boiling to simmering point. He was still frowning, but at least, Lina thought, he did not look as though he was tempted to pitch her straight out of the front door.

'Jewellery.'

'I don't have much,' she ventured.

'I've noticed.' He produced a leather-covered box. 'Left it all behind when you ran, did you? There should be something in here that is ornate enough to be convincing. Here.' He handed her pendant earrings with large misshapen pink pearls dangling from them, a pair of golden bangles set with more pink pearls and a fine gold chain.

'They are beautiful,' Lina said, holding up an

earring and staring at the strange pearl. 'But they look wrong with the blue.'

'Exactly. They will look thoroughly vulgar,' Quinn said, fastening the chain around her neck and twitching it until it fell sinuously between her breasts. 'They are Baroque-set freshwater pearls and ought to be worn with something subtle to show them off. If you wear them now it will give the impression of a woman determined to flaunt her lover's latest gift regardless of taste.'

'I understand.' Lina nodded; she had seen women like that on the arm of their lovers as they strolled in the park or drove in their new barouches, scandalising passers-by at the fashionable hour for the promenade. 'I cling, I flirt with you, but I also assess Inchbold rather obviously, then dismiss him as beneath my notice. I pout if I do not have your attention all the time and I have no idea what is going on.'

'Exactly,' Quinn said with a sardonic glance. 'One would think you did this all the time.'

'I do not,' Lina began. Quinn silenced her with a wave of one hand.

'Of course, your speciality is playing the virgin, is it not? Don't forget, I saw how you experimented with flirtation at the beginning—innocent one moment, knowing the next—until you settled on the part you were to play for me.'

That was close enough to the truth to make her blush, and he saw it. 'Quinn, I need to explain—'

'You can try later, if we aren't in the local lock-up by midnight,' he said as the dressing gong sounded. 'I need to get changed. You had better go and do your hair, as differently from that day as possible, and then go down to the salon—and don't talk to the staff; I do not want them implicated in this.'

Lina opened her mouth to argue, to somehow make him understand. But Quinn was already unbuttoning his waistcoat with one hand and yanking at his neckcloth with the other. She gave up the attempt and left.

Trimble blinked at her as she descended the stairs and Michael frankly goggled before he got his face back under control. Tight-lipped, Lina swept into the salon and sat down, trying to understand what Quinn was doing.

He did not believe her and yet he had not handed her over to Inchbold. Why not? She fought the urge to get up and pace like a caged cat and told herself that she had to trust in Quinn. He was not cruel, she knew him well enough now to believe that. Her safety depended on a man who felt angry and betrayed, and with good reason, and on her own ability to hold her nerve and act in a way that was utterly alien to her.

You are observant and intelligent, she told herself. *Think about those women, think about what the girls taught you of flirtation. Become a courtesan in your head.*

When Quinn entered the room she got to her feet with a smile and went to him. 'How handsome you look tonight,' she said, looking up at him from beneath her candle-black thickened lashes. She laid her right hand on his forearm, stroking along the thick green silk of his coat. 'Inchbold will never have seen anything like it.'

Quinn turned to walk with her back to the sofa and the long skirts of the coat parted for a moment. There was a dagger in the sash that cinched tightly around his waist. Lina glanced down and saw the small knife he always wore in his boot was still there and as she bumped against his side she felt the bulk of a pistol.

'You are armed?'

'Yes. The woman you are playing would have made a suggestive remark at this point, complimenting me on my magnificent weaponry,' he added.

'I am sure it is a very large and powerful pistol,' Lina responded, opening her eyes wide.

'Resist the temptation to giggle as you say it.'

'I have never felt less like giggling in my life,' she assured him as the dinner gong reverberated from the hallway.

As Michael pulled out Lina's chair for her, Quinn went to the windows, unlocking each one. She saw him turn the handle of the door at the rear of the room as he passed it. *He is making sure we have escape routes*, she thought, a fresh pang of fear cramping her stomach.

The meal passed in a dream. Lina forced herself to keep eye contact with Quinn whenever possible, to react to everything he said with smiles and nods, to offer no opinions of her own and to let her hands flutter close to her scandalously plunging *décolletage* at every opportunity.

He responded by holding her gaze until she felt the colour stain her skin. His voice became deeper, slower, his lids heavier as he watched her. When she glanced away, and it was always she who could not hold the look, she found herself staring at his hands, the long fingers caressing his wine glass, or dextrous on the carving knife. The scratches left by her nails had healed, faster than she had feared, leaving red marks that she wanted to soothe with her fingertips.

Her breath became shorter and a strange, disturbing heat began to build low down in her belly. Lina tried not to shift restlessly on her chair, but her breasts felt full and tight and there was a disconcerting, intimate pulse between her thighs that made her flustered and uneasy.

The meal ended after what seemed an eternity and Lina began to rise, to leave Quinn to his port. 'No, stay,' he said. 'Our visitor will be here shortly. Michael.' The footman set the decanters on the table and waited, attentive. 'That is all for the present. When Mr Inchbold calls, announce him at once.'

The man went out, leaving them alone, and she closed her eyes, seeking some relief from the intensity, the tension.

'Come here,' Quinn said, taking a tiny jar from his pocket and unscrewing the top. He dipped his forefinger into it and it came out red. 'Pout for me, Celina.'

Reluctant, she stood beside him while he touched colour to her lips as though painting an intricate picture. The touch was assured and disturbing as the cream caressed her lips, lingering over the fullness of the lower, gliding across the upper. 'There.'

Through the open window the sound of carriage wheels penetrated even the heavy curtains. Lina tried to step back to return to her seat, but Quinn took her hand and stood. 'Just one finishing touch,' he murmured, bent his head and kissed her, right on her painted mouth.

Chapter Twelve

Lina gasped, pulled back, but found herself held tight in arms that gave her no freedom to do anything but arch her back, pressing her lower body intimately against Quinn's blatant arousal. His mouth roamed over hers, his tongue pushed between her painted lips and into her panting mouth with complete assurance. If he remembered that she bit, it did not appear to concern him now.

There was no possibility of struggling, hardly any air to breathe, only the heat of him, the thrust of his tongue into the quivering moistness that seemed to arouse him so much, the strength of his hands, flat against her spine, the fingers splayed on her bare skin of her shoulders.

She wanted him to stop, she was frightened of her own response, the torrent of utterly undisciplined, alien feeling that swept through her—and yet when

Quinn did lift his mouth she put her hands up to pull his head down to her again.

'Oh, no, my passionate little *virgin*,' he said, his voice husky even as his eyes mocked her. 'There is no time for that now.' He took a napkin from the table, touched around her lips with it, then dragged the back of his hand over his own mouth, leaving a betraying smudge on his cheek. Quinn turned her to face the overmantel mirror and Lina stared at the pair of them. Her mouth was swollen and pouting, red from rouge and kisses. Quinn's eyes under the heavy lids were bright, alert, aroused. 'We'll do.'

He sat down in his chair again and pulled her back on to his lap. 'Ready?'

'After that?' Lina stared into the green eyes so close to hers and tried not to pant.

'Pretend you want to wheedle the nice big diamond I've got in my room out of me,' Quinn suggested, low-voiced, as the door opened.

'Mr Inchbold, my lord.' Lina did not dare look at Trimble, but she was sure that the butler's perfectly modulated tones faltered when he saw them.

'Show him in, if you please.' Quinn raised his head from nuzzling her bare shoulder and pushed her to her feet. 'Go and sit down, there's a good girl. You've had the pearls; I'm selling the diamond.'

Lina turned in a swish of silken skirts and sat

down, thankful her chair was so close. Whether it was that kiss or the appearance of the Runner, she did not know, but her knees felt like jelly. She put her elbow on the table, her chin in her hand, pouted her lips, and looked down the length of the table at the doorway.

Inchbold was a solid man, not tall, but broad across the chest. He had a face that looked as though it had been in many a fight and would be quite happy to engage in a few more. He was dressed like a countryman of the middling sort: neat in good cloth of a plain cut, but with pockets that bulged and boots that looked as though they had moulded themselves to his big feet.

'My lord. Miss Celina.'

He was looking to see how she reacted to the name. Celina let her eyes stray over him in a leisurely assessment, then merely nodded.

'Take a seat, Inchbold.' Quinn waved a hand at the chair opposite Lina. It was a considerable concession to a man like Inchbold to offer him a chair at table. Lina wondered if Quinn intended to disconcert the other man, but he merely nodded his thanks and sat stolidly on the broad satin seat. *Experienced and not easily intimidated*, she thought, her stomach churning.

Quinn poured two glasses of port and pushed one

across. 'Now then, this is my Miss Haddon. Are you going to tell me she is a witch who is able to be in two places at once?'

Inchbold reached into the breast of his coat and produced a sheet of paper, which he unfolded and spread out on the table, flattening it under one meaty hand. 'The footman who let the Shelley woman in is reckoned to be a bit of an artist,' he said. 'Seems this is a good likeness, by all accounts.'

Lina glanced at the sketch that had been strongly done in charcoal and pastels. The man had caught her perfectly: wide-eyed with fear, her mouth a thin line as she pressed her lips together to stop them trembling. Now she maintained her sultry pout and let her lids droop. As she tipped her head on one side a loose ringlet brushed her cheek, quite unlike the simple arrangement she had worn at Sir Humphrey's.

'Who says that's me?' she demanded petulantly, copying as nearly as she could the London tones overlain with gentility that Dorinda, one of the girls at The Blue Door, used.

'Information laid locally as a result of the notice in the *Morning Chronicle*,' Inchbold said, continuing to look at the drawing and then back up at Lina. *Mrs Willets*, she thought. *Mrs Willets and not my letter to Mrs Golding after all.* 'We knew you—'

Quinn cleared his throat ominously '—this Shelley female was seen at the Belle Sauvage, Ludgate Hill, so it seemed likely she caught the Norwich coach—'

'Or Bath or Bristol or Cambridge or...'

'Yes, miss. Quite.' The Runner glowered at her. 'It was *possible* she caught the Norwich coach, so a respectable source local to here saying that a mysterious female had turned up aroused our interest.'

'Who are you calling a mysterious female?' Lina demanded.

'You, my dear, are as mysterious as Woman always is,' Quinn said, reaching out a hand and running one finger possessively down her cheek.

Lina nuzzled against his hand like a cat seeking caresses and Inchbold's scowl deepened. 'You know London, do you, miss?'

'Course I do.' She tipped up her chin and gave him a saucy look. Goodness, but this was scary— and exhilarating. She would not think about Quinn, not yet.

'Know the house of The Blue Door do you?'

'All the girls know that one. Class place, that is. Not that I need a house, I like to be independent. You know, have my own gentleman, exclusive.'

'And what were you doing in France?'

'My last gentleman fancied seeing Paris, now we're at peace with them again. Lost all his money in the Palais Royale at *vingt-et-un*, didn't he? So he dumped me.'

'And I picked her up,' Quinn said. 'I don't believe in leaving a gaming house except with money in my pocket and a pretty girl on my arm.' He reached out and picked up the sketch, looking from it to Lina and back again. 'Inchbold, she's blonde, she's blue-eyed—as so many blondes are—and she's a young lady of an accommodating disposition. But otherwise, where's the resemblance? And delightful as it is to share a glass of port with you, I have to confess there are things I would rather be doing with my evening.'

The Runner frowned. 'Looks like I've been led on a wild goose chase.'

Don't show relief, don't faint, don't laugh... 'Looks like you have,' Lina said with a sniff. 'And I know who sent you on it, too. That sour-faced old bat, Squire Willets's wife.'

'Taken against you, has she?'

'Thinks I'm not respectable,' Lina said.

'Actually, she's taken against me,' Quinn interjected. 'I have a certain reputation and Miss Haddon here does not take kindly to being given the cold shoulder. The ladies have had a set-to and one of them appears to be of a vindictive disposition.'

The Runner eyed Quinn's exotic evening attire and cleared his throat, then tossed back his port and got to his feet. 'Aye, well, I'm sorry to have troubled you, my lord. Miss. And I thank you for your co-operation. There are those who would have taken umbrage.'

'You're just doing your job,' Quinn said, his eyes cold and steady on the other man. 'I have no quarrel with that. Just so long as you don't exceed your authority and you know when a trail's gone dead.'

Inchbold nodded, clearly understanding the message he was being sent. 'I'll be off back to London tomorrow, my lord. You'll not be troubled by us again.'

Quinn waited until the front door shut, then rang for Trimble. 'Trimble, send Jenks to me, would you? And, if you could intimate to the staff that Miss Haddon's state of dress and behaviour is in the nature of a masque? The Runner was on a false trail, but it was hard to prove it without some subterfuge. There will be gossip.'

'We do not listen to gossip, my lord,' Trimble said loftily. 'I'll send for Jenks.'

'Thank you—' Lina began, but Quinn held up one hand for silence. 'Not here.' He began to walk around closing windows until the groom knocked and came in.

'There's two of them, my lord. The other's been in the village and up along as far as Cromer. Interested in comings and goings here, by all accounts. I'll have a word with Tomkin and get him and the underkeepers to keep an eye out round the house, shall I, my lord?'

'Yes, do that. If anyone asks, it is a case of mistaken identity, but there is no need to go out of your way to volunteer anything. Thank you, Jenks, goodnight.'

Quinn was looking at her, Lina realised, pulling herself together. Inchbold had gone, her letter to Aunt Clara had not been intercepted, she could breathe again.

But not, it seemed, for very long. 'Upstairs, I think,' Quinn said in a voice that brooked no argument. 'I do not want to be overheard.'

He held the door for her, allowed her to precede him up the stairs with perfect courtesy and then took her firmly by the elbow, steered her into his bedchamber and turned the key in the look.

'Now then…' Quinn put the key in his pocket '…did you take that sapphire?'

'No!'

'Did you have anything to do with the man's

death?' He began to undo the knotted-silk buttons down the front of his long tunic.

'No—I—' Lina broke off, honesty warring with the desire to just forget every detail. 'He got very excited. I think he had a stroke. Or a heart seizure.'

'Did he, indeed?' Quinn threw the tunic on the chair and began on the shirt buttons. 'You lied to me.' His eyes slid over her, cold and detached. 'I do not like being lied to. You told me you were married and hiding from a husband who abused you.'

'You guessed that, I did not correct you. I did not think you would believe me if I told you the truth.'

The shirt joined the tunic and Quinn sat down on the end of the bed and began to tug off his boots. 'Yes, you were in a state, that first night, weren't you, Celina? Trying on roles until you found the one that fitted. Efficient housekeeper, meek young lady, flirtatious demi-rep.'

She bit her lip. It was difficult to look away from the muscled, bare torso. She had seen him naked, she reminded herself, but that did not help; in fact; it merely inflamed the confused feelings of fear and desire.

'I must admit, when you settled down to fugitive wife, you did it very well,' he said with the air of a man awarding praise for style. 'You chose something that you realised would gain my sympathy. What lies did you tell Simon?'

'None. I told him the whole truth. He knew my aunt, a long time ago. I think he may have loved her in his way.'

'And who is your aunt?' Clad only in his trousers, Quinn stood watching her, his hands on his lean hips, his bare feet flexing slightly in the deep pile of the carpet. She dragged her eyes away from them and up to his face.

'She is Madam Deverill, the owner of The Blue Door.'

'Not a pious spinster sewing hassocks, then.' His face was so expressionless that Lina knew he was furiously angry. 'She has imprisoned you there? You want to escape from her cruelty?'

'No, she has been everything that is kind to me, I love her—' She could not make Aunt Clara out to be the villain of this, even though that would perhaps win his sympathy. But if she could just get a word in, explain about Makepeace—

'You were under my roof, enjoying my protection. I do not like being made an unwitting accessory to a crime, Celina. Especially not a capital crime. Do I look like a man who would tolerate being lied to? Being forced to lie?'

No, he does not. No wonder he hates lies—look what that girl did to him with her falsehoods. Honesty in a woman must have become a very sensitive thing for him. 'I told you, I haven't committed a capital—what are you doing?' His hands were at the fastenings of his loose trousers.

'Undressing. We are going to bed.'

'*We*? I am not going to bed with you, Quinn.' She backed towards the door, realised too late it was locked and began to edge towards the pile of discarded clothes. *Which pocket did he put the key in?*

'You want to make even more of a liar of me? I told Inchbold that you were my mistress.' The heavy black silk fell to the floor and Quinn stepped away from it. Naked. Lina closed her eyes, but not before she saw just how aroused he was. This was no overweight middle-aged man, red in the face and groping for her. This was what she had been pretending to herself for days that she did not desire: a fit, handsome, athletic man in his prime. Liquid heat coiled in her belly. *Simple, instinctive lust*, Lina thought, dizzy with desire.

'I am sorry,' she protested. 'I do not want to be your mistress, I told you.' *Liar, liar.*

'Oh, yes, I recall now. You do not want to be bought, you want to be loved for yourself. Money is so sordid, is it not?' He had not moved, she realised, listening to his voice, fighting the urge to simply open her arms and give in. And she wanted to give in. Why? Because she desired Quinn, or because she wanted him to go on protecting her and if she became his mistress she was buying that protection?

That was an uncomfortable thought, that she could barter her virginity for a bodyguard. *And if I am not a virgin I have no value to Makepeace.* Another reason to give in to what she so desired.

Then I will be ruined. But I am ruined now. Or I might get with child—I could ask him to be careful...

'Tell me, Celina. When I kissed you after dinner, were you hating it? Did you want me to stop? Was I forcing you?'

'No,' she admitted, dragged out of her confused thoughts. She could not lie about that. He had known she was responding, known she was aroused.

'Tell me you do not want me to make love to you and I will open that door. I told you, I do not force women, even ungrateful, lying demi-reps.'

The silence stretched on. She could hear her own breathing, hear the blood rushing in her ears. 'I...I cannot tell you that.'

She thought she heard him make a sound, a sigh perhaps. 'This is your profession, Celina. You cannot afford to lose your nerve because of an unfortunate experience with one client. I'm not an overweight old man who needs help to perform and I do not need you to pretend to be a virgin. I would like you to enjoy yourself, too; it is not much fun for me if you do not.

'But don't stand there looking like a martyr waiting for the lions to come into the arena. I realise that is what you usually have to do and that you cannot relax and enjoy yourself under those circumstances, but you do not have to gull me into thinking you're a virgin by screaming the place down and using pigeon's blood and alum.'

'I cannot tell you that I do not want you,' Lina managed to say at last, focusing on the one thing that mattered to her, hardly hearing the cynical words about manufactured virginities. She opened her eyes.

Quinn walked to the pile of clothes and dug in the tunic pocket. 'Here.' He came closer and held out the key to her. 'Take it and then tell me again what you want.'

'You,' Lina said baldly, holding out her hand. Quinn laid the key on her open palm, she twisted her wrist and let the key slide to the floor.

'I warn you,' Quinn said, closing the space between them and laying his hands on her shoulders. 'I am angry with you, Celina. I am not sure still if I forgive you. I am not in the mood for sweet nothings, for wooing, for games. I need a professional and no frills. You understand me?'

'Yes, of course,' Lina lied with no idea what he meant. 'I am yours.' She smiled, and felt as though she had stepped from the top of a tall tower into space. She was falling, but there was no terror, only the consciousness that she had made an irrevocable decision.

If I am not afraid, if I don't show fear, he will not know, surely? she thought. *No, that's another lie. I must tell him.*

'Quinn, you ought to know, it isn't what you think, I really am—'

'Later,' he said, his voice husky as he began to unfasten her gown. 'Now is not the time for talking.'

'But—' And then the gown slid from her shoulders and he bent his head and took her right nipple in his mouth, sucking through the fine lawn of her shift and Lina felt her protest vanish in a gasp as sensation lanced through her from breast to groin. Quinn's fingers were busy with her laces even as he switched from one aching bud to the other, tormenting, licking, soaking the lawn until it moulded to her breasts.

Her stays fell away and he lifted the chemise and once again she was naked in front of an aroused man. Panic seized her, then she looked up and met his eyes, clear, green, intent, and the fear changed into a quivering apprehension laced with need and desire. *Not quite naked*, she thought, biting her lip against the wild laughter that was bubbling up, trying to escape. *I still have my stockings, my garters, my shoes.*

Quinn knelt, took her left foot and eased the soft kid slipper off, then took the other and removed that too. Lina caught her breath as she looked down on the dark head, bent so that the long hair parted, exposing his nape. He looked curiously vulnerable and she touched his head, a feeling of tenderness she had never experienced before sweeping away the shocking urgency of her desire.

This is why women yield, she thought, no longer trying to understand why she was doing this. Expediency, desperation, the need for protection all vanished in the overwhelming need to be touched, to be loved, by this man. Then he leaned in, kissed her right leg above the garter, his hands stroking down over her hips to hold her, and any trace of tenderness melted into the desire.

The bare skin was sensitive where it was constricted by the garter and Quinn's questing mouth felt scandalously intimate as he licked upwards. Lina groped behind her and found the bed post, seized it gratefully and hung on, waiting for him to stand. But the soft kisses, the wet, luxurious licks, kept travelling higher, higher until she gave a little scream as his tongue flickered into the moist secrets between her thighs.

She had seen pictures of this in the wicked little books that were scattered around at The Blue Door, but she had never imagined that a man would do that to her the very first time they were together. Nor had she imagined it to be anything but embarrassing and strange.

It was strange, yes. Her head fell back against the post as her hands reached out to cradle Quinn's head, to hold him, to prevent him ever stopping this shameful, wonderful thing that was turning her into a quivering, liquid creature of flame and passion.

'*Yes!*'

'Yes,' he agreed, standing up in time to catch her as her knees gave way. 'But time for that later. Show me, Lina. Show me those skills you have been keeping so secret.'

Chapter Thirteen

He wants me to make love to him? Lina closed her eyes on the sudden alarm. *I want him, I want to pleasure him...but he will guess, surely?* Or would he? Could she counterfeit enough skill from what she had heard, observed, read in those explicit little pillow books? She had begun to understand her own body now, what pleased her, what made her shudder with terrified delight. Could she use that understanding to make love to Quinn?

He was standing there, his hands supporting her, waiting. She opened her eyes and studied him under lowered lashes. He was beautiful and she wanted to touch him, to taste him. She licked her lips and saw his eyes following the movement, saw the effect that whatever was in his imagination had on his arousal.

Lina turned, bringing him with her until his back was against the bed post, then she caught his hands and put them behind his back, making a pretence of shackling his wrists with one hand. She was so close that their bodies rubbed together intimately, sending heat spiralling through her. She was wet with desire for him already, she realised, trembling with daring at what she was doing.

Quinn's eyes on her face burned with desire, with demands she could only guess at. Trembling, Lina bent her head and swept her tongue over the flat muscles above his right nipple, tasting salt and musk and man. The kick of delight surprised her, then the tip of her tongue found his nipple and she teased it, closing her eyes at the sensation, feeling it knot under the laving strokes.

He groaned, deep in his throat, and his hands shifted as he gripped the bed post as though she had truly tied him there. She licked her way across to the other nipple, tormented that until he was shuddering, then slowly slid to her knees, her tongue trailing down to circle his navel.

Lina put her hands on his narrow hips, more to steady herself than to hold him and Quinn shifted his feet apart as she realised where she was going, where this was leading, what he expected. Her shyness, her fears, seemed to have vanished. Lina stroked her cheek against the hot, hard length of

him, fascinated at how soft the skin was, intrigued
to feel the reaction to her slightest touch.

'Lina.' It was a plea and a gasp and a groan and
she reached for him, took him in both hands, felt
him shudder. 'More...'

There was that book that had shown... Dare she?
Her grip tightened as she thought it, drawing a
groan from Quinn's throat, and she tried a tentative
stroke, up, down. It was so arousing, so overwhelming. Yes, she dared. Lina bent her head to him and
let herself drown in the sensation of pleasuring a
man. This man.

His hands came to grip her head, she could feel
his whole body shuddering with the effort not to
thrust, then he freed her, bent and caught her up.
Lina felt herself being laid back on the bed. The
mattress dipped, his hands slipped under her but-
tocks, raised her and then, before she had time to
understand what was happening, Quinn entered
her with one long thrust.

It was shocking, so much faster and harder and
more than she had been expecting. Lina, even as
aroused as she was, gasped, *'Quinn!'* Her body
arched beneath his, fighting to accommodate him,
searching instinctively to make the joining possible. But the shock was not the pain—she had
expected that and it was fleeting, unimportant.

The shock was the pleasure. She had not realised how he would feel within her, how she would be completed by his body, how the sensation of being filled almost to the point of endurance could be so terrifying and so wonderful all at once.

Her body quivered and almost instantly she felt it yield, to begin to caress him, to open to him. Sensation flooded her, even through the lingering discomfort, the consciousness of her own clumsiness as she tried to mould herself to Quinn's long body and the drive of his hips.

'Hell!' Lina's eyes flew open as Quinn pulled away from her, out of her, the heat and weight of his body vanishing to leave her bereft and confused. He flung himself to one side of the wide bed and lay there breathing like a man who had run hard and fast.

'Quinn?' Lina reached for him and he rolled away and off the bed to stand with his back to the wall as though she had gone for him with a knife.

'Quinn?'

Quinn fought his way past the string of swear words that was all his brain seemed able to produce and managed to articulate. 'You were a virgin.'

He had just taken a virgin with the briefest of caresses, hard, fast, without care. *Dear God, I have ravished a virgin.* His mind filled with the nightmare images that still tormented his dreams: the huddled, bleeding figure in rags that flinched away when he tried to touch her, her eyes glazed over in pain and anguish. He had bought the girl when he bought Gregor, two broken, abused pieces of human wreckage. Gregor had fought back to life, had tried to help him with the girl—they never discovered her name—but men, any men, simply terrified her. The fourth night she killed herself as they slept.

For weeks afterwards Quinn had not been able to bring himself to lie with a woman. Gradually the revulsion against his own desires became rational again. He did not behave like that to women and he had done his best for her. But the experience had left him, he knew, with reservations that were not shared by most men of his age and class. He had paid for a night of frustration before now when he had realised that the apparently willing professional in his arms was being forced by a pimp. The idea of buying a virgin nauseated him.

And now, because he was aroused and angry, he had taken Celina as he would have an experienced Cyprian. He had expected her to behave like one, she had taken him in her mouth as a result of his demands. How could he have done that, how had she managed to overcome the revulsion she must surely have felt? What had he become if he had not even realised?

She was lying there just as he had left her, Quinn saw as he turned his head. As he stared at her, the image of the slave girl cleared, replaced with Celina's slim, pale body. His brain struggled with the confusion: she admitted she came from The Blue Door, that her aunt was a Madam, that she had been with a man, intimately, before he died of what sounded like a stroke brought on by excitement.

But she was a virgin. Don't make excuses. There are no excuses for what you have just done. Celina looked back at him, her eyes wide and dark with questions and confusion.

'You were a—'

'Don't you want me?'

They spoke together and answered together. 'Yes,' Celina admitted.

'Yes,' Quinn said between clenched teeth. She looked vulnerable and soft and infinitely desirable and he wanted, more than anything, to take her back into his embrace and love her—love her gently and sweetly and with skill, as a virgin deserved from her first man.

'Then, why have you stopped?' she asked and he realised that, much as he wanted to make love to her, he was losing his temper as comprehensively as he ever had in his life and that he really did not feel safe touching her. Which was a good thing, he concluded grimly, because he should not be touching her, gently or otherwise.

'Do you really have to ask?' Quinn demanded as he snatched up his robe. There was blood on his body, a smear. Hers. 'I do not deflower virgins—or I did not until you lied your way into my life.' He belted the robe and flicked one side of the coverlet over Celina as she sat up.

'But...' She paused and he saw her collect herself, fight the after-effects of unsatisfied passion, just as he was doing. 'You are upset because I did not tell you. But I tried—'

'Upset?' He stalked over to the dresser and poured himself a large glass of brandy, thought about it, poured another and went back to the bed and handed that to Celina. 'Yes, I would say I am upset. And all I can say is that you did not try very hard, Miss Shelley. In fact, you deceived me, did you not?'

'Yes,' she said, chin up. She was not defiant, he realised, feeling a sneaking admiration for the fact that she was making no effort to placate him or wriggle out of this. If his body would only stop admiring her too...

'Did you think it would not matter to me?'

'I realised I would not be very good at making love and you might be disappointed,' Celina began and Quinn saw red. 'But men seem to like—'

'I do not force women,' he snarled between gritted teeth as she flinched away. 'I do not deflower virgins—but I have just done so because you, I presume, thought you had better attach me in some way to ensure I do not hand you over to the authorities after all. Which means that I have somehow given you the impression that you cannot rely on my word any more than I can rely on yours.'

'No!' Celina protested, sitting bolt upright and letting the silk coverlet slide down to her hips with devastating, innocent, effect. 'I wanted you to make love to me because I desired you.' The wide blue eyes vanished as her lashes came down in confusion. Quinn winced at the stab of ridiculous, treacherous pleasure the words gave him. He could not trust this woman, yet his own instincts threatened to betray him.

She was acting again, of course, and he was coming to believe that this wide-eyed protestation of innocent desire was her best performance yet. Miss Celina Shelley was a courtesan in training being groomed to take over from her aunt one day. She had been about to lose her virginity very profitably to Tolhurst when he had keeled over and, while it cannot have been anything but a very unpleasant experience, it was difficult to believe that she had been a prisoner of her own aunt, a woman she said she loved, or had been forced against her will.

There was no other explanation for her willingness to make love to him as she had, to be as bold and as sensual.

'I should have told you, but I had no idea you would take on so,' she finished with a gasp of indignation. 'You are a rake, you told me so yourself. You have a shocking reputation. I thought rakes did that sort of thing all the time!'

'Well, *I* don't,' Quinn retorted. 'Where do you think I would draw the line if you believe that of me? Abduction? Rape?' He threw himself into a chair at a safe distance from the bed—and the temptation to wring Miss Celina Shelley's delightful neck. 'And cover yourself up, I am not made of iron.'

She grabbed for the edge of the coverlet in confusion while Quinn tried to calm down. At least there was no risk he had got her with child, not that he would not have been careful in any case, he thought, resting his aching head on the chair back and glaring at the ceiling.

'I suppose that being wrongfully accused of seducing Lord Sheringham's daughter would have made you sensitive to such things,' Celina ventured. 'And being the victim of lies would give anyone a strong dislike of falsehood. I did not mean to deceive you out of any malice.'

Quinn looked at her curled up now against the pillows, swathed in the lush green silk of the bedcover. The picture of the perfect mistress, if it was not for the frown on her forehead and the anxiety in the wide blue eyes. And that lovely, kissable lower lip that just now she was biting in distress.

He let go of the anger as best he could and listened to his reason. Yes, she was telling the truth now: she had not deceived him about her identity for any motive other than fear. He was still not certain why she had wanted to come to his bed. He had a fair idea of his own worth, women appeared to find him attractive, but it took more than that surely, for a virgin to go so far?

Then he reminded himself what had triggered this whole chain of events—she had been in the act of selling her virginity to Tolhurst, so giving herself to him to secure his protection had to be an easy choice. And Celina's instinct that once he had slept with her it would tie him to her emotionally was not wrong, either. Could he blame her?

He tried to be fair. She was at risk of her liberty, if not her life.

'Won't you come back to bed?' she asked.

'No! Celina, I have told you—'

'No virgins, I know. But I am not one any more.'

'You are as good as,' Quinn said, trying not to recall the feel of her, hot and wet, tight and silken around him.

That provoked a snort of rather desperate laughter. 'I do not think I can be just a little bit of a virgin, Quinn.' He glared at her and she sobered immediately. 'Isn't it very painful for a man to stop like that?'

'It is not comfortable,' he said, hoping to sound repressive and merely, he feared, achieving fractious. 'It will get better in time.' She really was the oddest mixture of innocence and knowledge. 'Especially if you leave. You should go to your room. Are you…are you all right?' Damn it, he should have checked at once. He had hurt her, for heaven's sake, there had been blood. His damnable temper. Quinn felt a pang of guilt, then shoved it away. He was feeling bad enough as it was and it was all her fault.

Celina shifted a little, then bit her lip. 'I'm sore. Just a bit,' she hastened to assure him.

He now felt worse. She was being brave. Shouting at her was not going to help and he could hardly just throw her out of the room. 'You need a warm bath,' he said, in an attempt to deal with this practically. 'With salt in.' He got up, gathered her scattered clothing together and went to the door. 'Stay there.'

If nothing else, he could cope with physical hurt even if he had no idea how to deal with the distress she was inevitably going to feel in the morning when the reaction to the danger of the Runner's visit and the eroticism of that heated coupling subsided and she realised just what had happened.

Lina blinked back tears. She could not collapse and weep all over Quinn, not after what she had done. He was furious with her for lying, for entangling him with the authorities and for not telling him she was a virgin. She had thought, if he realised, that he might have found whatever pleasure other men did in that, but, apparently not. The very idea had angered him.

How had she got into this situation? If she had known she could trust him from the beginning, then she would have told him about the Tolhurst Sapphire. But she had not known and everything had followed from that, every tangled lie, every pretence.

Quinn came back, her robe in his hands, a night-gown over his arm. 'Here, put on the robe and go into the dressing room.' He turned away as he handed it to her, walked to the bell pull and stood with his back to her even when he had tugged it.

His respect for her modesty had the opposite effect to the one he had intended, Lina thought, blushing at the memory of her utterly wanton behaviour. The trouble was, she brooded as she scrambled off the bed and into her robe, Quinn's reaction only made her want him more. He was chivalrous as well as intelligent, attractive, desirable… Lina knotted the sash and went into the gloomy little chamber that did service as a dressing room.

It was not until she shut the door behind herself that she wondered what she was doing there and what Quinn had rung for. Surely not to have her bath brought at this hour? It would utterly compromise her in the eyes of the staff. She should go back to her own room, but there was only the one door and she could hear him speaking to someone.

Lina sat down on the *chaise* and looked round, feeling rather blank. Soon, she would have to think about what had just happened, about how she felt about Quinn and how she was going to live day to

day with him now. The triumph and excitement she
had felt at Inchbold's retreat, his acceptance that
she was not the woman he was looking for, was
ebbing away. That immediate danger was past, but
it was very clear that the authorities still believed
her guilty and were not looking for anyone else.
How was she ever going to clear her name?

The sounds from outside were still continuing.
Lina curled up on the *chaise*, wincing slightly at
the unaccustomed intimate soreness. There was a
little blood and she wished she could wash. She
put her head on the bolster at the end and closed
her eyes, too weary to try to think any longer.

She must have dozed off, she realised as the door
to the bedchamber opened, and she blinked against
the sudden flood of light. More candles had been
lit and, in the corner, steam was curling up from
the marble sarcophagus.

'You rang for that to be filled at this time of
night?' Lina walked stiffly to the doorway. Towels
were spread on the edge of the bed and Quinn was
rolling up the sleeves of his robe.

'I did. Highly inconsiderate of me, I know. I also
made the point of warning the footmen to tiptoe
past your bedchamber door as I assumed you would
be asleep,' he added, shaking what she assumed

must be salt into the water. 'Come and get in and soak a while. It will make you feel better.'

He sounded briskly practical, but he looked grim as he moved to put the screen around the big marble container and she realised he was afraid he had hurt her.

Protesting was embarrassing. Lina smiled a nervous *thank you* and slipped round the screen. She shed her robe and climbed the library steps that had been pressed into service. It was easy to get over the side and she slid into the warm water with a splash and a sigh of pleasure at the way she could sink up to her neck.

'Are you all right?'

'Yes, thank you.' Silence. Something prompted her to keep talking. 'Such luxury! No wonder you use it daily. But I am sorry that you will appear so inconsiderate as to have demanded a second bath and at this hour.' It was easier to talk without being able to see him. How strange that they could speak like this when only a short while before she had lain in his arms, their bodies joined. The very thought of it made those rippling waves of sensation run through her again, and she saw with surprise that her nipples had hardened despite the warmth of the water.

Even the new aches and soreness were pleasurable,

Lina found, as she cupped the water in her hand and let it trickle over her body. How could her body feel like this when there was so much wrong, so much to fear?

'Lina?' It sounded as though he was pacing.

This was no time to hide in the bath tub. Lina found the soap and washed, wishing she was not rinsing away the scent of Quinn as she did so. She stood up, then realised that without the steps she could not climb out. 'I'm stuck, Quinn. My legs are not long enough to get out.'

'Here.' He came round the screen, eyes closed, holding out a large bath towel. 'Wrap yourself in that.'

It seemed ridiculous to be shy after what had happened, but she was grateful for his tact. 'I am decent now.'

Quinn opened his eyes. She wished he would smile, but he still looked grim as he put his hands around her waist and lifted her out.

'Quinn, are you tired?'

His eyebrows lifted. 'I am not sure how to take that—I will try not to feel insulted.' Lina felt herself blush; he was talking about their short-lived lovemaking. 'No, I am not tired.'

'Then let me tell you who I am, how I came to be

at The Blue Door, what happened at Sir Humphrey Tolhurst's house. Everything.'

'Get dry, then, and put on your robe.'

When Lina emerged Quinn had lit the fire and tidied the bed. The room looked innocent and comfortable and safe. 'Curl up on the bed,' he suggested. 'I'll sit here.' She wondered whose protection that distance was for. 'Now, tell me it all. Honestly.'

'I was brought up in a vicarage in the Suffolk countryside,' Lina began, flushing at the implication that she would tell him any more untruths. The pillows were soft yet firm and smelt of Quinn as she tried to make herself relax. 'I have two sisters— Arabella and Margaret—and our mother died when we were children. Our father is very strict, very puritanical…'

Chapter Fourteen

'…and Lord Dreycott took me in,' Lina finished, perhaps half an hour later. 'I have heard nothing from my aunt, so I wrote to Cook, who lives out, the other day, but there has been no reply from there either. Now I do not know what to do.'

'So this man Makepeace forced you to go to Tolhurst?' Quinn was looking decidedly sceptical.

'Yes! What choice did I have?'

'Run away.'

'Where to?'

'Back to Suffolk,' he said as though it should have been obvious.

'My father would have thrown me out.' She was not convincing him, she could see. 'And my sister had gone, too.'

'And you say Makepeace told you that and you believed him?'

She had not thought that the man had lied, Lina

realised. Of course, that was the sort of lie he would tell. Then the way Quinn was phrasing his questions hit her. He thought she was telling another pack of lies.

'Your father is a vicar,' he persisted. 'Am I to believe he would be seen to throw you out? He would be angry, I have no doubt. Had he ever struck you?'

'No,' she admitted. He had whipped Meg, but never her or Bella. 'But he shouts—'

'Are you telling me that being shouted at by your father is worse than being deflowered by Tolhurst?'

'No, of course not. But Makepeace was demanding the money. If he didn't get it, he would do all those dreadful things at The Blue Door.'

'He would do them anyway. You are an intelligent woman, you would know that.'

'You do not believe me, do you?' she demanded.

'I believe that you are being groomed as your aunt's successor by both her and her business partner. You would not welcome the encounter with Tolhurst, but you accepted it as a necessary evil. After that, yes, I believe that you are not responsible for the theft.'

'Why should I lie to you now?' Lina wanted to weep. She thought that she had Quinn's support.

Yes, he was right: her story was full of holes if it was looked at objectively, in cold blood. But how to convince a confident, courageous man that at the time she had felt terrified, trapped, without any option but to submit?

Perhaps if she had thrown herself on his mercy right at the beginning, he would have believed her. But now she had lied to him, deceived him, shown herself less than chaste.

'For the same reason you wanted to be my lover once I had heard Inchbold's story—because you need me.'

'I see.' Lina felt too miserable even to protest. She lay back against the pillows and closed her eyes. 'So, what happens now?' He could not throw her out because of the will. They were tied to each other.

'We must both go to London,' Quinn said, startling her so much she sat bolt upright. 'Letters are too dangerous.'

'We? You will take me? You will help?'

'Of course.' Quinn was staring back at her. 'Do you think I would abandon this—you—now?'

'But it will compromise you even more if I am caught,' she protested. 'If they come back, you can say you were mistaken in the dates or something, but if you do something active, then it makes you an accessory, does it not?'

'Yes. So we will not be caught.'

We, Lina repeated to herself. *We. I am not alone any more.* 'Thank you,' she murmured. 'I do not know why you should, after I lied to you, but I am just so grateful.'

'I dislike injustice as much as I dislike lying,' Quinn said. Lina dropped her eyes from the look in his. He was disappointed in her as well as angry, she realised. 'We will go to my town house—the one I have purchased and spent one night in so far—and establish you as my mistress, just in case the Runners are still taking an interest. I will write to Gregor tomorrow, tell him to work faster to open it up and employ servants.'

'The will,' Lina recalled, and her heart sank. Of course, there had to be a reason why this would not work.

'There is no reason that you must stay here. You are entitled to, but I do not read that codicil as compelling you to remain here. If I cannot clear your name in six months, then I will send you abroad until I can.'

'Abroad?'

'Better than Newgate, wouldn't you say? But that's academic—we will face it if we have to.'

The relief that he was not abandoning her made it difficult to think straight, but she still felt so guilty. 'You would do all this for me after I embroiled you in it, lied to you. How can I repay you? I…I led you on to make love to me when you believed I was not a virgin. But I am not any more. If you still want me, then I will be your mistress, Quinn.'

Even as she said it, Lina knew she was making a mistake. Quinn's face hardened and his hands closed into fists on the arms of the big chair, but when he spoke his voice was calm. 'If I give you money for sex, you say that makes you a whore,' he said. 'If you give me sex for protection, what does that make me?'

'A bodyguard?' Celina ventured, her cheeks flaming. Pride, male honour, this man's honour. She understood none of it well enough, it seemed, and now she had blundered again.

Quinn felt the anger and the tension dissolve. He wanted to laugh for what seemed the first time all day, and controlled the impulse, afraid if he began he would not stop. His innocent courtesan-in-training had managed to put her dainty foot in it, yet again. And this time, he was convinced, she had meant it as a genuine gesture, offering him the one thing of worth she possessed: herself.

He wished she would put some real value on herself, he thought. But perhaps the prospect of the gallows made everything else—honesty, virtue—unimportant. She knew too much, including how to lie and how to act, but she was still too innocent for her own good. He could not stay cross with her any longer, even if letting go of his anger made him vulnerable to the physical attraction that had him aching for her. But he would not trust her over anything but the fact she had no idea what had happened to that sapphire.

'Celina, have you ever desired a man physically before?' he asked, seeing the pink turn to deep rose as she shook her head. 'I know you enough to realise that you will be sorry if you waste that first experience with someone you don't have strong, real feelings for, someone who docs not feel like that about you. You are a romantic. I am flattered you are attracted to me, but I do not sleep with romantic virgins.'

He was wasting his breath, wasting the emotion with which he tried to convince her of the importance of what he was saying. She probably thought he was a complete hypocrite, a rake lecturing a woman he had just been with on the importance of romantic love, of chastity and waiting for the right man.

But he could recall what it had been like to feel that the act of love was sacred and he knew the bitterness of romantic youth on having that belief shattered. His entire adult life had been turned around because of one young woman's lack of honour and the disillusion it had brought. In his anger he thought of revenge on any society female careless enough to put herself in his power, but he knew in his heart he would never do that. But the men who had trapped and traduced him—they would pay.

'But I am not a—'

'Yes, you are, in here.' He touched his forehead as she frowned at him. 'You had convinced yourself that you could separate whatever happened with Tolhurst from what is inside you, but, believe me, you cannot.'

She looked away, biting her lip.

'You have my word that I will help you, Celina. I do not need paying with anything—except truth.'

There was no response, just a tiny shake of her head, so Quinn pressed on with the practicalities, working it out as he spoke. 'Tomorrow I will write to Gregor to expect us, tie up the loose ends here and you will practise with the macquillage until you can fool a lady's maid into thinking you use it all the time. Then the day after we will leave for

London by post-chaise. And I want you to write down every single thing you can remember from the moment you agreed to go to Tolhurst until the moment you arrived back at The Blue Door. Everything, every tiny detail. Describe it as though you had to paint a picture of each scene. Do you understand?'

'Yes.' Celina nodded. 'You are looking for clues about the sapphire.' She yawned hugely, transformed before his eyes from a desirable, beautiful, dangerous creature into a tired young woman with too much to bear on her slender shoulders. 'Oh, I am sorry.'

'If you tell me you are sorry one more time, I will turn you over my knee,' Quinn threatened. He was tired of gratitude, he just wanted honesty. Then he wished he had not spoken, as the image of her squirming in his lap while he stroked that perfect peach-like bottom had the inevitable result. 'Go to bed.'

Celina scrambled off the bed. 'Goodnight, Quinn.' She leaned in as she passed him and dropped a hesitant kiss on his cheek as he was off guard getting to his feet. 'Thank you.'

Hell. There goes a night's sleep. He was not certain whether he dreaded the inevitable erotic dreams or the familiar nightmares most.

* * *

'How can you read with the carriage swaying about like this?' Lina asked, clutching at the strap with both hands as the post-chaise lived up to its nickname of *yellow bounder* over a particularly rutted piece of road. 'I would be sick in an instant.'

'You get used to it. It is worse reading on camelback,' Quinn said, his eyes fixed on the sheaf of papers she had given him that morning as they set off for London.

'Really?' Images of camel trains trekking across boundless deserts filled her imagination. *Oh, to be away from here, away to somewhere strange and wild and free. With Quinn.*

'It is like being on a ship in a swell. It rolls back and forth and side to side at the same time and you are a long way off the ground,' he said, his eyes still fixed on the page as he removed a pencil from behind his ear to make a note. 'Is this Makepeace a man of means?'

'He's a crocodile,' Lina said, the camels merging into a vision of the River Nile, its banks covered in evil, grinning reptiles. 'Have you ever seen the Nile?'

'Yes. And the crocodiles,' Quinn added, looking up and smiling. 'But has he money?'

'I have no idea. He is very anxious to get his teeth into The Blue Door and to do disgusting things that would make higher profits. Why? Surely he could not have stolen the sapphire?'

'I agree. I don't think he would risk alienating a good client by staging a theft while one of his girls was on the premises.'

One of his girls. That is me, Lina thought, trying not to be hurt by Quinn's choice of words. She had to accept that he classed her as a courtesan. He had taken her virginity and that, she knew, put her on the wrong side of the wafer-thin line that divided decent women from their fallen sisters. One thrust of that hard body and she was ruined, but for him she had been lost before that, ruined from the moment when she had chosen to stay and not flee from Makepeace.

It was strange being shut up with him in the post-chaise. Yesterday's flurry of activity had given her little time to reflect on the events of the previous evening, yet now she was alone with the man who had taken her virginity, the man she still wanted with a passion that she knew she did not have the vocabulary of words, or actions, to express.

The rake had vanished. So had the man amusing himself by playing the country gentleman. This was the traveller and the adventurer now, planning an expedition, heading into danger. And she could see the scholar, too, in the concentration on her story, the search for clues, the precise notes.

'I need to get inside The Blue Door and talk to your aunt,' he said, frowning at the page. 'I imagine that will not be difficult?'

'It will not be, provided she is well,' Lina agreed. 'But she suffers from a stomach complaint that sometimes lays her low for days at a time. She was ill with that when I left.'

'Then you must tell me how to reach her rooms. Makepeace will want to help clear the smear from the name of the establishment, but I am assuming he does not know where you have gone and we cannot risk him deciding to ingratiate himself with the authorities by betraying you.'

'So you accept I have reason to fear him?'

'Of course.' Quinn raised one eyebrow. 'Brothel keepers are rarely people of finer feeling or elevated moral standards.'

'I had better come with you,' Lina said, pushing away the logical conclusion that he classed her, and her aunt, in the same category. 'The house is a maze.'

She expected him to refuse, point blank. Instead he looked at her, while he pushed a lock of tawny hair back behind one ear. 'It would be dangerous.

Besides the risk of you being captured, there is a strong probability that I will run foul of the doormen and you could end up in a fistfight.'

'I have no doubt that you would deal with them.' And without hesitation, either. He was used to living where violence was an everyday occurrence and, even if she had not overheard Michael's awestruck comments about the training sessions in the barn, she knew he was hard and fit.

'Do I frighten you?' Quinn asked, startling her out of her recollections of his naked body.

'Yes,' Lina said. '*Yes*. You are outside society, outside convention. You are free in a way I do not understand.' *And I love you*. The realisation drove the breath from her lungs and the blood from her face. In all her daydreams it had never occurred to her that her true love might be utterly out of her reach.

'I would never hurt you,' Quinn said as he reached for her hands, obviously thinking her reaction was alarm. 'Not more than I have already,' he added under his breath.

'I know.' Lina let him take her hands, curled her fingers within his for a second before freeing herself. She must not indulge her need to touch him, for she *was* frightened now with the vision of their parting all too plain in front of her. What was she going to do, feeling like this about a man who would be gone from her life within months? 'I…' *Love you. I will always love you.* 'I trust you, Quinn.'

'Then rest, relax. We will defeat the dragons together.' He went back to reading her narrative for what, she was convinced, was the fifth time. *Dragons. My knight, set on a quest to rescue a very tarnished damsel. And he said* together. *Does he really mean that? Can he possibly mean to treat me as an equal partner in this when he does not entirely trust me?*

'Of course we will,' Lina said. 'Although I am not very experienced with adventures,' she added. 'Or dragons.' It was only fair to warn him. 'My sisters always said I was the timid one.'

Quinn stared at her. 'Timid? I hardly think so. You ran away from home and got yourself to London. Had you ever travelled by yourself before?' She shook her head. 'Then you climbed out of a window to escape from Tolhurst's house and got to Simon. You coped with the shock of his death and my arrival.'

Lina bit her lip at the satirical tone in his voice when he said that. Her subterfuge was not forgiven. 'I—' Well, yes, she had done those things. Perhaps she was not totally lacking in courage.

'You stood up to the Runner, too, even though you were so frightened. That takes nerve.'

'I did not do it very well,' Lina muttered, thinking how utterly she had relied on Quinn. Without him she would have simply collapsed, she was certain.

'Rather too well, perhaps,' Quinn said, his eyes on the papers. One corner of his mouth twitched, just a little.

What would he do if she changed seats, curled up next to him and kissed that provoking hint of a smile? He would probably pick her up and deposit her firmly back where she was now, she concluded, not certain whether that was a good thing or not.

His actions had meant that, even though she had lost her virginity, it was, perhaps, not as bad as it sounded. There was no risk that she was with child, she had acquired none of the experience of a lover, even though he had seemed to find her attempts to caress him convincing. If there ever was another man, perhaps he would believe her a virgin still. *More lies.* And besides, she could imagine wanting no other man but Quinn, ever.

But now he certainly appeared well able to resist whatever it was about her that had so aroused him when he thought to make her his mistress.

Of course he could. She had lied and had put him

in a position where he had to lie, too, or betray her. And then she had let him make love to her believing she was a woman of experience, a woman who had been married. *Instead he finds himself deflowering a virgin and that obviously outraged his honour even more than the lying. It is a good thing I was already ruined by my association with The Blue Door or he might have felt honour bound to—to marry me?*

Oh, yes, that is likely, Lina mocked herself. It was better to jeer at the thought than to take it seriously, even for a moment, for the pain of dreaming was just too great. The daughter of an obscure country vicar marrying a baron? Even if she had been utterly respectable, it was highly unlikely. But now, she was quite impossible. Quinn had enough of a problem with his own reputation and retrieving that, without involving himself with her. He would need to make a careful, well-judged, marriage to someone of the utmost respectability who would not mind when he took himself off on his travels for months at a time.

'Don't sigh,' he said without looking up. 'You must not get despondent or you will lose your will to fight and you need every drop of that.'

'I'm not despondent, exactly,' Lina said. 'But how is getting into The Blue Door going to help?'

'One thing at a time.' Quinn tapped his teeth with his pencil and frowned at her notes. 'You told your aunt that you could not recall whether Tolhurst had been wearing the ring when you arrived, but now you think he was?'

'I was in such a state when I got home that I could hardly think straight,' she admitted. 'But writing everything down like that, I began to recall. He made me undress and he was... I tried not to look at him but he was taking off his own clothing and I saw a blue flash, which must have been the ring catching the light.'

'Which side?'

'The left side. And it was the left hand that Reginald Tolhurst, his son, lifted to feel for a pulse. But I must have been wrong, imagining things, because the ring was not there then. He laid his father's hand back on his chest and his fingers were in plain sight.'

'I see. Reginald is not the heir?'

'No, his elder brother George has inherited. He was away, I think.'

'Good,' Quinn said, as though that confirmed something he had been thinking. He folded the papers and set them aside. 'Do you play chess?'

'No.' Lina watched apprehensively as Quinn removed a small box from the valise on the seat beside him and opened it to reveal a travelling chess set. 'I do not expect I will be any good.'

'No, Celina.' Quinn shook his head at her as he put the board on the seat and began to set out the pieces. 'No defeatist talk. You can do anything. Now, this is a pawn...'

Chapter Fifteen

Chess lessons were one way of taking her mind off her troubles, Lina thought, even if one of those troubles was sitting opposite her maintaining a scrupulous distance and patiently explaining for the fourth time what the difference between a rook and a knight was.

They were in London now, rattling over cobbled streets she did not recognise, working their way south towards Mayfair. Quinn had told her the address: Clifford Street. Not one of the great squares, but a very respectable, obviously fashionable, street running east off Bond Street. Just how wealthy was Quinn? she wondered, eyeing his plain breeches and coat. He had gems and silks, business affairs in Constantinople and now there was the house they were drawing up in front of, which, if it was not rented, had cost him a pretty penny.

'That is Gregor's next door.' Quinn nodded to an

identical portico with plastered hood and elaborate ironwork.

'You both bought one?'

'Yes. Seemed a good investment,' he said, helping her down. 'Now I am going to spend time here, then I will buy more property. London is expanding by the day.'

'Welcome.' Gregor stood on the top step of his own house, grinning at them. 'You have brought me some excitement, just when I was getting bored with London.' He ran down the steps and joined them on the pavement, his eyebrows lifting comically as he took in Lina's changed appearance. '*Madame!* A masquerade?'

'Good afternoon, Gregor.' She dropped a slight curtsy, making his grin spread wider.

'No, this is not a masquerade,' Quinn said and she saw the Russian's eyes narrow at the edge to the words. 'Come, we will walk and talk where we cannot be overheard.'

'I would like to go inside first,' Lina said. The idea of walking, in broad daylight, without checking that her disguise was intact gave her palpitations. In fact, she was not certain she had the nerve to do it even then.

'Of course, I should have thought.' Quinn obviously thought she needed to retire for more intimate reasons.

'Shall we all go in and have a cup of tea and then go out?' she suggested and to her relief the men followed her past the butler and through the front door, almost cannoning into her as she stopped dead in the front hall. 'How wonderful!'

And it was. A lofty hall with a great hanging lantern, a dramatic sweep of stairs with wrought-iron banisters and an array of massive panelled doors. 'So large and grand.'

'I am intending to entertain,' Quinn said, much as he might have announced he was about to declare a small war. Lina cut a sideways glance at him and saw his expression; he looked grimly amused.

Now what is that about? she wondered as Gregor introduced the new butler, a middle-aged man called Whyte, to Quinn. 'I'll speak to the rest of the staff later,' he was saying. 'Tea in the drawing room now and please send Miss Haddon's maid to show her to her room immediately.'

Gregor had selected a pleasant, plain, young woman who had an air of discretion and common sense about her. 'Prudence, ma'am,' she said, bobbing a curtsy. 'This way, please, ma'am.'

The bedchamber, after the Gothic eccentricities of Dreycott Park's furnishings, seemed modern and airy and luxurious. Lina sat before the dressing-table mirror patting rice powder into her cheeks and touching up tiny smudges of candle black under her eyes while Prudence dealt with loose hair pins. Lina wondered what the girl thought of serving someone who was all too obviously the paramour of her master.

They drank tea in the elegant drawing room, the men exchanging news about business matters, some new publications, domestic trivia that Gregor had dealt with. He was discreet about how he had spent his time otherwise, Lina noticed, although she suspected he would be less inhibited when she was absent.

'Berkeley Square,' Quinn said, grounding his tea cup. 'You would like an ice at Gunter's, I am sure, Celina.'

And if I said no, *I would find myself there anyway,* Lina thought, not sure whether to be amused or irritated. The men escorted her punctiliously, leaving her feeling rather like a small prisoner between two large, if unlikely, jailers. She kept her head down, expecting a Bow Street Runner to jump out at any moment and point an accusing finger at her.

'Nervous?' Quinn asked as they paused at the kerb, waiting to cross Bond Street.

'No…yes. Yes, I am,' Lina admitted.

'Well, stop looking as though you have something to hide or are going to faint with nerves,' he said. 'You are behaving like a girl about to make her come-out dithering on the edge of the dance floor. Remember, you are my mistress and act like it.'

'But I am not, am I?' she shot back. 'So it is quite hard to imagine the role. But I will do my best to act as brazenly as you would wish.' Gregor, she saw, was biting the inside of his cheek, presumably in an effort not to laugh. What had Quinn told him in the time she had been upstairs? They were as close as brothers—did that mean they shared everything, even her intimate secrets?

Lina tightened her grip on Quinn's arm, put up her chin and looked around her with frank, defiant, curiosity. In some ways, that was easy to do; she had never ventured this far into the exclusive world of Mayfair and in such a fashionable lounge as Bond Street there was the chance of seeing almost any member of the *haut ton*, including the Prince Regent.

The shops were dazzling. Lina saw Savory and Moore, where her aunt obtained the fine milled soap she insisted on using at The Blue Door. 'I would like to go in there, one day,' she said, slowing down, then saw the advertisement in the bow window: *Newly arrived, the renowned Seidlitz Powders, exclusively to be had of Savory and Moore. An infallible cure for every digestive distress or obstruction.* Or perhaps not, certainly with a masculine escort.

Quinn turned into Bruton Street. 'We must certainly shop. You have your image as an expensive ladybird to establish.'

By the time they emerged into Berkeley Square Lina was feeling thoroughly out of charity with Quinn. Ever since they had arrived he had been more autocratic and less sympathetic. Perhaps the full enormity of the problem had only dawned on him as they reached London, or perhaps he was simply regretting taking up her cause. *I am a fool to love you*, she thought, deliberately pouting at him before batting her eyelashes at a passing gentleman. The young man smiled and slowed, then focused on her formidable escort and hurried past.

It was easy to see where Gunter's was. Rows of open carriages were drawn up, each with one or more ladies sitting inside, their male escorts leaning against the carriage doors or the railings that enclosed the central rectangle of gardens, while waiters in huge white aprons hurried back and forth with trays laden with ices and sorbets.

'We will sit under the plane trees, not being in possession of the requisite fashionable carriage,' Quinn said, walking through the gate. 'What would you like, Celina? An ice or a sorbet?'

'Lemon ice, please.' She unfurled her parasol and stared around while Gregor went to place their order. 'What is wrong, Quinn?'

'Nothing,' he said and smiled. Lina blinked. No, nothing was wrong, he was simply vibrating like a tuning fork with concentration and excitement, tightly reined. He was enjoying this, the danger, the challenge, and his sharpness with her was like the orders of an officer just before battle. She was one of his troops and he wanted her obeying commands and with all her weapons in perfect order. She wondered if he had forgiven her for her lies; she suspected not, but it did not seem to spoil his enjoyment of the fight now they were in it.

Gregor came back, a waiter at his heels. When they were seated, with no-one within hearing, he said, 'Now, tell me what this is all about, my friend. You give me mysterious instructions, send me to an expensive brothel—I do not complain of that, you understand—and now Miss Celina arrives looking delightful, but not quite as a respectable *jeune femme* should and with an air as though the devil is after her.'

'Quinn, if we tell Gregor, then we are implicating him, too,' Lina said. 'I should have thought of that.'

'Indeed. Gregor, do you object to being made an accessory to a capital crime?'

'Who committed it?' the Russian asked. 'You have murdered your husband, Celina? Did he deserve it?'

'I do not have a husband and I have not done anything wrong. At least,' she corrected with scrupulous care, 'I have not committed any capital crimes. I am unjustly accused of one.'

'Of course. So tell me. I think we are here to prove you innocent, no?'

'Yes, but if we fail, then you and Quinn will have been seen to help me.'

'So? There are many other countries in the world where I can live, quite happily. Tell me.'

She should not be happy that yet another innocent person had become embroiled in her troubles, she knew, but the thought that Gregor's formidable presence would be at Quinn's back made her feel much safer for both of them.

'Celina lives at that brothel I sent you to,' Quinn said. Lina waited for the change in Gregor's expression. He would think less of her, she knew, treat her differently. But he just nodded and settled to listen as Quinn told the story, including the events as she had described them in her notes. Although he did not spell it out, she knew the Russian would be quite clear that she had gone to Tolhurst's house deliberately to sell her virginity.

I will not behave as though I am ashamed, she thought. *I have nothing to be ashamed of. Except lying to Quinn, embroiling him in this, not telling him I was a virgin and falling in love with him*, her conscience reminded her. She made herself concentrate on what Quinn was saying.

'We need to talk to Celina's aunt, Madam Deverill, and discover what she has been able to find out and what she has done to clear Celina's name. She may still be too sick to have done anything—did you see her when you were there?'

'I did. A lady of great personality,' Gregor said. 'In her day, which was not so very long ago, I think, she would have been one who wove magic—an enchantress.'

'So my great-uncle thought, I assume,' Quinn said. 'She is well?'

'She looked fragile, like glass. But formidable. Now I hear the story I can see she is under great strain, but she hides it—almost.'

'I have a back-door key,' Lina said. 'We could

let ourselves in and make our way to Aunt Clara's rooms.'

'No.' Quinn shook his head. 'I want to see Makepeace in action if he is there and I want to walk in through the front door legitimately so if we are found wandering about we may plausibly be lost.'

'Then I will go in at the back door,' Lina said. 'I still do not understand what Makepeace has to do with this.'

'He is a loose end I want to snip off,' Quinn said, infuriatingly vague. 'No, we all go in the front door.'

'But I cannot!'

Gregor looked across her at Quinn and laughed. 'Aha! Our young friend the prince incognito?'

'Exactly. I have the clothes in my baggage.'

'What are you two talking about?' Lina demanded.

'Let me explain,' Quinn said. 'Once we had reason to remove a young lady from a place where she was not happy to be.'

'A harem?'

'A staging post on the way to one. We could not walk out with a young woman, so we left with—'

'A youth!' Fear and a thrill of excitement made

her laugh out loud. 'But could I pass?' Quinn's gaze swept down over her bosom and she coloured up. Her breasts were not impressive, she knew that, but perhaps, now, that was a blessing.

'By the time I have finished with you, you would pass for the Shah of Persia,' he said with a grin.

It was certainly a high-class establishment, Quinn thought as they mounted the steps of The Blue Door at half past eleven that evening. The deep blue paint was offset by gleaming brass fittings, torchères flamed with brazen disregard for discretion and elaborately clipped shrubs in tubs lined the wide steps.

He looked for the spy hole and saw it blink with light for a moment before the door swung open. 'Monsieur Vasiliev.' The big man inside spoke politely, even as his eyes flickered over the two figures beside the Russian. 'Welcome back. And your friends also. You will sign the book?'

It was all part of making this seem like an exclusive club, Quinn thought, signing *George Arbuthnott* with a flourish. Doubtless the book was full of more pseudonyms than genuine signatures. He stood back and the slim youth at his side bent his turbaned head over the book and produced an elaborate flourish. It had taken Quinn half an hour to teach Celina how to write something short but very rude in Arabic.

'Gentlemen, the salon.' Celina took a step forwards and he reached to touch her arm, then she must have realised her own mistake, for she dropped back, gazing around as though in wonder at what must be very familiar surroundings indeed. The doorman gestured towards a wide arch hung with blue-velvet curtains. 'Mr Makepeace will be with you at once to enquire your pleasure. Refreshments will be brought.'

They sauntered through. Celina he could feel quivering slightly—fear or excitement? He suspected both, but he had confidence that she would act her part. With her hair concealed under a turban, her curves by a long jacket of heavy silk with a long brocade waistcoat over the top and full trousers caught at the ankles, she made the perfect youth. Her skin was stained to a warm gold, her eyebrows and lashes blackened and her blue eyes subtly ringed with kohl to make them seem darker. Cotton pushed high inside her cheeks changed the shape of her face and she had spent the afternoon following Gregor around trying to walk like a man—an exercise that had them both in fits of laughter.

Now she was serious, staring about her with a

good approximation of a cocky youth rendered nervous by his first exposure to the sins of the flesh. Perhaps she had seen enough young men receiving their initiation here under the aegis of older brothers or even fathers to know what to do.

There were half-a-dozen young women in the room and four men. A swift glance reassured Quinn that he knew none of them. Two of the girls fluttered over, all pretty silks and low cut gowns. 'Gentlemen.' A redhead with bouncing curls took Gregor's arm. 'Oh, you've come back and brought some friends, Mr Gregor.'

'Friend,' Celina said in Arabic. Her accent was atrocious, but with any luck no one here would speak the language.

He had taught her three words. *Friend* for those she knew would not betray her, *enemy* for those who might and *unsure.*

'Ooh.' The redhead giggled. 'Who is the young gentleman?'

'A very *special* young gentleman,' Quinn said with heavy emphasis. 'He speaks no English and those who serve him would be very anxious if they knew he was out. But young men will be young men, hmm? And we think it is best he sows his wild oats with us and not by slipping off and getting into mischief.'

'I'll help him keep out of trouble,' the redhead said with a smile, fluttering her lashes at Celina, who ducked her head and wriggled in convincing embarrassment.

'I think we would all like to stay together,' Quinn said. 'Perhaps some of your friends would like to join us?'

'Ooh, yes. I'm Katy and this is Miriam.' The brunette gave him a look that promised a night of smouldering pleasures. 'And there's Daphne, just come down.'

'Unsure,' Celina said after a swift glance at the statuesque blonde.

'How about someone more our young friend's size?' Quinn asked.

'Paulette?' Katy looked at Miriam, who nodded. 'She's ever so sweet and she's tiny.' Katy's hands waved about five foot from the floor.

'Friend.'

'He likes the sound of her,' Quinn said.

'I'll just get Mr Makepeace and find a nice room.' Katy fluttered off, leaving Miriam to press glasses of champagne into their hands and lead them to couches on the far side of the room from the other group.

Wedged between himself and Gregor, Celina was safe from Miriam's wandering hands that just now had settled one on his thigh, the other on his shoulder as she curled up on the sofa next to him. He was in proper evening clothes after a hectic afternoon at the tailor and shirt maker and the skilful caress was hard to ignore through thin knitted silk.

He could have worn his own eastern clothing here, but the first part of the evening had taken him to the Society of Antiquaries. He had membership, originally because old Simon's influence had overruled any qualms about his reputation and latterly because of his own fame amongst men who valued travel and scholarship above tales of society scandal.

Now he had a handful of introductions, some renewed acquaintances and two invitations. His own campaign of revenge and reinstatement was running very well alongside Celina's adventure. But there was no time to think of that now; the man approaching them across the room was more than sufficient distraction from Miriam's wandering hands.

'Here is Mr Makepeace,' she said. Quinn decided that the man's taste in waistcoats alone was a crime.

Chapter Sixteen

'Mr Vasiliev, Mr Arbuthnott, er...' he frowned a little at the crown of Celina's turban, which was tilted towards him '...sir, welcome.'

Quinn could feel Celina pressing closer to his side. Tension was radiating from her and he could see why she disliked this man so much; now he was showing them an unctuous servility, but the crocodile was visible beneath the surface. The urge to put an arm around her was strong and quite impossible. He wondered at how protective he felt.

'Gentlemen. May I offer you any supper yet, some more wine? Or perhaps you would prefer to retire upstairs immediately? The room is ready. There are menus tucked in that folder should you wish to enjoy any of our other facilities.' He offered the small leather file he carried and Quinn opened it to see the cost of the room and the girls they had chosen set out. The price was high and the options available had him raising his eyebrows. Something for everyone except those who preferred flagellation or their own sex or, he noticed as he got to the end of page three, young girls.

Even as he thought it Makepeace remarked, 'If there is anything that you gentlemen desire that is not on the list, do, please enquire. I will do my best to obtain it. I hope, very soon, to expand the range of the delights to be had at The Blue Door.'

Celina was grinding her teeth. Quinn got to his feet. 'Thank you, but what we have ordered will be sufficient. We may be some time.'

'But of course! Just ring if you need anything.'

'*A nasty piece of work,*' Quinn observed in Arabic, apparently to the slender young man climbing the stairs at his side.

'*The male staff are armed,*' Gregor answered from behind them.

'Here we are.' Katy threw open the door to a room with a vast four-poster bed with a scantily clad young woman lying in wanton invitation in the middle of it. There were mirrors all around, a *chaise*, and marble sculptures of classical beauty and startling obscenity. Celina, he saw, did not turn a hair. No wonder she was immune to the weirder archaeological remains scattered around at Dreycott Park.

Quinn locked the door behind them and walked to the *chaise*. 'Are there any spy holes in this room?' The girls shook their heads in unison. 'Then, ladies, may I rely upon you not to shriek?'

'Only if you want us to,' Katy said with a wicked twinkle. She perched on his knee and wrapped an arm around his neck, a sweet-scented soft bundle with a wicked tongue, which she proceeded to use on his ear.

'Katy, Miriam, Paulette—it is me, Lina,' Celina said, pulling off the turban, and the three girls abandoned any pretext of interest in the men.

'Oh, my Lord!' Katy gasped, throwing her arms around her. 'You're safe! Where have you been? We haven't dared ask Madam in case that toad Makepeace is listening. You didn't take that sapphire, did you?'

'Not that I'd blame you if you had,' Miriam chimed in.

'Ladies, please.' Quinn held up his hands. 'Not so loud. Let us sit down and Celina will tell you all about it.' She shot him a sideways glance, her darkened skin strange in contrast to the tumbling blonde hair. 'A short version,' he added.

'...and Lord Dreycott wants to talk to Aunt Clara,' Lina finished. It felt so good to be with her friends again. Miriam and Katy sat either side of her with their arms around her waist, Paulette sat on the floor, gazing up at her open-mouthed.

'Can you prove her innocence, my lord?' Katy demanded, her eyes fixed on Quinn with fierce loyalty.

'Yes,' Quinn said with quiet confidence. Lina wanted to get up and hug him, but she made herself stay still. He was seeing her in what he thought of as her natural surroundings at last; his opinion of her would be set in stone by now. 'Can you bring Madam here, or can Celina and I get to her without Makepeace knowing?'

'Best to go to her,' Miriam said. 'Paulette can stay here with Mr Gregor just in case Makepeace puts his ear to the door.' Both Gregor and Paulette looked enthusiastic about that suggestion, Lina noted. 'Katy and I can cover both ends of the corridor—we'll say we've come out for more wine or something if Makepeace or one of his bullies comes along.'

In the event they reached Aunt Clara's door without any alarms other than a patron chasing a squealing girl out of one room and into another. Lina scratched on the panels and after a moment the key turned and the door opened.

'Lina!' She was in her aunt's arms, both of them

sobbing, hardly aware of Quinn behind her propelling them both firmly into the room and locking the door behind them.

It took a while for both of them to regain their composure, but eventually she was able to introduce Quinn.

'Of course, the new Lord Dreycott. Thank you so much for taking care of Lina,' Aunt Clara murmured, turning her handsome blue eyes on him. 'I was so grateful to Simon for taking her in. I received the letter you sent to Cook, my dear, but I haven't been able to get anything out. That wretched man watches like a hawk and I did not dare do anything to give away your hiding place.

'I am never going to forgive him for what he has done to you,' she added fiercely. 'To sell you to Tolhurst like that and then for this to happen!'

'It was Makepeace's idea to introduce Celina to Sir Humphrey?' Quinn asked.

'Of course it was! Do you think I would do such a thing to my niece? The swine took control when I was so ill and forced her by threatening me and everyone here. He knew that her only role here was as my companion and to keep the books, but he threatened all of us, so she felt she had to obey him.'

There was silence as Clara twisted her handkerchief

between her hands. Lina looked at Quinn. 'I am sorry,' he said, directly to her. There was regret and a sort of anger in his eyes. 'So sorry.'

'I had lied to you,' she said, meeting his gaze, holding it. 'I understand.' She hated that he had misjudged her, but she understood why, admired him for his immediate apology. A lesser man would have justified what he had thought, what he had said, but Quinn was too honest for that. Perhaps it was why she loved him, that fierce honesty.

Aunt Clara was looking puzzled at the exchange and her frown deepened as Quinn turned back to her. 'How much do you owe Makepeace?'

'A thousand pounds. He controls one-tenth.'

'Would you prefer a different investor, Madam? Myself, for example? I would be a sleeping partner—I have no desire to interfere with your management of the establishment.'

'You? Yes, of course,' Aunt Clara said, an incredulous smile spreading across her face. 'But how would you make him sell?'

'You cannot,' Lina interrupted. 'Just think what an outcry it would make if it became known! Lord Dreycott, part-owner of a brothel? You cannot afford more scandal if you wish to re-establish yourself in society, Quinn.'

'Why should it become known? And besides, the

name of a front-company would be on the papers. It would take a determined investigation to find the truth and why should anyone bother?'

'But how will you persuade him? He enjoys running a brothel.'

'Gregor and I have friends who, shall we say, walk on the shady side of the street. And they have been hard at work for us for several days. It seems Makepeace has been involved in transactions that verge on the treasonous and I think he would be very glad to take a thousand pounds and the opportunity to distance himself from them if he is warned that not to do so will result in him being betrayed to the authorities.'

'It would be a vast relief—' Clara broke off at the sound of raised voices outside the door, then relaxed when the speakers moved on. 'To be rid of the loathsome creature would be bliss. But this does not help Lina's predicament.'

'That is the next problem,' Quinn said. 'Is Reginald Tolhurst an *habitué* here?'

'Why, yes. He seems to bear no grudge for the circumstances of his father's death. I wish he was more prompt in settling his account, I must confess—I suspect he has not inherited much to set beside his debts.'

'Is he here tonight?'

'I believe so.' Aunt Clara got up and opened the door that led to the passageway to her secret gallery. Laying a finger on her lips, she motioned to them to follow and Lina found herself once more in the familiar darkness, peeping down through the grill at the salon below. Makepeace was greeting a group of noisy new arrivals, girls flitted back and forth, for all the world like a flock of exotic butterflies and men lounged, drinking, laughing, joking. 'There,' she whispered, pointing and Lina stiffened at the sight of the man who had accused her.

As he stood at her side Quinn slipped his arm around her shoulders and pulled her to him. His lips grazed hers, warm, gentle, conveying trust and regret as much as any physical desire. It was so quick she had no time to react before he was leading the way back to the drawing room. Lina felt comforted, strengthened. He believed in her now, even if he would not be able to forgive her for lying to him at the beginning and embroiling him in this scandalous crime at a time when he must, surely, be wanting nothing but social acceptability for himself.

'I need to get to know him,' Quinn said. 'I'll go down now—will it be safe for Celina to stay with you, Madam?'

'What about Gregor?' Lina asked The thought of some time to talk alone with her aunt was bliss, but she could hardly abandon the Russian.

'I imagine he is getting our money's worth out of a large bed and the undivided attention of three young ladies,' Quinn said with a grin that took several years off his age and had her laughing back at him.

'What a fascinating man,' her aunt observed when the door closed behind him. 'I do not blame you for falling for him. I did not know Simon until he was a good thirty years older than your Quinn is now, but I can see him so clearly in his great-nephew.'

'He isn't *my* Quinn,' Lina protested, but she could hardly deny that she had fallen for him, not with the way Aunt Clara understood her. 'But I wish he was.'

'Why is he doing this for you, if he is not?' Clara asked. 'I know about the old scandal—he does not need to court more trouble. Are you lovers?'

'No. I should not say it, but I wish we were.' What had happened between them did not count, she told herself. 'He is angry with me for not telling him the truth from the start, for putting him in a position where he had to lie to the Runner.'

'He does not show it. Are you sure, my dear?'

'Yes,' Lina admitted. 'He hates lying. And liars,'

she added. 'I should have seen that I could trust him, but I did not. He is doing this for me because I think he would never stand back and see an injustice. He bought Gregor when he was a slave, almost dead, and nursed him back to life, gave him his freedom. I think he is a very fine man,' she added, appalled to find herself almost in tears. 'I just do not think he values himself so much.'

'You are in love with him. That means only heart-break for women in our world, my dear.' Her aunt came and sat beside her, putting her arm around her shoulder.

'Am I of this world? I suppose I am and society would condemn us all and never see the good in you, in the girls here,' Lina said, all the excitement of the evening, all the hope, draining away. 'I love him. I dream of marrying him, and I know how impossible that is. And he will not take me as his lover, so I cannot even have that.'

Quinn lounged against a pillar, smoking one of Reginald Tolhurst's inferior cheroots, and let the man talk, looking for his opening.

'Only thing wrong with this place is that there's no gaming room,' Tolhurst observed.

'You know, you're right. What's your game?'

'Whist, piquet, whatever's going,' Tolhurst drawled. 'I'm a fair hand at all of them.'

No, you are not, or you'd not boast of it, Quinn thought. 'Friend of mine recommended a place just round the corner. I haven't played there myself, mind, which makes me a trifle wary.' He looked uncertain and saw the interest in the other man's eyes. 'I'm not used to town hells, if the truth be told—I've been abroad too long.'

Tolhurst smiled patronisingly. 'I fancy I'm up to snuff. Why don't we try it tonight? If you're finished here, of course.'

'I'll be right with you,' Quinn said, all eagerness. 'Just let me go up and drop off a note for the fellow I came with.'

We both believe we've caught a pigeon, Quinn thought as he went upstairs and knocked on the door of the room he had left Gregor in. After a moment it opened a crack and Paulette peeped out. 'Give this to Gregor, will you? And make sure he reads it.' He scribbled on a page from his pocket book—*Easier than I thought. Going to the hell now. Be there in two hours, send C. home in a hackney*—and handed the note to the girl. Then he went to tap on Madam Deverill's door.

When she opened it he saw no sign of Celina. 'You're being careful, I see. Gregor will come and collect Celina shortly and send her home in a carriage.'

'And you?' Celina appeared just behind her aunt. Her eyes were red, he noticed.

'I am going to play cards with Tolhurst, who thinks he is going to rook an innocent from overseas.' Celina's eyes widened in alarm and he grinned. 'I didn't tell him I learned to play cards in the Palais Royale.'

When he saw Gregor stroll through the salon at the discreet little hell in Pickering Place, Quinn was just throwing down his hand in disgust. 'Damnation! Well, that's me for the evening. Good sport, Tolhurst—I hope you'll give me the opportunity for my revenge another day soon.'

'But of course, my dear fellow.' Tolhurst was raking in the banknotes and coins with ill-disguised delight. It seemed the intelligence that Gregor had gathered, that the man was near bankruptcy, was correct. 'My card.' He handed over the rectangle of pasteboard and accepted Quinn's in return. 'Goodnight to you.'

Quinn got up and went to the door to collect his coat and hat, then waited in the small courtyard of Pickering Place until Gregor came out. 'That's got him. He thinks I'm a pigeon for the plucking and he'll be far less wary next time.'

'Can he play?' Gregor followed Quinn through the narrow alleyway and out into St James's Street. To their left the great Tudor palace blazed with light. They turned right and began to walk uphill towards Piccadilly.

'He's superficial. He isn't good at calculating odds and once he starts to lose he throws more money after it in a panic. I can have the shirt off him. We'll give him a couple of days to convince himself that he's better, and I am worse, than he recalls and then…' Quinn slammed his clenched fist into the other palm. 'We'll have him.'

'Celina has gone home,' Gregor said. 'I had a very good time with her friends—such nice girls!'

'Yes.' Quinn felt a jolt of guilt. He had been avoiding thinking about it, but there was no escape from the fact that he had not believed Celina when she told him that she had been forced to go to Tolhurst. She had accepted his apology with grace, which was like her, but he suspected he had wounded her deeply and that disturbed him.

The fact that he had taken her virginity was even more of a disaster now. He had not simply reduced the value for which she could sell herself, he had ruined her. When the shadow over her was lifted and she was cleared of the theft, then, with the legacy from old Simon, she could establish herself respectably. But if a man came into her life, courted her, wanted to marry her, what did she tell him? Did she lie and hope her husband did not notice that he was not the first or did she tell him the truth when he proposed and have him almost inevitably leave her?

'She does not belong there,' Gregor said abruptly. 'Those are nice girls, but not good girls. Celina is a good girl.' The sideways look he gave Quinn was as close as he had ever come to a criticism.

'I spent the night on the *chaise* with her,' he said, trying not to sound defensive. 'She was having a nightmare.' Gregor was silent. 'Hence my hands.' He did not tell him about the night that Inchbold came.

They stopped at the kerb, the traffic in Piccadilly heavy, even at that late hour. 'A thousand pounds is a fine dowry for a young lady, I think,' Gregor remarked.

'Yes.' Quinn strode out into the road, ignoring the shouts of the hackney-carriage driver who had to steer round him.

'That is good.' Gregor caught up with him as he turned into Old Bond Street. 'Will you find her a husband?'

'Certainly not,' Quinn snapped. 'Do I look like her mother?'

'No,' the Russian agreed. 'But you pick up stray lambs, do you not? And she is one.'

'I picked you up, and you are not a lamb, are you?' *You appear to think you are my conscience, damn it.*

'No,' Gregor said. 'I am a wolf, and you are my friend. So what are we going to do about the lamb?'

'Nothing,' Quinn said, meaning it. 'This is not the Mani, or the middle of Anatolia or the backstreets of Constantinople. We prove her innocent and that is that.'

He dug in his pocket as they reached the steps to his front door and pulled out the key. Gregor dogged his heels in through the front door.

'We sort out Tolhurst,' Quinn said over his shoulder. 'I continue to acquire invitations to polite gatherings until I get in a position to corner Langdown and then I fight the duel. After that—' He turned and found himself face to face with Celina, still dressed in her youth's clothes, but bareheaded.

'You do *what*?' she demanded.

Chapter Seventeen

Over Quinn's shoulder Lina saw Gregor beating a hasty retreat. The front door slammed, leaving them alone. 'I've sent the staff to bed,' she said, blocking the way to the stairs. 'Why on earth do you want to fight a duel? Who with?'

'Langdown, Sheringham's son,' Quinn said. She thought for a moment he was going to pick her up bodily and set her aside; instead he turned into the drawing room. Lina followed.

'After ten years?'

'It is a matter of honour. I wanted to fight and he would not. I was left with the choice of staying in England, branded as a seducer of an innocent young lady, or leaving the country. They took my good name, spat on my honour, tore up my career and my plans with as much conscience as they would have in swatting a fly. Now I will challenge

Langdown and he can refuse and be branded a coward or he can give me my satisfaction.'

'He might give you your death,' Lina retorted. Her stomach felt as though she had bolted ten of Mr Gunter's ices one after the other. How could he risk everything like that?

Then she made herself think about him, and not about how she felt, and understood the gnawing anger and shame of that old scandal. This was a man for whom truth and honesty were vital. His instinct was to protect women, to care for the weak and defenceless, and he had been branded a man who would ravish an innocent and abandon his own child.

'I am too good for him to kill me,' Quinn said arrogantly, glaring down his nose at her.

'He might be better,' she pointed out, unable to let it go.

'I doubt it.' He walked away to the sideboard and splashed brandy into a glass. 'Forget that, there is something more important. I am sorry. I should have believed you when you told me you had no choice but to go to Tolhurst.'

As apologies went, Lina thought, pushing aside her fear about the duel, she had heard more gracious ones. He was probably tired; although he hid it well, he seemed to have his head filled with a half-dozen intricate plots all at once and he was not used to having to apologise for anything. Timid Lina of a few weeks ago would have been grateful for the expression of regret and would not have dreamed of challenging a man about his plans.

This new Lina threw herself down in a big winged chair and curled up, momentarily distracted by how comfortable the loose trousers were. 'You had your preconceptions about me. It doesn't matter now.' But it did, and the fact that it had taken her aunt's words to make him realise the truth stung. She was probably being unreasonable—after all, she had lied to him about who she was, what she was, why she was there—but she did not feel in the mood to be fair.

She tipped her head back, shook her hair straight and began to plait it into one heavy braid; it gave her something to do with her hands other than hitting him, or dragging him to her for a kiss. Quinn was silent while she worked, brooding into his brandy glass as he leaned against the sideboard. Lina tied the end of the plait with her handkerchief for want of anything better.

'You want to begin your return to society with a scandal?' she demanded.

'It has a pleasing symmetry to it. I left it with one, after all.' He knocked back the brandy in one gulp and put the glass down. 'I will deal with Reginald Tolhurst by the end of the week. Makepeace, too. When that is straightened out with the authorities you can emerge as Miss Shelley once more, so it is probably best if you are not seen with Gregor or me. My courtesan idea is not a good one, not now I realise the truth of your situation.'

'I stay here, hiding away while you two superior males *deal* with the situation?'

'Yes.'

'And then what am I supposed to do?' Lina demanded.

'You can hardly go back to The Blue Door, not now your circumstances have changed, so you had better return to Dreycott Park for the remainder of the six months and then you will have your thousand pounds and can do what you want.'

A few weeks ago that would have seemed like a miracle. Now the prospect made her miserable because Quinn would be here, living his new life, far away in every sense of the word, and she wanted to be with him, always. Which was impossible. He was a baron who was about to recover his reputation, provided he survived this insane duel he was plotting; her only hope of respectability was to retire to some out-of-the-way market town and trust that her chequered past never caught up with her.

'Thank you,' she said blankly.

'What is the matter?' He came and stood in front of her as she sat there, curled up in her exotic boy's clothes. 'I told you everything will be all right. Your name will be cleared, we'll get Makepeace out of your aunt's life and you will have your own money.'

Lina shook her head. What could she tell him except the truth, that she loved him? Even the new, braver woman that she was baulked at that. Quinn would want to run a mile—he was not a marrying man, beside anything else. Perhaps one day he would fall in love, but she thought it far more likely that he would find a complacent wife to give him his heir, keep his house and leave him free to do exactly as he pleased.

'It is the other night, is it not? When I took you.' She saw the way his eyes darkened, just thinking about it. She winced. *Took you* sounded so brutal for something that had been, for a few moments, so wonderful.

'I do not consider it,' she said. *There I go, lying to him again.*

'Then you should do. It is going to be damned awkward if you want to marry.'

'Why? I can always deceive him,' she said, feigning lightness. 'I am sure the girls can tell me all the tricks I would need to use.'

'You would lie to your husband?'

'No,' she admitted. 'Not if I loved him.' *I will never find another man I can love, so that does not matter.*

'Hades,' he swore, turning away. She watched him, enjoying the sight of his lean elegance, the masculine strength of him, even as she struggled with the misery that threatened to sweep over her. He turned back, intent on her expression. 'Well, there is only one thing I can see that would square this circle. Marry me.'

Lina felt the blood drain out of her face. 'No. Absolutely not. Impossible.' Quinn opened his mouth, but she swept on. 'You are a baron. Even before all this, I was simply Miss Celina Shelley from an obscure country vicarage. I cannot possibly marry you—with your history you need a wife of the utmost respectability, not a nonentity who has lived in a brothel, been accused of theft, was found in a naked man's bedchamber... Oh, yes, and not only is my aunt a courtesan, so was my mother, although I do not believe my father ever discovered that.'

There, surely that was enough to stop this

madness. But, no, she saw as she watched him, it was not. 'It sounds eminently sensible to me,' he remarked, folding up neatly on to the carpet to sit cross-legged at her feet as easily as if he was wearing his Eastern clothes. 'I get a wife who is not going to cavil about my past. I know the worst about you. No secrets. We will be good in bed,' he added, watching her from under hooded lids.

'Is that all you think about?' Lina demanded, furious to find he was putting outrageously tempting thoughts into her head. Sex should not matter. Love should and Quinn's future and reputation.

'Certainly not. I am thinking about Simon's memoirs, Makepeace, Tolhurst, throwing a party, the duel, selling the Park, buying clothes, whether or not I can leave my business in Constantinople for six months or whether I need to send Gregor back there to supervise... And taking you to bed.'

'Oh!' Lina dragged the cushion out from behind her back and threw it at Quinn. It hit him in the chest and he laughed and rolled with it, sprawling back on to the carpet, over six feet of elegant, desirable, hard man spread at her feet for the taking.

'I don't know why I didn't think of it before,' he said, sitting up again without using his arms.

His stomach muscles must be like iron, Lina thought. 'Because it is a ridiculous idea. I have no intention of sitting at home, sewing a fine seam, dusting your library and bringing up the children while you career off around the world with Gregor. Marriage ought to be a partnership.' *Children. Our children.* She could almost see them.

'Ah, yes, you want love in marriage, do you not?'

'Yes,' she said, staring back into the amused green eyes.

'And you will either have to lie to the man you love or lose him,' Quinn observed.

'Why are men such hypocrites about sex?' Lina demanded. 'You are not a virgin.' He grinned. 'And that is not supposed to worry me.'

'A man likes to know who the father of his children is,' he observed. 'And, yes, we're hypocrites. Jealous and territorial. You would get the benefit of a great deal of experience and the knowledge that I'll fight to the death for you.'

'I wouldn't want you to!' It was a shamefully exciting thought, even as she denied it. 'Even if you survive this idiotic duel you are intent on provoking. And as for experience, I am sure that is overrated.' As soon as she said it she knew it was a provocation too far. Quinn looked at her through slitted eyes for a moment, then reached out, seized her wrists and pulled her out of the chair and down on top of him so they both ended up on the carpet with her on top.

Lina gasped, almost winded, her senses full of the impact of hard muscle and the scent of hot man, cigar smoke and brandy. He rolled before she could get free and she found herself trapped, his elbows on either side of her, his thighs bracketing hers and the very clear evidence of his arousal pressing into the junction of her thighs with devastating effect.

'Get off! You said you do not force women—or doesn't that count if they are not virgins?' They were almost nose to nose. He had only to lower his head a few inches and he could take her mouth. Take anything.

'It will not be force and I promise you will not end up any less of a virgin than you are now,' Quinn said. 'Don't you want to know what you are turning down?' He angled his head and trailed his tongue-tip along the line of her jaw. 'Give me one minute and then, if you want to, say *no*. How dangerous can one minute be?'

'Lethal,' Lina said, trying not to pant.

'Sixty seconds. Start counting.' His mouth covered hers and his tongue slid between her lips, opening them, opening her, to heat and moisture and the taste of him.

One, two, three… He tasted of brandy and spice

and what must be just himself and the thrust of his...*five, six*...tongue was blatant and demanding and her own tongue met it, licked against it, tangled...*nine, ten*...found the hardness of his teeth, found the soft inside of his cheek...*twelve. Oh, I cannot...fourteen.* His hand was moving, she felt buttons give way and long fingers probing the bandaging around her breasts.

Quinn gave a grunt of frustration, freed her mouth and lifted off her enough to tear open every button on the long silk coat. *Twenty, twenty-one...* He dug under his own coat at the back and produced a slim knife. 'Keep still.' Her heart thudded as the blade glinted in the candlelight. It slid, warm from his body, between skin and wrappings, then slashed up and he was peeling them back, exposing her to his hot, intent gaze.

Thirty? It was difficult to concentrate, to count. Lina stirred, restless, pressing up against the hard length that promised so much, that her hands ached to caress, and he growled, deep in his throat, tossed the knife aside and bent to lave her breasts with his tongue. *Twenty-nine...no, thirty...thirty-four?*

'Lovely,' he murmured, capturing a nipple and tormenting it with his lips and teeth until she was whimpering. 'Patience. Are you counting?'

'Yes,' she gasped. 'Forty...I think.'

He smiled against her skin, the evening beard fretting against the soft swell of her breast and she moaned, a sound that turned into a gasp as he pulled at the drawstring of the loose trousers and slid his hand down, over her belly, over the soft mound of curls, parting her as he rolled sideways to give himself better access to her body.

Numbers swirled in Lina's mind. *Sixty, a hundred?* She lost time and reality as one finger slid into the moist folds. She could feel she was wet with desire for him, beyond shame, her legs falling open to let him do what he wanted, whatever he wanted.

His thumb found that part his tongue had tormented in the bedchamber, the sensation bringing her hips up off the hard floor in shock. He slid one finger, two, inside her and she clenched around him as his thumb moved. Everything whirled together, his touch, his scent, the hard floor under her, the heat of his body against her and his mouth, murmuring against hers. She was falling, flying, wanting—and then breaking, breaking into a million shards of pleasure and behind her closed lids the black velvet darkness was shot through with colours.

'You forgot to keep count,' Quinn's voice said, rumbling under her ear. Lina blinked and opened her eyes. He was still lying on the floor with her held against his chest, and she was naked except for the crumpled silk coat. Words, she found, were beyond her. 'Are you all right?' He sat up, bringing her with him until she was cradled on his lap, her head on his shoulder.

'I am beyond all right,' she murmured. 'Quinn, that was…overwhelming.'

'Good.' He sounded content, and tender too, and the combination made her quiver with longing. 'You see—there are some benefits to marriage with me.'

Of course, that was what this was all about. *Convincing me to say* yes, *so his honour and conscience are satisfied.*

'There are benefits to being made love to by you,' she said as she sat up, pushed the hair back from her eyes and tried to drag the coat closed over her exposed body. 'How could I deny how much pleasure you just gave me? But it does not change anything. I am not going to marry you, Quinn.'

'You will,' he said, making it sound more like a threat than a promise. 'You must go to bed now.' He stood up and helped her to her feet, waiting while she pulled on the trousers and buttoned the coat, getting it completely awry. 'Here.' He reached out and redid the fastenings as though she were a child, his voice husky with suppressed impatience.

Or perhaps frustration. 'Quinn,' Lina said as he guided her unsteady steps towards the door. 'That is the second time we have lain together and you have not… I'm sorry. Should I—?'

'No,' he said. 'That would not be a good idea. We will wait until we are married.'

'But I am not going to—'

'Bed.'

Lina found herself on the far side of a firmly closed door. She leaned against it, trying to summon up the energy to climb the stairs to her room. Stubborn, stubborn man! Oh, but his mouth, his body, those hands. Not just his body, but the man himself, his mind, his courage, his humour. All of him.

Marriage would be a disaster, she told herself as she stumbled upstairs, so much worse than living with a man for whom she felt merely liking and respect. There would be no messy emotion then, no yearning for something she could not have, no expectations, constantly disappointed. And if Quinn ever realised how she felt, then there would be the humiliation of knowing he was being kind and pitying her.

Thank goodness she had sent the servants to bed,

Lina thought as she gained the sanctuary of her bedchamber. She did not even think of snuffing out the candles; what remained of the night was going to be long and wakeful.

Quinn pushed himself upright away from the door and went back to the decanters. If he could bring himself to do it, the sensible thing would be to follow Celina to her room and make her his once and for all. But the sensible thing was not the honourable thing and she had to be persuaded into doing what was in her best interests, even if that involved seduction.

A wife had not been in his plans, at least, not until the point in his life when he decided honour was satisfied and he was ready to settle down a trifle. Someone intelligent, he had thought, when he had thought about it at all. Someone who would not sulk at being left for half the year to her own devices, or expect to drag him out to balls and parties every night when he was home and working—a capable girl she would need to be, one who could make her own friends and entertainment. A good mother, for there was the title to think of and, he supposed, he was not establishing his fortune just for the sake of it.

And now, thanks to his conscience, he was faced

with the prospect of marrying an obscure vicar's daughter from somewhere in the depths of the country. A girl with dubious relatives, a scandalous past and possessing a curious blend of innocence, ignorance and shocking knowledge. A young woman who did not, apparently, want to marry him.

He could appreciate her scruples, honour her for them even, he thought, sitting down and nursing his glass on his chest while he did his best not to think about the ache in his groin and the tension in his belly. But she was supposed to tell him of her worries, listen to what he had to say and then be convinced and marry him, not answer back, dig in her heels and refuse to be swayed, even by lovemaking.

He had gone as far as he felt he could; now all he could try was a war of attrition, reminding her with touch and murmured words and intense looks what had passed between them and what was to come—if she saw sense.

If only Celina had not heard about that damn duel—it had alarmed and upset her. Doubtless she thought him not a very good prospect as a husband if she feared he would end up flat on his back in some field on the outskirts of London with a doctor, irritable at being dragged out of bed at an ungodly hour to participate in an illegal activity, prodding at his wounds. She would not believe him if he told her he was unlikely to get killed; he could quite see that a woman would prefer her fiancé to assure her he was definitely *not* about to do something fatal.

Quinn mentally added *Marry Celina* near the top of his list of things to be done and crossed off *find wife* from the bottom. He knocked back the brandy in his glass and stood up, suddenly not so concerned about the prospect after all: Celina was going to be a delight in bed. And she made him laugh. And she would make him comfortable. And she had guts. Yes, his conscience was not so inconvenient after all.

Chapter Eighteen

Lina met Quinn's eyes defiantly at breakfast the next morning. She could feel she was blushing, and she knew the dark circles under her eyes would betray her lack of sleep the night before, but when he bent low to drop a kiss on her nape in passing she swivelled in her chair and hissed, 'Do not do that and do *not* mention marriage again.'

She had to stay angry with him or she would simply melt into his arms. The wretched man had discovered a weakness and she could only hope he did not realise that the way she responded to him owed as much to her own feelings for him as to his undoubted expertise in making love.

'There is no need to whisper,' Quinn said, calmly helping himself to the buffet as though they had not lain entangled in each other's arms on the drawing room floor only hours before. 'I have told the staff that I prefer to eat my breakfast without a footman hovering. We can ring if we want anything.'

'I want you to stop this nonsense.' She poured him coffee, strong and black as she had learned he liked it. He took the cup with a murmur of thanks and a look that curled her toes. 'I am not going to marry you and that is that. Now, what are we going to do today?'

Quinn did not respond to her statement, but neither did he agree. He cut into his steak and said, 'I am going to the Society of Antiquaries, then I am making some visits, taking up invitations to call.' He smiled, although without humour. 'Insinuating my foot into respectable society. Then I will meet Gregor and we will see if the rumours we have picked up about Makepeace can be forged into a lever to get him out of The Blue Door.'

'How have you discovered anything about him in such a short time?' Lina asked. 'We have only been in London two days.'

'Gregor has been here longer, don't forget. But I wrote from Norfolk to my agents and to some rather less respectable sources. I may not come to England often, but I trade and that means I have a network of acquaintances in many ports. Makepeace has the air of a man who has reinvented himself; I suspect he would rather take my money for his share in

The Blue Door and vanish than confront his old life. We will see.'

'That will be a great relief for Aunt Clara,' Lina said, making herself eat the bacon in front of her. Picking at her food was senseless.

'But you are wondering what I am doing about the sapphire?'

'Yes. I have to confess it would be a weight off my mind not to expect arrest and worse at any moment,' she said, trying for a lightness she did not feel.

'I will meet Reginald Tolhurst tomorrow night and then I hope to discover what he did with his father's ring.' Quinn buttered bread lavishly as though he had not just dropped a bombshell.

'Reginald? But why do you think he had it?'

'Who else?' Quinn raised an eyebrow at her bemused expression. 'Sir Humphrey was wearing it when you were undressing. You did not take it and you were in the room up to the point it was found to be missing. Reginald took his father's left hand to feel for a pulse and then *discovered* the ring was gone.'

'But why would he do such a thing? It is very valuable, but well known and difficult to dispose of, surely?'

'That puzzles me, I have to admit,' Quinn agreed.

'Did he know his father's will left him insufficient funds to cover his obligations? Or perhaps he just could not resist the opportunity to take it and then had to worry about disposing of it afterwards. He is obviously a gambler and not a wise one. But if it was cut up for safe disposal, even a big sapphire would be greatly reduced in value.'

For a moment Lina was breathless with relief, then reality hit—this was a theory, nothing more. 'But how will you prove it?' she asked.

'We set a trap, bait it lavishly and make sure of our witnesses.' Lina shivered. Quinn reminded her of a hunting cat all of a sudden: sleek, focused menace.

'I want to come, too.'

'No.'

'I see, your word is law. That attitude is hardly an inducement for me to marry you, you know,' she pointed out sweetly. 'I want more from a marriage than to sit at home meekly doing what my husband tells me. I expect a partnership.'

'Does that mean you are going to see sense about this?'

'About marriage? Maybe.' Lina cast down her eyes so he could not see the defiance in them. 'If I thought I might see more of you than a glimpse at breakfast and interludes in the bedchamber.'

'This is dangerous,' he began, then, to her amazement, he hesitated. 'It seems unfair that he has made you suffer so much and you cannot see the end game. Yes, you may come along, but only if you promise to do as you are told.'

'I swear it! Thank you, Quinn.' She looked up, smiling, enchanted that he would do this, overrule his own judgement, because he felt it was fair. *I love you*, she thought, and then saw him frown as he studied her face. What had she betrayed? 'I want to see him get his come-uppance,' she added, hoping her glowing pleasure would be read as delight in revenge, not directed at him.

'You had best wear your Oriental disguise,' he said after a moment. 'It is the best thing to hide your hair and this time I can explain you away as a servant if you are seen.'

Quinn found Celina's face kept coming back into his mind throughout the day, distracting him while he had serious discussions about Crusader castles at the Society of Antiquaries, interrupting the smooth flow of his small talk while he took tea at the homes of those gentlemen who had extended invitations, making him vague when Gregor spoke to him in the carriage taking them to The Blue Door late that night.

'Are you ill?' the Russian demanded.

'No.' Quinn sat up and made himself focus. Perhaps he was sickening for something because otherwise, why could he not get the infuriating woman out of his head?

'In love, then?'

'Of course not. But I have asked Celina to marry me,' Quinn said abruptly. 'It seemed the best thing.'

'So, I am to be the best man? I like the idea,' Gregor said with a grin.

'She says she won't have me,' Quinn admitted, gratified by the way his friend's jaw dropped. 'And I have told her she can come with us to trap Tolhurst.'

'You are mad, both of you. But we are here now, you can tell me later.'

Makepeace was in the salon when they arrived. His smile of welcome faded when Quinn said, 'A word with you in private, sir?' but he guided them through to an office and shut the door.

'You have some complaint, gentlemen?'

'Not at all. I merely wish to purchase your share in this establishment.' Quinn could see no merit in beating around the bush.

'It is not for sale, Mr Arbuthnott. I cannot imagine

what can have given you the idea that it was.' He sat
behind his oversized desk like a spider in a corner
and eyed them warily.

'We are both sailing under false colours,' Quinn
remarked. 'I am Lord Dreycott and you, sir, are
Henry Foxton, wanted by the authorities for arms
dealing with the enemies of the Crown.'

The man froze. 'Nonsense. I have my papers in
this drawer, letters from my attorney—'

'And you also have a pistol in there, no doubt.
Really, Foxton, do we look that easily gulled? I am
insulted. And armed.' Quinn brought his hand out
of his pocket and rested it, and the small pistol it
held, on his crossed knee. The man calling himself
Makepeace froze. 'There is no need for drama.
I will not betray you to the magistrates if you
will take a fair price for your interest here—and
disappear.'

'Why?' Makepeace blustered. But Quinn could
see from the calculation in the small brown eyes
that he had already decided to cut his losses.

'Because I have a fancy for the place and it is an
insult that men who have fought for their country
should be entertained here by scum like you. I have
money and a deed of sale; our business can be dealt
with here and now.'

Gregor took the wad of banknotes out of the

breast of his coat and tossed them across the desk. Makepeace thumbed through them, his eyes flickering back and forth between the money and the gun. 'Here.' Quinn pushed a document across the desk. 'Drawn up by my attorney today. You take the money and your personal belongings. You leave the keys and you walk away tonight. If you are seen here again, I will have the magistrates on you. Agreed?'

Makepeace looked from the money back to Quinn, then nodded abruptly. He reached for the pen in the standish. 'Your real name,' Quinn said softly.

Quinn signed and Gregor witnessed the document. 'Now,' Quinn said, handing the pistol to Gregor, 'you will pack and leave. Give me the keys.' He held out his hand. 'My friend will see you out.' The dark, sly eyes sent him a look of pure venom, but he had to give the man credit for sizing up the situation and knowing when to cut and run, not stay and bluster.

Makepeace pushed a bunch of keys across the desk. 'Mr Vasiliev will search you before you go,' Quinn added, getting to his feet. A second key appeared from an inner waistcoat pocket. 'Thank you. Good evening. I trust we are never going to meet again.' The look he received in return promised a slow and painful death, but Quinn merely nodded and left the room.

The salon was busy now, warm and fragrant with perfume, powder, the scent of flowers and candle wax. Quinn wove his way through, smiling at the girls he recognised, and made his way upstairs to tap on Madam Deverill's door.

'Lord Dreycott!' She put a hand on his arm and drew him inside. 'Is anything wrong with Celina?'

'No, nothing is wrong.' She did not look well this evening, even frailer than the night before. Knowing that her niece was in London, even closer to danger, could not help. He handed her the papers. 'These are for you. Makepeace will be leaving very shortly.'

She read them, sinking down on to a *chaise* as she did so. 'I am free of him? Truly?'

'Yes.' Quinn told her what had happened as he stood by the window, the curtain drawn back a little so he could see the street below. 'Come, see,' he said after a few minutes. Light spilled out as the front door opened and the figure of Makepeace emerged on to the pavement, a valise in each hand. Gregor followed, carrying another bag. He signalled for a hackney, bundling both man and bags inside. As he did so two other figures detached themselves from the shadows and entered the vehicle, one on each side. Gregor spoke to the driver and it moved off.

'What has just happened?' Madam Deverill asked. 'You promised him his freedom, but—'

'I promised not to give him over to the authorities. I said nothing about putting him in the hands of a certain sea captain who is going on a long voyage east. The captain's an honest man, after a fashion. Makepeace will keep his money, and his life. He may even start a new career, a long way away. I do not like men who seek to make money at the expense of their own countrymen's lives. He was dealing in weapons with our enemies during the war.'

'Thank you.' She turned and took his hands. 'Thank you so much. You will want to see the figures, of course, so you know how much return you might expect every month—'

'That is a gift,' Quinn said, taking the papers from her hand and going to her pretty ormolu desk. He wrote across the bottom and signed it. 'I intend marrying Celina and I would wish her to have no anxiety about your position.'

Madam Deverill's thin face went so pale that the subtle macquillage she wore stood out against her skin, then she smiled and held out her hands. 'I am so happy for you both! You love her, then?'

'I feel it is only right, given the circumstances, which have, you will agree, compromised her utterly,' Quinn said, trying not to wince at *love*. Why did women have to imagine that every man was capable of such softening of the brain? Marriages could be perfectly comfortable without all this damned emotion. He took her hands and dropped a kiss on one.

'Hardly through your own fault,' Madam said. 'I honour you for doing the right thing despite your lack of feeling for her.'

'I did not say I held Celina in anything but affection and regard,' Quinn said, unaccountably irritated. He liked Celina. In fact, he was very fond of her, she had spirit and a sense of humour and intelligence. She was loyal and affectionate. She would, he was certain, make a good mother. And she would certainly be passionate in bed. Why should her aunt assume he felt nothing for her if he did not feel love? 'I must persuade her of that, however.'

'I wish you every success,' Madam Deverill said with a faint smile. 'And I thank you for my freedom from Makepeace.'

* * *

'You will do,' Quinn said. Lina stood in front of him, once more in her boy's clothes, her hair concealed by the turban, but without any of the discreet jewels he had given her to wear the night before. 'Stick to Gregor like glue; if anyone speaks to you, say something in broken English. You're a servant, remember.'

'Yes, lord,' Lina said in imitation of the subservient tone Gregor had used that first night at Dreycott Park.

Quinn grinned at her. 'Here, take this money. If anything happens, if someone recognises you, leave at once, run, and take a hackney back here.'

She was still dizzy from relief at hearing that Makepeace had sold up without difficulty and was on his way to a new life in the East, although Quinn was strangely reluctant to explain why the man had allowed himself to be so easily persuaded. He had been brusque when she had tried to thank him.

He is keeping things from me, she thought. But now her aunt was safe her way was clear to leave London and take advantage of her legacy, just as soon as the sapphire was discovered. She would find herself a cosy home, a few servants and search for Bella and Meg. And in time she would learn to live with the hollow feeling inside her, the knowledge that Quinn was somewhere in the world, living his own life, an adventurous, satisfying life that did not include her. And which would, she was certain, include a large number of other women.

That is another reason for not marrying him, she concluded, curling up in a chair while Gregor and Quinn played a hand of cards, passing time until the hour when Quinn had arranged to meet Reginald Tolhurst in the Pickering Place hell. Could he possibly ever be faithful if he married without love?

They set out at last. St James's Street was busy with men moving between club and gaming house, chop house and brothel, some alone, more in convivial groups. In amongst them the women moved, some elegant, refined, accompanied by a maid on their way to an appointment. Others were coarser, more obvious as they caught at sleeves and made their offers.

Gregor and Lina remained in the carriage as Quinn got down, put on his tall hat and sauntered down the passageway next to Berry Brothers and Rudd's shop. Even this late Lina could smell the coffee wafting from its cellars.

'Now we wait,' Gregor said, settling back. They sat in silence for a while, watching the crowd. Lina felt her eyelids droop; even the anticipation of what the evening would hold was not enough to counter inaction and an almost sleepless night.

'Why will you not marry him?' Gregor asked suddenly.

'Because he thinks he should wed me,' Lina said, startled out of her doze and speaking before she thought. 'He doesn't love me.'

'And you love him?'

'No, of course not!' she lied, hating denying how she felt to this man who was so close to Quinn and who must understand him so well. It would be wonderful to talk to Gregor about him, but she knew she could not do so without betraying herself. 'I am quite unsuitable for a man of his rank, and he knows it. But whether I was or not, I believe in love in marriage and I do not want to end up wed to a man who will feel shackled for ever as a result.'

'You think you could shackle Quinn?' Gregor gave a snort of laughter. 'I would like to see a woman try.'

'So he would marry me and then carry on doing just what he wants, would he? He would spend most of his time abroad travelling, taking lovers while I sat at home like a good little wife? Forgive me, but I do not call that marriage.'

'Many women do,' the Russian pointed out.

'I am not *most women*,' Lina retorted. 'I would not tolerate infidelity for a start!'

'He is a man of passion,' Gregor remarked. In the lights from the street she could see he was amused.

'Then he could be passionate with me,' she snapped. 'He would have to come home if he could not be celibate.'

'Ah! I would like to be a fly on the bedchamber wall,' Gregor chucked.

'Gregor! Of all the outrageous things—'

'It is time I went in. Are you coming or do you stay here?'

'I am coming.' She just hoped her blushes were not visible under the paint on her face.

'Follow me closely then.' Gregor strode off into the mouth of the passageway, Lina on his heels.

The courtyard was lit by flambeaux and the door to the gaming club stood open, noise and light spilling out of it. At the doorway Gregor shed his outer garments, snapped his fingers at her and wandered into the room.

It took her a minute to see Quinn, sitting at a table in the middle of the room. Her heart contracted in panic as she saw the man opposite him: Reginald Tolhurst. The last time she had seen him he was shouting that she was a thief, that she would be hanged, that—

The hot, smoky room swam before her eyes. *I shouldn't have come. I can't do this.*

Quinn looked up and saw her and she knew she was about to confirm all his doubts about bringing her. She was not capable of being an equal partner in his adventures, she was just timid Lina again, terrified of her own shadow. She dragged a panicky breath down into her lungs and braced herself to run.

Chapter Nineteen

I must get out of here. Tolhurst will see me, he will know...

Quinn's eyes held hers, then something changed. She did not understand what, his expression remained aloof, focused, and yet those hard green eyes softened, looked directly into her and she seemed to hear his thoughts. *It is all right. You will be all right.*

Lina gave a shaky nod and he looked back at his opponent and the cards and the panic ebbed away, leaving her shaken but determined. *He believes in me.*

'Here.' Gregor thrust a bottle into her hands and wandered vaguely in the direction of Quinn's table, taking a swig from his wine glass as he went. A rowdy group was playing a game she did not recognise with much slapping down of cards and exchange of money; Gregor stopped close by and watched along with several other men. Lina pressed up behind him, careful not to knock into a table beside them where two sombre men were engaged in a silent game.

She shifted her position so she could see the table from the shelter of Gregor's shoulder and found that Quinn was close enough for her to overhear. He had a sizeable pile of guineas and banknotes on the table in front of him and Reginald Tolhurst was sweating.

'Mine, I think.' Quinn swept the stake money towards himself. 'Another hand? You'll be wanting to win some of this back, I'll be bound. Your luck must change sooner or later; I'm amazed at how well I'm doing. We'll have a new pack, shall we?' He sounded almost naïvely enthusiastic.

'Yes. My luck's bound to change.' Tolhurst opened the pack and shuffled.

'Double or quits?' Quinn said. 'I've always wanted to be in a position to say that!' He took what appeared to be an incautiously large swig of wine and waited.

Is Tolhurst the fool Quinn thinks he is? Lina wondered, seeing how he was luring the man into taking one giant incautious gamble.

He was, it seemed. 'I'll have to give you a vowel,'

he said. At Quinn's nod he scrawled *IOU* and paused. 'What's the sum?'

Quinn made a show of adding up the money in front of him. 'Four hundred.'

'Eight, then.' Tolhurst's hand shook, but he tossed the note into the middle as Quinn pushed his winnings and a further four hundred pound notes out.

'Good thing I went to the bank this morning,' Quinn remarked.

There was silence as they began to play. Gregor turned and strolled up to watch over Tolhurst's shoulder and Lina shifted to keep behind him and to one side so she could see both men's faces. They were playing whist, she saw, the hands falling reasonably equally at first. Then Quinn began to win and, as he did so, Tolhurst became visibly more anxious, his judgement clearly affected by the tension.

When the last card fell he stared at the tally of points, white-faced. 'Your...your game.'

'So it seems.' Quinn raked the money towards him, stowing it away in his pockets. 'I must thank you for an entertaining evening. The only thing is...' he picked up the IOU between thumb and forefinger '...I'll need to ask you for this in a day or two—I'm going over to France for a bit. Could I have your direction?'

Tolhurst stared back white-faced. 'I… By the end of next week?'

'No, sorry. As I said, I'll be leaving. There's no problem, is there?' Quinn let the mask of amiability he'd been wearing all evening slip as he stared at Tolhurst and Lina shivered. She would not want him to look at her like that.

'Goodness, no!' Tolhurst pulled out his card case and handed one over. 'No problem at all.' His hands shook.

Quinn stood up, ignored Gregor, nodded to Tolhurst and walked out. As he went out of the door Gregor shifted so he was alongside Tolhurst. Lina ducked further into the shadows to watch. He pulled a handkerchief from his pocket and blew his nose while apparently gazing with interest at the next table. With the handkerchief came a ring that landed on the baize, spinning in the candlelight. Tolhurst's hand shot out, flattened over the gem and drew it back. He looked around, his gaze sliding over Lina as she watched him from the corner of her eye. Gregor, apparently bored with the game, stuffed the handkerchief into his pocket and wandered over to the door, Lina scurrying behind like a servant who has been taken by surprise.

'He's taken it,' Gregor said as they moved out of the door and into the small courtyard of Pickering Place.

Quinn came out from behind a pillar. 'Now he'll need to get it off his hands fast. It is too big and too distinctive to take just anywhere, if he fenced the sapphire, he'll take this to the same place.' He led the way back down the passage and climbed into the carriage. 'Now we wait.'

Lina wished they were alone. She wanted to confess how frightened she had been, how the message in Quinn's eyes had steadied her and given her courage, but she could not say that in front of Gregor and after a moment she realised she could not say it to Quinn, even if they were alone—he would take it as encouragement, a sign that she was weakening. She swallowed the words, clasped her hands together tightly around the wine bottle against the urge to reach out and touch him, and closed her eyes.

'Nervous, Celina?' Quinn asked, his voice sounding like a caress to her ears. 'I will not let him hurt you.'

'Just apprehensive,' she said. *Just wanting you.* 'I have been so frightened, it is hard to believe this could be the end of it.'

'It is.' His voice was deep and certain and she

was conscious for the first time in many days of the slight foreign intonation. *He is the adventurer again, not the English gentleman.* 'Why are you clutching that bottle?'

'Gregor gave it to me.'

'Then let us all have a drink.'

She passed it to Gregor, who tipped it up for a good swallow, wiped the neck and gave it to Quinn. He drank more moderately, wiped it in turn and handed it to Lina. She put it to her lips and drank a little, imagining she could feel the heat of his lips on the neck, remembering with sudden and shocking vividness how it had felt when she had taken him into her mouth.

It was such an outrageous thought that she choked. Gregor grabbed the bottle before she dropped it and gave her a firm buffet on the back.

Lina let her spluttering coughs last far longer than necessary, aghast at her own wanton imaginings and glad of an excuse for being red in the face. The door opened and the two sombre men who had been sitting at the card table next to Quinn's opened the carriage door and climbed in. She swallowed, braced for action, but they were obviously expected.

'He is leaving,' one said without preamble. 'He made no effort to declare that he had found a lost ring. I think he waited to see if you came back, Mr Vasiliev, and now feels safe.' He seemed to register Lina's presence as he spoke. 'Who is this, my lord?'

'My servant, Hassan,' Quinn said. 'Ah, here comes Tolhurst.' Lina was left in ignorance of their companions, but she supposed Quinn could hardly be expected to introduce them to a servant, whoever they were.

Tolhurst emerged from the passage, hailing a hackney as he did so. Quinn rapped on the roof and after a moment their carriage moved off, down St James's Street and left into Pall Mall.

'A bad business, if you have the right of it, my lord,' the man observed.

His companion nodded. 'That is very true, Sir James. His elder brother is a fellow magistrate which makes it all the worse. If he proves to be responsible for this, it will be painful to ask Sir George how he wants this handled.'

'I would rather think you should ask the unfortunate young woman who has been falsely accused,' Quinn said with a sharpness that had the magistrate staring at him.

'When Mr Trevor here approached me as your attorney with this accusation and your novel suggestion for testing it, I did not ask what your concern with the case is, my lord,' Sir James said. Lina forced herself not to shrink back. Not that there was anywhere to go—she was wedged between Gregor's shoulder and the side of the carriage.

'I am acting on behalf of Miss Shelley's aunt. I am part-owner of The Blue Door.'

'Indeed!'

'An unusual investment, I agree,' Quinn said. 'But one that gave me an interest when it was obvious an injustice had been done.'

'And where is the young woman at the moment, might I ask?'

'I have every reason to believe she is in London,' Quinn said readily. 'Certainly that is where I last saw her.'

'We are going into the City,' Gregor remarked and Lina made herself breathe.

The carriage stopped and the driver got down and came to the door. 'The other 'ackney's stopped— what do you gents want me to do now?'

'Wait here,' Quinn said, passing something that clinked. 'There'll be more when we return and we may be a while.' He turned back to his silent companions. 'Now, very quietly, there are a lot of us to go falling over each other's feet.'

They got out, staying in the shadow of the carriage. Peering around Quinn, Lina saw a figure descend from another hackney and walk off down an alleyway. Quinn followed, Gregor soft-footed at his back, the attorney and the magistrate behind them. Lina stayed on the magistrate's heels; if she was out of his sight she might also be out of his mind, she thought, wondering just how perceptive he was.

The alley opened out into a narrow street. There was a public house on one corner, brightly lit and busy. A little further along the light reflected on three golden balls. 'Pawnbroker,' Quinn said with an air of satisfaction. Tolhurst was standing at the door and they could hear his knocking from where they stood.

There was only a faint glimmer from the shop, but the light wavered and intensified as someone within approached the door. It opened, there was a low-voiced conversation and then Tolhurst went inside.

Quinn waited until the light had vanished again before leading his four companions forwards over the greasy cobbles. 'Locked,' he murmured as he tried the handle. Gregor stooped to the lock. 'I suggest you look elsewhere, Sir James,' Quinn added.

'I am sure he is merely checking it as a concerned

passer-by,' the magistrate whispered back. 'And look, it is open. I feel it our duty to investigate.'

Gregor eased the door wide and went in, followed by Sir James and Mr Trevor. Quinn bent to Lina's ear. 'Stay behind me. When he finds himself cornered, he may be dangerous.' She looked up and he kissed her suddenly, pulling her to him, his mouth fierce and possessive on hers.

When he released her his eyes held hers for a long moment. It was a look of possession, she recognised, the look of a warrior about to go into battle, fired up, needing to assert his ownership of his woman before the fight began. She found herself responding to it, her blood heating, her tension and fears swept up into that one focus of mouth on mouth, the primitive claiming.

They stared at each other, Quinn seeming as shaken as she was, before he gave himself a shake and followed the others to the back of the cluttered shop.

Lina stood for a moment, her hand pressed to her lips, everything—the shop, the danger, the closeness of a magistrate—all swept away by that one kiss. When she managed to regain her focus she saw that the others were grouped on either side of a door that stood slightly ajar. Light spilled from inside and the smell of someone's supper perfumed the air with a rich aroma of onions.

'…if it's another of those bloody sapphires, you know what you can do with it, Tolhurst,' a voice said. 'I haven't shifted the real one yet, need to get it to Amsterdam once the heat's died down. And as for that paste ring—if you expect more than the guinea I gave you for it, think again. Best I can hope to do with it is sell it to some travelling theatre troop!'

'This is real, I'm sure of it,' Tolhurst said. 'A diamond, for all that it's an odd cut.'

'Oriental,' the other man said with a grunt. 'Give it here.' There was silence. Lina could hear several clocks ticking, the crackle of firewood. Something brushed her ankle and she started, reaching out for Quinn without conscious thought. He caught her hand and grinned as the battered tabby cat abandoned her and went to twine around his legs.

'It's a diamond, I'll give you that. But it's another flaming stone that'll have to be recut before I can sell it safely. Why can't you nick something simple for once?'

'How much?' Tolhurst demanded. The other man was muttering, apparently working the price out. 'What? How much? I need more than that! I was taken by some damned sharp I mistook for a pigeon to the tune of eight hundred tonight and the bastard wants paying on the nail like some merchant. He's no gentleman.'

Lina saw the flash of Quinn's teeth as he grinned.

'Another twenty-five then, and that's your lot. And don't bring me anything else until I've got those sapphires off my hands.' There was the sound of a key grating in a lock. Quinn nodded to Gregor, let go of Lina's hand and the two men shouldered through the door, pistols in their hands.

'What the—'

'You are under arrest on suspicion of the theft of the Tolhurst Sapphire and of a diamond ring belonging to Mr Vasiliev. I am Sir James Warren, magistrate. Do not attempt to resist.'

Squashed behind Mr Trevor, Lina could see the pawnbroker throwing up his hands, his face bitter with anger as he glared at Reginald Tolhurst. 'You cack-handed idiot!'

Tolhurst looked around wildly then, to Lina's amazement, sank down on a chair, buried his face in his hands and burst into sobs. 'Where is the Tolhurst Sapphire?' demanded Sir James.

The pawnbroker rummaged in his safe, which stood with the door swinging open, and came out with a small bag. He tipped it out into the magistrate's hand and they all stared at the deep blue stone burning with cold fire in the palm of his hand.

'And the ring?' Quinn asked. The man produced a ring, its stone the exact replica of the unmounted one except, seeing them together, there seemed something less vivid about the stone in the ring to Lina's untutored eye.

'Who brought you these?'

'He did—Reginald Tolhurst. Brought me the genuine article a month ago and I bought it in all good faith,' the man said. The magistrate snorted. 'Then he turns up with this paste version, saying he'd substituted it when he stole the real thing and now his father's died and he daren't have it found to be a fake. And the next thing I knows, the papers are full of the ruddy Tolhurst Sapphire.'

'It did not occur to you that an innocent young woman was being accused of stealing something that was in your safe?' Quinn's voice was like ice.

'Just some bawd, weren't it?' the pawnbroker said and the next moment was flat on his back on the rag rug in front of the fire.

'My lord! We need him with his jaw unbroken to give evidence,' Sir James said. He produced his card case, scribbled a note and passed it to

Mr Trevor. 'Perhaps you would be so good as to take the hackney to Bow Street and send me three Runners and a secure wagon. We will have this place searched.'

Trevor hurried out and Gregor hauled the pawnbroker to his feet and set about tying him to a chair. 'What about this one?' He jerked his thumb at Tolhurst who looked up, his red-rimmed eyes glassy with fear.

'I am hoping he is going to make a run for it.' Quinn ran a finger down the barrel of his pistol.

'We must take him to Sir George and see what he wants done,' the magistrate said with a warning shake of his head.

'That is not justice.'

'It is the best way to avoid scandal. I imagine Sir George will make his brother's life hell for this—stealing his father's ring, replacing it with paste and then stealing the paste version from his father's hand as he lay dying so he might not be discovered? Despicable.'

'It could have been murder, if Miss Shelley had been hanged,' Quinn said. 'I know a man who trades with the British penal colony in New South Wales. I will tell Sir George Tolhurst that he can arrange passage there for his brother or I will make a scandal that will rock the Tolhursts to their foundations.'

Reginald burst into tears again. Lina found she could not stand it. This pitiable excuse for a man had almost been the death of her, had given her weeks of fear and nightmares; now he was revealed as a pathetic, greedy, selfish creature not even worth hating.

She pushed the door open and stumbled out of the stuffy little parlour into the crowded shop. She wanted to run away, away from here, away from the torture of seeing Quinn every day. She wanted to go back to the peace of Dreycott Park, but she would not even be able to go to church or the village shop without running the gauntlet of hostile villagers.

She wanted her aunt and Katy and the other girls, but she knew now that their world would never be one she could be happy in. She wanted to go home to Martinsdene and find her father had forgiven her and that Meg and Bella were there, too, but she was certain he never would and that there was no one there for her now.

Lina knew she wanted Quinn as a starving woman wanted bread—not because it tasted good but because her life depended on it. But she could not have him. He did not love her and her soul would wither between the brief interludes when he came home to be kind to her, to rub the salt in her wounds. He would find adventure and interest and other women on his travels and then he would come home to a world of scholarship women were not allowed to share.

If she told him how she felt about him, she was certain those intervals at home would be few and far between. He was free and wild and independent and he could not change for her. Nor, she realised as she stared blankly at a bad oil painting in the gloom, would she want him to. To love someone truly was to love them as they were, not want to change them.

'Lina?' It was Quinn. He moved like a cat through the dark cluttered space and put his hands on her shoulders. 'Are you all right?'

'Yes. Thank you. You have probably saved my life,' she said, turning so that she was against his chest. It was weak and self-indulgent, but she thought she could stand there, hold him, hope for his embrace and he would suspect nothing but that she was overcome with relief and gratitude. Which she was, but it was neither that made her shed silent tears into the linen of his shirt. 'I am sorry I did not trust you with the truth at first. What will happen when that Runner, Inchbold, finds out about this? He will know you deceived him.'

'I will talk to him, apologise. I hope he will understand that it was a matter of life and death. With the true culprit identified and Sir James involved, he will see there was little choice.'

It would not be easy for him, she knew. Lina rested her hot cheek against Quinn's shirtfront and imagined this proud man having to confess that he had lied to an officer of the law. It touched his honour. As she thought it he said, 'Just Langdown to deal with and we can get married.'

Protesting about marriage was pointless; he was implacable, she could sense it. 'Why must you risk your life?'

'To draw a line, to retrieve what I lost ten years ago,' he said. 'Will you accept that, Celina, and not seek to persuade me against what I have to do?'

She thought of moral blackmail, of asking him tremulously what she would do if he was killed and did not marry her. But her own sense of honour revolted against that. Live or die, she would not be his wife, and to suggest anything else was to lie to him.

'Yes,' Lina said. 'I will not mention it again.' But in her heart she knew what she had to do.

Chapter Twenty

'Could Gregor take me to The Blue Door?' Lina asked Quinn as the Runners piled into the pawn-shop bringing light and noise with them. 'I would like to be with my aunt for a while.'

'Of course.' He was distracted by questions Sir James was asking and not concentrating on her, she saw with relief. 'Ah, there is Inchbold. Best you are out of the way before I speak to him.'

Gregor was enjoying himself, she could tell, and not best pleased to be sent off to fetch a hackney and take her to the brothel, but he put a good face on it.

'Thank you,' Lina said when they were settled on the musty seats. 'You'll be able to get back quickly, I am sure.'

He grunted. 'It is interesting to see how your law and order works here. It is different in Constantinople.'

'I am sure it is,' Lina said with some feeling. *We do not allow people to own slaves and flog them to death here, for a start.* 'Gregor, will you tell me when Quinn challenges Lord Langdown?'

'Why? You want to stop him?'

'I cannot stop him. I just wish to know.'

'Very well.' He shrugged. 'Tomorrow, I think. There is a reception that is being given at the Society of Antiquaries for some ambassador or another who has written a book. They say Langdown will be there. If he is, then Quinn will challenge him.'

'And when the challenge is issued, will you tell me where, and when?' When he hesitated she added, 'I will not make a scene or try to interfere.'

'He will kill Langdown, there is no cause for worry.' Gregor sounded amused, as if at feminine weakness.

'Then he will have to flee the country,' Lina said. 'It is illegal to duel, let alone kill your man. Will you please try to stop him doing that, at least?'

'I can try.' Gregor still sounded amused. Lina wanted to box his ears.

'Then please do so.' The carriage drew up outside The Blue Door and Lina opened the door and jumped down before Gregor could help her. 'Thank you, Gregor.'

She was still fuming over the idiocy of men—she

could understand why they felt the need to avenge an insult to their honour, but not why they thought it enjoyable—when she reached Aunt Clara's rooms.

Her preoccupation with Quinn vanished when she saw her aunt. 'Oh, you look so well!' She flew into her arms and hugged her, her turban toppling off. 'Is it not wonderful that Makepeace has gone?'

'Wonderful indeed.' Clara hugged her back. 'But what of the sapphire?'

Lina pulled her to the *chaise* and told her the night's events in detail. 'Sir James is going to speak to Sir George Tolhurst. Tomorrow it will be made known that I am innocent, but I do not know what explanation they will come up with to satisfy both the law and the Tolhursts.'

'And then you will be free to marry Lord Dreycott,' Clara said. Lina thought she detected a question in her aunt's expression.

'No. I will not wed him. Yes,' she said as Clara opened her mouth to speak, 'I told you I do love him, but he does not love me. Nothing has changed. And what kind of life would that be if I did wed him? Besides, it would be an unequal match, even though I am cleared of the theft. And then to add the fact that I have been living here—it is impossible.'

How calm and logical it all sounded, how strange that she could be explaining it so clearly while inside she was weeping with the misery of it. 'Quinn is seeking to rejoin society, to base himself in London, even though I do not expect him to spend much time here. Marriage to me would only handicap him further.'

'But if he loved you?' Her aunt took her hand in hers and pressed it gently. 'What then?'

'If wishes were horses, beggars would ride,' Lina said with a bitter laugh. 'I would still be an impediment as a wife. But there is no point in speaking about it, for he does not, and there's an end to it. He likes me, I think. That is all.'

'But he is determined to marry you,' Clara pointed out.

'He has spoken to you? I might have known. He feels responsible for me, just as he does Gregor, or an injured animal he rescued. He is a man for whom honour is everything and his honour must override my happiness, although I doubt I could ever get him to see it like that.'

'So what will you do?' At least her aunt did not seek to persuade her that Quinn was right, although she looked as sad as Lina felt.

'I must get right away from him, or he will spend all his time and efforts attempting to dragoon me up the aisle. In six months' time I may claim my legacy from old Lord Dreycott and then I can devote myself to finding my sisters, for surely, by then, Quinn will have realised that I cannot, and will not, marry him. But until then—will you lend me a little money? Just enough to find a respectable lodging away from London and a maid to give me countenance?'

'Oh, my dear.' Her aunt regarded her with exasperated affection. 'He is such a fine man, one your mother would have been glad to see you wed to. But if you will not have him, then we must contrive. Now I no longer have to pay Makepeace I could give you his share every month and enough for travelling and establishing yourself. Where will you go?'

'Norwich, I think,' Lina said. 'I saw a little of it when I was going through on the stage—it looked a pleasant, respectable place and large enough not to be noticed in.'

'Then let me give you some money now. You can write and tell me when you are settled and we can arrange the rest with a local bank. It will be soon? I shall miss you.'

'And I you. Thank you, Aunt. I will call tomorrow and say goodbye to the girls; perhaps I will know then.'

* * *

Quinn felt the familiar tightening in his gut and the sensation that every nerve in his body was alert for danger. He glanced around the crowd of gentlemen, talking quietly, greeting friends, drinking in moderation from the glasses being circulated by attentive footmen. Few places seemed more remote from a desert oasis where an ambush lay, or the back streets of Constantinople with footpads in the shadows. Yet he was braced for danger, for a fight. His right hand clenched, and he made himself relax it—there was no rapier hilt to hold. Not yet.

The crowd of gentlemen, united by their antiquarian interest, parted as the ambassador who was guest of honour entered. The volume of conversation increased.

'He is not here?' At Quinn's side Gregor, too, was dressed in immaculate evening wear, indistinguishable from any of the gentlemen around them. This was what he wanted, to appear one of them, not the exotic outsider. Langdown and his father had attempted to trap one of their own kind; now he had returned in the same guise, only older, more experienced. More dangerous.

Oh, yes, much more dangerous. For some reason he thought of Celina and the anticipation turned, inexplicably, to something more like apprehension.

Gregor shifted, impatient, and he dragged his mind back to the present. 'Not yet.'

'You'll recognise him?'

'Oh, yes. In fact, here he is.' Viscount Langdown was in his mid-thirties now, his face a little thinner, his blond hair a little darker, than Quinn remembered him. They were of a height, he reckoned, getting a grip on the flare of temper that flashed through him at the sight of the man. Langdown looked fit and moved well. He could well be a competent swordsman.

Quinn hoped to be challenged, not to be the challenger. It would give him the choice of weapons and he would select rapiers. There was less chance of killing his man with a sword than a bullet and, besides, there would be the pleasure of the fight, of looking into his eyes at close range.

Celina's face came into his mind, her voice as she had said she would not mention the duel again, the warmth of her tears soaking into his shirt. Why had she agreed to stop talking of it? Nothing, in his experience, stopped a woman nagging if it was something she felt strongly about. And Celina felt strongly about this, he knew. Impatient, he shook his head. He had to stop thinking about her.

He wove through the crowd until he was standing in front of Langdown. Quinn knew he had changed in ten years and it was obvious the man did not recognise him at first. He had filled out from the lanky twenty-year-old he had been; his face was harder, tanned, his shoulders broader. He knew, too, that the inner change from shy young scholar to experienced adventurer showed in his face.

'Langdown.'

'Sir, you have the advantage of me.' The viscount spoke pleasantly enough, relaxed in the convivial company.

'Quinn Ashley, Lord Dreycott.'

He saw the recognition hit the other man and with it, just for a second, a flicker of apprehension. *Wise*, he thought. *Or just guilty?*

'They said you had skulked back,' Langdown said.

'I do not skulk,' Quinn replied, keeping his voice pleasant. No heads turned yet. 'I have returned because of the death of my great-uncle and to establish my home in England.'

'I will see you blackballed from every club in the land,' Langdown snapped.

'Why? Because I was the youthful victim of your family's plotting and lies? An interesting approach, Langdown, to threaten the victim of your own wrongdoing. But then, you always were a lying bully.'

'How dare you!' They were drawing attention now, men were looking. A few drew back a pace or so, Gregor amongst them, leaving the two in a small circle of open space. 'You made my—'

'Hush, Langdown! You may be enough of a black-guard to mention a lady's name, I am not, and I never was. Nor would I dishonour one. I repeat—and in front of quite an audience, I note—you are an underhand, lying bully.'

'Damn you! You will meet me for this.' Langdown had lost both his supercilious sneer and control of his voice. He was almost shouting now, livid with anger. 'Name your friends.'

'Mr Vasiliev.' His only friend here, or at all, In London. *Except for Celina.* The thought almost took his focus off the man in front of him. *Celina,* a friend?

'And you may count upon me.' It was Sir James Warren, unexpected and more than welcome. Quinn bowed and the magistrate nodded, a tight smile at the corners of his mouth.

Langdown had two men at his side in earnest discussion. 'As soon as may be,' Quinn said to his two supporters. 'And I choose rapiers.'

'Leave it to us,' Sir James said. 'Mr Vasiliev will bring you news of what has been decided. I expect you will want to return home now?'

'Be damned to that,' Quinn said. 'I want to speak to the ambassador about the Gobi Desert.' *And do not want to go home and have to face Celina,* he realised as he made his way towards the grey-haired man who was holding court in front of a table spread with copies of his book. *I'll face a man trying to kill me at dawn, but I cannot cope with one stubborn female. Just let me get married to her. I'll keep her in bed for a week and there'll be no nonsense after that.*

But something was making him uneasily aware that it would not be as simple as that. She wanted to be loved, even though he suspected she would perish rather than admit it. *And so do I,* he realised, startling himself so much he stopped dead and almost upset a footman with a tray of glasses. *Well, we will just have to make do with good sex, friendship and humour. What if she falls in love with someone when we are married?* He would not tolerate her taking a lover, whether he was in the country or not, he knew that. *But sauce for the goose is sauce for the gander. I'll have to be faithful too. Hell.*

But even as he thought it he realised that being faithful to Celina would not be such a strain. He would make vows and he would keep them because not to do so would be to live a lie and he would not do that to either of them.

The ambassador was turning. Quinn made himself think in French and stepped forwards, disconcerted to find himself having to struggle to think of something coherent to say. Yes, the sooner he married the woman and got his life back on an even keel, the better.

Dawn tomorrow, Hampstead Heath. It took Lina a while to decipher Gregor's handwriting on the note that had been slipped under her door. *The right fork at Jack Straw's Castle,* she read. *Swords.* She rang the bell for Prudence and, when the maid came in, asked, 'For what hour has his lordship's and Mr Vasiliev's shaving water been ordered?'

The girl seemed to find nothing strange in the question, nor at being summoned at midnight to answer it. 'For quarter to four, ma'am.'

That seemed right. Sunrise would be about five o'clock and she supposed they would not take more than coffee for breakfast; she could not imagine anyone fighting on a full stomach. Fifteen minutes to wash, dress, drink, then an hour to get to the Heath, which was enough time to allow for any delay on the road.

'Wake me at that time, too, please,' she said. 'I

want to make sure they get away all right. There is no need to tell them, I hate to be seen to fuss whenever his lordship goes on a journey.'

'Of course, ma'am.' Prudence bobbed a curtsy and took herself off to bed, leaving Lina to blow out the candle and lie staring up through the darkness, wondering if Quinn could possibly be able to sleep facing a lethal fight in the morning.

She was woken by Prudence in darkness. It seemed she had slept after all, although the fleeting memory of her dreams were filled with blood and threatening shadows.

'I've brought your hot water, ma'am, and your chocolate and a sweet roll,' the maid said, setting them down.

'Thank you, Prudence. If you will just help me dress, then you can go back and have a rest; I shall not need you again this morning.' She put on a simple walking dress and then, when the girl had gone, delighted at the thought of a lazy morning, she found stout shoes and a plain cloak and took up her station at the window.

A few minutes later a chaise appeared and the men came down the steps and got in. She watched Quinn avidly, all too aware that next time she saw that elegant, loose-limbed stride he would be facing bare steel.

As soon as they were out of sight she ran downstairs. The butler was just walking away from the front door. 'Whyte, a hackney, please, at once.'

'But, ma'am—'

'His lordship has forgotten something important,' she said, waving her reticule as though it contained the item in question. 'I must catch him up.'

'Yes, ma'am, of course.'

The driver he found looked alert; presumably this was his first hire of the day and both he and his horse were fresh. 'Take me to Jack Straw's Castle,' she said quietly to him. 'As fast as possible. Then stop and I will have further direction for you.'

She climbed in and found herself with nothing to do but worry. Her own terrors over the sapphire and what might have happened to her seemed distant now, as though they had happened to another Lina. All that mattered was Quinn and the threat to his life and freedom. *It is all your own fault, you stubborn man*, she scolded in her head. But in her heart she knew the fault lay with Lord Sheringham and his son all those years ago. They had shattered Quinn's trusting nature, wounded his honour and made a hardened adventurer out of a naïve young man. He had to bring this to a close, with blood if need be. *Please, not your blood*, she prayed.

They were climbing the long slope of Haverstock Hill now, she saw. The outline of buildings were beginning to show against the sky. Hampstead soon and then the Heath. How far was she behind? How quickly would they begin to fight? Would she be there in time?

Lina was almost frantic with the inaction of just sitting, waiting, by the time the driver drew up. 'Jack Straw's Castle,' he announced.

Lina looked out of the window. There was the bulk of the big old coaching inn with the morning bustle beginning around it, but no sign of the chaise. 'Take the right fork,' she said. 'And look out for a chaise. There will be at least one other vehicle with it.'

'A duel, is it?' The man leaned down from his perch. 'Going to stop it, are you, miss?'

'No. I want to observe it without being seen. Can you manage that?'

'Aye, I'll do my best. Don't want your husband to see you, eh?'

'Yes,' she agreed, wishing she had thought to put a veil on her bonnet. 'That is so.'

The hackney took off at a brisk trot, then she

heard the man bang on the roof of the cab as they passed three carriages drawn up together, one of them the chaise Quinn and Gregor had taken. They trotted on past, round a bend and the carriage drew up. 'There you are, ma'am. Won't see us here.'

Lina got down. 'Will you wait, please? You'll be well paid.'

'I'll wait,' the man agreed as she ran back up the road to a clump of bushes on the corner. There, as though on a distant stage, the lethal dance was about to begin. She could see Quinn in his shirt sleeves standing with his blade held down. Facing him some yards away was another man. Gregor and Sir James and two others she did not recognise were in an earnest huddle, presumably discussing whether an apology might be forthcoming. To one side stood a black-coated individual with a servant holding an ominous bag at his back. The surgeon.

The knot of seconds broke up and went to their principals, then stepped away. One of them spoke, Lina thought, for the two swordsmen walked forwards, raised their weapons and took guard.

I will not faint. Lina reached out for support and took hold of a handful of thorns. When she looked back, sucking her fingers, they were already fighting. Elegant, deadly, they parried and feinted, lunged and swayed, advancing back and forth over the rabbit-cropped turf.

Langdown was taller than Quinn, and, to her untutored eye, as strong a swordsman. Then Quinn did something so fast she could not quite make it out and Langdown jumped back with blood on his shoulder. The seconds hurried forwards, but the viscount waved them away; honour, it seemed, was not satisfied.

The fight became intense, the men close, their blades flickering in the light of the rising sun. Then she saw the blood on Quinn's sword arm. Again the seconds, again Langdown waved them away, this time with a gesture she had no trouble interpreting. *To the death.*

Chapter Twenty-One

Quinn's sleeve was soaked, but the mark on the viscount's shoulder was the size of a man's palm and growing no bigger. Lina fell to her knees, hands clasped to her mouth so as not to call out. He would bleed to death if this did not stop soon.

Then Quinn lunged, twisted, seemed to change the direction of his thrust at the last moment and Langdown's rapier went flying and the man was on his back, the point of Quinn's sword at his throat. The moment stretched on, an eternity, everyone frozen, waiting to see whether Quinn would finish his man. Then he stepped back, raised his rapier in formal salute and reached out his left hand to pull Langdown to his feet.

He is going to refuse to take his hand, Lina thought. *Is this never going to end?* Then the fallen man was standing, his hand still in Quinn's. Their bodies were stiff; this was no instant reconciliation, but she could see that something was being said and that Gregor was smiling.

The surgeon hurried forwards, Langdown waved him away and went to join his supporters while the man turned to Quinn, who was already ripping up his sleeve to expose his arm.

Dizzy with relief, Lina made herself turn away. She wanted to run to him, but she knew she must not put herself into a situation where he might feel he had to defend her honour. 'Your man all right, then?' the driver said as she reached the carriage. She nodded. 'Which one? Husband or lover?' he added.

Which one? The carriage seemed to sway and shift; Lina grabbed at the door, sick to her stomach.

'Here, have this.' The man passed down a flask and Lina took a mouthful, the ardent spirit burning clear down to her stomach like fire. She handed it back with a nod of thanks. 'Back to Clifford Street,' she said, and then collapsed on to the battered seat.

Quinn sat on the folding stool that the surgeon's assistant produced and submitted to having alcohol poured over the slash down his arm while the surgeon threaded an ominously large needle.

A hackney carriage passed, going towards Jack Straw's Castle, and something about it had him narrowing his eyes at it. The things were as like as peas in a pod from a distance, but the horse was skewbald, not a common sight, and one of the same colouring had passed them just before the duel was beginning.

He glanced at Gregor and saw his friend was watching it, too, a faint smile on his lips. 'Gregor?' The surgeon chose that moment to take the first stitch. By the time Quinn had unclenched his teeth Gregor was looking perfectly innocent, such an unusual occurrence that he must be hiding something. 'Who is in that hackney?' The surgeon stabbed again. 'Damn it, man, I'm not a piece of tapestry!'

'It is a very nasty cut, my lord. You were fortunate that an artery was not severed.'

Quinn growled and submitted to more stabbing. 'Gregor?'

'A young lady, I think,' he admitted.

'You told her? Of all the—'

'She asked. She did not interfere, did she?'

Without creating an interesting scene for the edification of the surgeon, his assistant and Langdown's seconds who were helping him into his carriage, there was not a lot to be said. Not here. Quinn gave

Gregor a look that promised words later and tried to relax while the surgeon finished.

Ten years of wounded honour should now, in theory, be healed. He supposed they were. Langdon had apologised, stiffly, it was true, but there had been a look in his eye that spoke of shame. When they met socially in future there would be nothing for anyone to observe, nothing to keep alive that old scandal.

All that was left was to marry Celina and begin the new life he had planned. The fact that she had been here meant, surely, that she was reconciled to the necessity to marry? Quinn found he was smiling—whether Celina was reconciled or not, he was.

'Will you be wanting me to come with you, ma'am?' Prudence asked as she folded the last of the items Lina had identified into the portmanteaux. 'Or will your aunt be lending you a maid?'

Lina thought about it. It would probably be better to be accompanied on the journey and she would need to take a room at an inn when she first arrived; having a maid with her would identify her as respectable and ensure that she received better treatment. 'Would you be prepared to travel a little, Prudence? I may need to go out of town.'

'Yes, ma'am.' Prudence looked a little puzzled, but willing. She had not commented that Lina's elaborate macquillage had disappeared, but she must have been wondering. She seemed discreet, Lina thought.

'Well, then, pack your bag. I will be going shortly after his lordship returns.'

A chaise drew up outside, much to her relief. She had told herself that they would need to spend time getting Quinn's arm dressed, then they would probably go to the inn for breakfast, so there was no need to worry that the wound was more dangerous than it had seemed, but it was still good to see the men come in.

Lina ran downstairs and found Quinn, his right arm in a sling, his coat over his shoulders, asking Gregor to step into the library. When he saw her he stood aside and gestured for her to precede them.

'You are all right? There is no damage to tendons?' Lina demanded as soon as the door was closed.

'A nasty, but clean, slash. It is stitched, it will scar, but that is all. And now, if the pair of you will kindly explain—what were you doing on the Heath, Celina?'

'I would have thought that was obvious,' she retorted. 'I was worried about you.'

'A duel is no place for a lady.'

'No,' she agreed, 'which is why I stayed well back. No one saw me, I did nothing to distract or interfere with anyone.'

'What were you thinking of?' Quinn demanded of Gregor.

The Russian shrugged and said something Lina did not understand.

'I am well aware that women are a mystery. I do not need you helping this one to be any more damned mysterious than she already is,' Quinn snapped. 'Would you excuse us now?'

Gregor went out, looking far from chastened, leaving Lina confronting Quinn. 'Your arm must be hurting,' she said. 'Can I get you a powder for it?'

'Are you trying to placate me?' he demanded.

'I am trying to help you, you infuriating man,' she retorted. 'Won't you at least go to bed and rest?'

'No, I am going round to speak to the vicar at St George's about a licence.' His eyes challenged her to defy him.

Lina shrugged. 'As you wish.'

'Indeed, as I wish. We will speak more of this after dinner.'

She wanted to shout at him, or box his ears. Instead she went and stood on tiptoe and kissed his cheek. 'You bull-headed man. I am glad you did not get yourself killed.' Then, while he stared at her, she walked out of the library and out of his life. The taste of his cold skin went with her on her lips, a fragile reminder that was already vanishing.

'Are you all right, ma'am?' Prudence appeared on the landing with a bag in her hand as she reached the top of the stairs. 'You've gone quite pale.'

Probably as the result of having no air in my lungs, Lina thought. She had known she must do this, but it seemed so physically painful now she had, that she wanted to cry. 'Getting up so early, I suppose,' she said, trying to banish the fantasy of walking down the aisle of one of the most fashionable churches in London with Quinn waiting for her at the altar rail.

She heard his voice in the hall and went to the banister rail to look down. Whyte was helping him ease into his coat while a footman waited, hat, stick and gloves in hand. *Goodbye, my love.*

St George's was not far away; she must move quickly now.

Within fifteen minutes she and Prudence and their bags were in the hall. 'I am visiting my aunt for a few days, Whyte,' she said, praying that Gregor was not about to come down. 'Prudence is accompanying me. Can you call me a hackney, please?'

'Yes, ma'am. What shall I tell his lordship?'

'Oh, he knows all about it,' she said, smiling brightly.

Prudence looked startled when Lina said, 'Belle Sauvage', to the driver and she realised she was going to have to take the girl some way into her confidence.

'May I rely on your discretion, Prudence?'

'Yes, ma'am, of course.'

'I am leaving Lord Dreycott without his knowledge.'

'Oh, lord, ma'am! And I thought him such a nice gentleman, too.' The girl looked aghast.

'He is. He wishes to marry me, I do not wish to marry him.' Prudence's mouth dropped open. 'A few months in Norwich should suffice for him to realise what a bad idea it is.'

'Yes, ma'am,' Prudence muttered, obviously convinced that her mistress was all about in her head. 'He's not going to be best pleased, ma'am.'

'I know,' said Lina, imagining Quinn's reaction when he found her gone. He was not easily going to accept his will being thwarted, but that would be all he would feel. He would recover soon enough from that.

* * *

'Where is Miss Shelley?' Quinn enquired as he and Gregor went into the dining room. 'There are only two places laid.'

'Miss Shelley left to visit her aunt this morning, my lord. With Prudence.' Whyte frowned. 'I had understood you were apprised of the fact, my lord.'

'Of course, it slipped my mind,' Quinn said. *Hades, the woman will have me in an early grave, never mind at the altar at this rate.*

He ate with no apparent haste, but rose without taking any port. Gregor got to his feet. 'The Blue Door?'

'There is no need for you to come,' Quinn said. 'Stay and do what you can to make this seem normal. I do not want talk amongst the servants.'

By the time he had reached The Blue Door he had calmed down a trifle. His arm hurt like the devil, which did not help his temper, but he reminded himself that women set store by things like weddings. He should have consulted Celina first about the venue. But it was not like her to flounce off in a sulk. Perhaps she wanted to do her planning surrounded by women.

'Good evening, Lord Dreycott.' Madam Deverill was in the salon, elegant in deep blue satin.

'Good evening. I wish to speak to Celina.'

'She is not here. No—' she raised a hand when he began to turn towards the stairs and gestured him into the office '—I give you my word, I do not know where she is just now and I have not seen her since yesterday evening.' Her fine blue eyes scanned him with the wisdom of one with long experience of studying men. 'Your duel went well?'

'It did. I have a flesh wound, but that is all. Celina was not happy about the duel and then I was clumsy over the arrangements for the wedding.'

'There are several things Celina is unhappy about,' Madam Deverill remarked. 'The marriage most of all.'

'You surely agree with me that it is the best thing for her?'

'Not if you do not love her. Celina is not a young woman who would ever tie herself to a man for security, or money or title. She has a sweet, affectionate heart and the sense to know what would break it. You would, it seems.'

'You want me to pretend to love her?' Quinn demanded, feeling something almost tangible slipping through his mind, just out of reach as he tried to catch at it. His stomach felt as though he had been punched in the gut. He had been so certain she would be here. He would have seduced her back to Clifford Street, seduced her up to bed and made love to her until she was incapable of saying anything but *yes*.

'Of course not! Lina wants no lies from you. Her parents' marriage was based on lies and that ended in tragedy. If you cannot love her, then leave her alone.'

'Love works two ways,' Quinn retorted, goaded. 'I am supposed to love her, but she…' His voice trailed away. Why did he feel dizzy? It must be the loss of blood. Celina's aunt just looked at him and said nothing. 'Where has she gone? I know that you know.'

'Come here.' Clara Deverill reached out and, compelled by something in those blue eyes, so like Celina's, Quinn stepped forwards and put his hands in hers. She drew him close, his nostrils filling with the same subtle and provocative scent that Lina used. She said nothing, simply stood and looked deep into his eyes. 'I hope she will forgive me if I am wrong,' she said at last. 'Do you give me your word that you will not seduce or bully or frighten her into marriage?'

'Yes. You have my word.' *Then how will I get*

her back? But he had sworn. Somehow he must manage with this handicap if it was the price he had to pay to find her.

'She has gone to Norwich on the stage. I believe there was one at noon.'

Quinn looked at the clock. Half past nine. He could not catch her on the road now. 'When does it get in?'

'It takes about twelve hours, so she will be there at midnight or thereabouts. I gave her money, Quinn. She will be able to stay at a respectable inn and then find decent lodgings. You will pursue her?''

'I cannot leave things like this. I must be sure she is safe, end this.' End what? Not an *affaire*, not even a friendship, although he wished it were. All he knew was that he missed her, and he worried about her and he wanted her happy, even at the expense of his own happiness.

Quinn went home, packed a bag, summoned a chaise and four with postilions and set out at midnight feeling more uncertain than he had done since he stepped on to French soil ten years before.

It was not until he woke from an uncomfortable doze to find himself in Thetford at half past eight in the morning that it occurred to Quinn to wonder how, exactly, this marriage had become a matter of his own happiness. It was the right thing to do, his duty, and it would certainly not be a burden to be married to Celina. But, *happiness*?

The nagging feeling that he was probably running a fever pursued him through Wymondham and into Norwich. He was not thinking logically, he could not seem to plan, and his emotions felt painfully raw. Where was she? Was she safe? How unhappy had he made her that she had to flee?

It was almost noon before the chaise drew into the yard of the Maid's Head, hard up against the walls surrounding the cathedral close. This, the postilions told him, was where the stage from the Belle Sauvage set down its passengers and it was also a most respectable inn, so with any luck Celina had decided to put up there. Quinn climbed down, favouring his arm, which was giving him hell. He set his teeth and walked towards the door, then had to catch the young woman who hurried out of it into his arms.

'My lord!'

'Prudence.' The realisation that he had found them swamped the pain in his arm and sharpened his voice. 'And where, might I ask, is Miss Shelley?'

'Up…upstairs, my lord. Third door on the right, my lord. A private parlour.'

Thank goodness for that. He had feared finding her in some common tap, her pocket picked, at the mercy of every rake and petty criminal in the place.

He flung the door open, all reasonable thoughts forgotten as the anger of relief took over. She sat by the window, looking out on to the busy street below, but she spun round on the chair as the door crashed back against the panelling.

'Quinn.' There were tear tracks on her cheeks and that only infuriated him further.

Why do you want to leave me if it makes you cry? Am I so bad that this is preferable? Quinn threw his hat and his gloves away from him. 'What the devil do you think you are doing?'

'Starting my new life,' she said with a calm that took him aback until he saw that her fingers were pleating the fabric of her skirts into tight creases.

'I have come to take you back.' He strode across the floor, pulled her to her feet and shook her.

'Don't do that!' she shouted at him. 'You will hurt your arm, you idiot man.'

'My arm be damned.' The fact that it was agony, and he suspected that he had burst a stitch, did nothing to calm him. '*I* am an idiot? What do you call careering about the countryside by yourself like this?'

'I was on a perfectly respectable stagecoach with a perfectly respectable maid and I am now in the best inn in Norwich. I am safe, I have money in my pocket and I do not need you.'

The last five words sank in as they glared at each other from a distance of perhaps a foot.

'Then why are you crying?'

'Because I am tired, and I have left my aunt, and it is just beginning to sink in that I am not in danger of being hanged and because I need peace and you will not let me have it.'

Celina twisted in his grip and he felt another stitch go. He should free her. Part of his mind knew that, but not the part that was in pain, and confused and needing...needing something he did not understand.

And it was there in her eyes, too. A question, a yearning. Conflict and desire. Quinn yanked her hard against his chest and took her mouth in an open, brutal kiss. Celina struggled, kicked him, drummed her fists on his chest and he ignored every blow, fixed only on the heat of her mouth, the taste of her, the erotic struggle of her tongue against his.

Without breaking the kiss he bent and lifted her

off her feet, an ungainly, struggling bundle of skirts and furious woman. He shouldered open the inner door and dropped her on the bed, falling beside her without care for boots or his arm or the fact she was trying to knee his groin.

He pinned her hands above her head, using his weight to subdue her and stared down as she lay panting beneath him. It was still there, the heat that was not anger, the trembling that was not fear. He kissed her deep and hard and without mercy. When she stopped struggling he lifted his head. 'Tell me you do not desire me. Tell me you do not want this.'

'How dare you force me?' she spat. 'How could you?'

'Was I forcing you?' he asked. 'You know how to bite me. You could have told me to stop. You could have screamed. Look.' He pushed himself up, bringing her with him. 'Look in the glass on the dressing table.' Their reflections stared back, his intense, his face pale, his mouth swollen, as hers was. She was wide-eyed and panting and the hard peaks of her nipples showed against the fine fabric of her gown.

'Fear,' Celina said. 'Anger.'

'Desire,' Quinn replied, brushing his hand against her breast. 'Need.'

It was as though all the fight had gone out of her. Celina turned from the betraying glass, turned from him. 'Whether I desire you or not has nothing to do with it. Nothing. Nor does the fact that it would not be a wise marriage for you to make. I do not want to marry you, Quinn, for reasons that are all to do with me, not you. Please.' She turned to him, imploring, and his heart turned over in his chest. 'Please let me go.'

Chapter Twenty-Two

Let her go? It was impossible. Quinn stared at Celina and the world came back into focus. Crystal clear, sharp and as painful as a shard of glass. It was impossible and that was why he had to do it.

'Yes,' he said and got off the bed. 'Yes.'

'You will let me go?'

It did not seem to give her much pleasure, he thought, struggling to read her face, realising that he had understood neither her, nor himself, for days.

'Yes,' Quinn repeated and finally understood why. He sat down again. He could feel blood soaking into his shirt under this coat sleeve, but it did not seem very important now. 'I love you. I cannot force you to do what I think is right. You mean too much to me.' He watched her face in the mirror, unable to look at her directly, as though her rejection would turn him to stone. 'I love you and so I will let you go.'

'Oh, Quinn.'

'Don't cry,' he said, helpless. It seemed even freeing her could not make her happy. 'Tell me what you want and I will do it, only do not cry.'

'Marry me? Please,' Celina said and saw the fact that she was smiling through the tears register at last. 'Quinn, I love you.' She knelt up and put her arms around his neck and finally he turned to look into her eyes. *There it is: love. Can he see it in my face, too? How did I ever hide it?*

'You love me? But why would you not marry me when I asked you?' He seemed more baffled than angry

'I could not bear to marry you, live a polite, civilised lie, knowing you were only doing what you thought you must,' she said, cradling his face between her palms, looking deep into his eyes. 'If I did not care it would not matter—I suppose we could have rubbed along, you would have your mistresses and your adventures, I would have comfort and security. But loving you—it would have broken my heart.'

'Celina.' He said her name like a vow as he kissed her, a feather touch, a caress. 'I did not understand what I was feeling. I have never been in love before. All I knew is that I wanted you so violently—I am sorry if I frightened you.' She shook her head. 'I told myself I must marry you for your own good and then, just now, I realised that if I really cared for you, and not for myself and my pride, then I must let you go. Because I love you.'

'I knew when you brought me to London,' she confessed. 'I realised on that journey. And I knew I had to hide it because I could not bear for you to have to pretend, or be kind or pity me.'

'Why did you stop trying to prevent me duelling?' he asked as he traced her brows with his finger, followed the whorl of her ear as though discovering her all over again. *My explorer. My adventurer and I am his new found land.*

'I almost tried moral blackmail, pretending I would marry you if you did not fight. I realised I could not do that to you, not if I loved you. Because your honour told you to challenge Langdown and your honour is everything to you.'

'*You* are everything to me,' he whispered, his voice husky. 'You have my heart and my soul and my honour in the palm of your hand. I have the licence. I told them at St George's that we would marry in a month because I thought you would want to buy bride clothes, plan properly. But we can wed where, and when, you want.'

'St George's,' Lina said, leaning in to touch her

lips to his. 'The first of June and there will be roses everywhere.' She felt suddenly shy through the happiness. 'Quinn, do you want…now, I mean?'

'To make love to you? Yes, I do.' He caught her back and kissed her hard, possessively. 'But shall we wait for our wedding night? I made love to you once before, lay with you. That filled me with guilt, but now I can remember those few moments when we were one with wonder—and anticipation. There has been no-one for me, since that moment, and now there never will be. Only you.'

'Only you,' she repeated, awed by what she saw in his face, the need for her, the control he would exert if she wanted that. 'Yes, I would like to wait, Quinn.'

'I love you,' he said as he lay back on the bed, arms flung wide, his face smiling and full of joy.

'Quinn! Your hand!'

'What?' He held out his right hand, grimacing at the blood. 'Damn, the stitches have gone. That must have been when I picked you up.' His grin was rueful as she jumped off the bed and ran to pull the bell cord. 'Perhaps it is as well that we are resolved on patience, I suspect I would not be able to do justice to just how I feel about you, my love.'

'I suppose there is no point in asking you to take

care, is there?' Lina asked. Life with Quinn would always be like this—she must just become used to it. A tamed wolf was only a lapdog; she wanted hers wild and free.

A maid put her head around the door. 'Find my servant, if you please, and have hot water sent up and the doctor called.' She turned back to the bed and helped Quinn off with his coat. 'Thank goodness you chose swords; at least it is a clean cut and not a festering bullet wound.'

Worrying about Quinn's wound helped bring Lina down to earth for the rest of that day and into the next morning. The doctor came and went, Quinn refused to be sensible and to rest, which she assumed was likely to be the pattern for their married life, and instead swept her out shopping, his arm in a dashing black sling. Prudence followed at their heels, organising packages to be sent back to the Maid's Head, carrying the precious Norwich silk shawl he insisted on buying.

They ate dinner in the private parlour, hardly speaking. Lina found herself reaching out to touch his hand, looking up to meet his eyes. It all seemed too wonderful, too precious to need words.

'I must go and find my room,' Quinn said at last when the clock struck ten. They had been sitting in the same chair, Lina curled up on his lap, her head on his shoulder. They were learning to be at peace with each other, she thought. 'You must sleep: we have an early start tomorrow.' It still took another half-hour of kisses before he left.

At the door he turned, laughter in his eyes. 'Do you think Simon was matchmaking when he added that codicil to his will?' he asked. 'I do, the clever old devil.'

Now, sitting in the chaise, with the luxury of four horses in the traces eating up the miles back to London, Quinn seemed more inclined to talk.

'Do you want me to keep the Park?' he asked.

'I really do not know. The people were so hostile. I do not want to run away, and I do love the place, but it will be hard to put that day in church behind us.'

'We can lease it out, make it part of the inheritance for the children,' Quinn suggested.

'Oh. Children.' She had not thought of that. 'You would like children?'

'The thought of yours is rather pleasant. One of each to start with and see what we think after that?'

'You cannot order them up.' She shook her head at him, amused. 'You have to accept what arrives.

But two would do nicely to start.' He would make a good father, if hair-raisingly inclined to involve the children in dangerous exploits, she feared. How old would a child have to be to begin riding on a camel? she wondered. She imagined a miniature version of Quinn outfacing a crocodile.

'I have to get down to finishing Simon's memoirs and getting a publisher,' Quinn continued. 'Is the London house all right or would you like to find something else? You must furnish it as you see fit, of course. It is yours.'

'It is perfect,' Lina said, a small doubt, like a puff of cloud across the sun, making her uneasy. 'How long will the memoirs take?'

'I must get back to Constantinople before the autumn storms make the Mediterranean difficult,' he said. 'I need to get my business out there organised. But actually, I doubt it will take me beyond the end of August if I employ a secretary and copyist. There was lack of order and linking passages are needed, that is all.'

So he was going abroad three months after the wedding. A three-month honeymoon in the company of old Simon's memoirs and then she would be alone again. 'How long will your business in Constantinople take?' Lina asked, trying to sound bright and interested. And she *was* interested only...

Naval wives manage, she told herself. *This is what he does, who he is. Do not try to make him someone else, someone less. Remember the wolf and the lapdog.*

'How long would you like?' Quinn asked her.

Lina stared, puzzled. She did not want him gone a moment longer than he must, of course. And then she realised what he was asking.

'I may come, too?'

'You thought I would leave you? You thought I *could* leave you?' It was his turn to stare now. 'Celina, I love you. That means I want to share my life with you. And you must tell me where you want to go, what you want to do. Constantinople is business, but after that, the entire world is ours. Do you want to see the crocodiles and the Pyramids? Cross the desert on a camel or buy silks in Samarkand? Do the Grand Tour or sail to America?'

'Everywhere, anywhere,' she said, laughing with relief. 'Anywhere that you are.' A sudden thought struck her. 'What about Gregor?'

'Gregor can find his own camel,' Quinn said, catching her in his good arm and kissing her until her smart new bonnet fell off.

Chapter Twenty-Three

June 1st, 1815

There was whispering going on in the corridor outside. Lina smiled; there had been whispering and laughter and the sound of running feet all morning. Last-minute preparations on a wedding day were always going to involve a bustle of activity, but add three pretty denizens of one of St James's most exclusive brothels, all dressed up and pretending to be young ladies of the *ton*, and mayhem was the result.

Lina had wanted her best friends and her aunt at the church and at the wedding breakfast. Quinn had agreed. But all four had refused. They would be with Lina beforehand and they would stand on the steps and throw rice and then they would vanish. 'Half of the male guests would recognise us,' Clara had pointed out and eventually Lina had to agree—it would be dreadful if one of the female guests found her husband chasing Katy round a spare bedchamber.

As it was, the intelligence that the young lady at the centre of the Tolhurst Sapphire scandal was Lord Dreycott's bride created endless gossip. Mr Reginald Tolhurst was so shattered by the discovery that he had falsely accused a perfectly innocent person that he had gone on an extended sea voyage, those in the know whispered. It was extraordinary, but the fact that Sir George Tolhurst was a wedding guest put paid to the more extreme speculation.

Miss Shelley, it seemed, had been thoughtfully returning Sir Humphrey's cane, which he had dropped in the street as he was hurrying home, feeling the first symptoms of the stroke that killed him. The sapphire ring had fallen down the side of a chair, the well informed were able to tell their friends in strictest confidence. So embarrassing after such a hue and cry!

'If you'll just bend your head, ma'am, I'll fasten the necklace,' Prudence said. The diamonds caressed her skin and when Lina looked up they sparked fire that dazzled her. Quinn had showered her in gems, it seemed. Earrings, the necklace, pins for her hair, the tiara that would secure her veil, the great solitaire on her finger. She had protested that brides were supposed to be modestly adorned with pearls, but he had shaken his head: his bride would shine.

In contrast the dress was simplicity itself—white silk satin for the bodice and underskirt and a gauze shot through with gold thread for the overskirt. The veil was lace so precious she had hardly dared touch it after Gregor had told her it was seventeenth-century Flemish work.

The whispering outside became louder. They were planning some surprise, Lina guessed, smiling. The door opened and she looked in the mirror to see two strangers, elegant young matrons in fashionable ensembles.

Lina rose from the stool and turned. 'I am sorry, you must have the wrong room…' They smiled at her and her heart stood still, then they ran, their arms outstretched, and she tumbled into their embrace. *'Meg, Bella.* You've found me, oh, you've found me!'

It had taken ten minutes for the weeping to cease and for the three of them to stop talking, all at once. At last they stood back and looked at each other and Lina thought she was almost too happy to bear it. 'How? How did you find me?'

'With Miss Celina Shelley all over the

newspapers?' Meg said. 'We have all been up on a visit to the Lakes, a holiday. It was only when we got back to Penrith from the little house that we had rented that we saw the papers—and by then, thank goodness, it was the news that you were cleared of all blame.'

'We wrote to Lord Dreycott,' Bella took up the story. 'My, isn't he gorgeous? And we arranged to be here as a surprise for you. The children are downstairs with our husbands, but there is no time to meet them now. We must stop crying and do something about the tearstains or we will never get you to church.'

In a daze, Lina submitted to cold cloths, rice powder, curling tongs and hairpins while her sisters told her the story of the years they had been apart. She almost wept again when she heard that Meg had been widowed after the Battle of Vittoria and had then found she had never been legally married at all. She was married now, to Lord Brandon—'Ross is wonderful,' Meg sighed—and had a baby son and had found Bella after she had run away from home, scandalously pregnant, to marry Viscount Hadleigh.

'And Elliott is wonderful, too, and so is our daughter,' Bella said. 'Oh, Lina, I have dreamed of this for so long, the three of us together again.'

'We must go to Papa,' Lina said, suddenly serious. 'We must try to be reconciled. He has grandchildren now.' The others nodded and all three linked hands. It would be painful, he would probably rebuff them, but it was right to try. She wondered, fleetingly, if she should tell them about Mama, and then decided that some truths were better unsaid.

'Time to go, ma'am,' Prudence ventured, breaking into the moment of reflection. 'The flowers are downstairs.'

'Are there enough for my attendants?' Lina asked. Sir James Warren, the magistrate, had been so charming when he discovered the true identity of Hassan the servant boy, and so assiduous in restoring her reputation, that she had asked him to give her away. But she had thought she must walk up the aisle without female support, had shed a tear for the absence of her sisters, and now here they were.

'Oh, yes, ma'am,' Prudence said with a smile that showed she had been party to the secret all along. 'Lord Dreycott ordered those.'

St George's was full, the wide galleries as well as the body of the church. Quinn had more friends than she had realised, men ranging from the antiquaries, through merchants to some very dubious characters who, he had promised her, would be on their best behaviour. There were two ambassadors, even. And they all brought their wives and families. Lina was aware of the people surrounding her, but she had eyes only for the tall, slim figure at the altar rail, the bulk of Gregor looming beside him.

'Celina,' Quinn whispered as she reached his side and Sir James gave him her hand. Throughout the vows his voice was strong and steady, but at last, when he lifted her veil, he had no words, although his eyes told her everything she would ever need to know about his feelings for her.

So she said it for both of them. 'I will love you for ever,' Lina said and raised her lips to his.

'Still dressed?' Quinn asked as he closed the bedchamber door behind him. 'No wicked nightgown to show for all your shopping?'

'I thought you might prefer to do the undressing,' Lina said. 'I seem to recall that you are very good at it.' She closed the distance between them, took the emerald pin from his neckcloth and began to untie the intricate knot. She was quivering with desire and with nerves, but tonight there was no doubt and no fear, only the bliss of expectation.

'Oh, yes,' Quinn agreed, shrugging out of his coat. She had the neckcloth off, unbuttoned his waistcoat and attacked his shirt before he caught her hands, laughing, just a little breathless. 'My turn.'

Prudence had removed all her jewellery except the wide gold band and he lifted that to his lips for a kiss before he turned her and began on the tiny buttons of her gown. His mouth followed his fingers, his breath hot. Gown and petticoats slipped off together and he had the laces of her corset free in moments.

Chemise, stockings, garters. Oh, yes, she remembered Quinn's way with stockings. Lina turned and slid the shirt from his shoulders, bending to kiss the healing scar of the duelling wound. There was time to touch him now, to place her palm against the spring of dark hair, to skim his nipples with a questing finger and find they responded just as they had before, hardening, and that the caress made him catch his breath.

He undid the fall of his trousers and she slid her hands inside, daring, exploring, finding the heat and power of him, using her soft hands to make him harder, longer. Hers.

Quinn growled and had her shift off, caught her in his arms and laid her on the bed and shed the rest of his clothes with an urgency that aroused and delighted her. As he stood beside the bed she rolled over, caught him in her hands again and kissed him, intimately, drugged with the feel of silken flesh against her lips, the musk of aroused man in her nostrils.

'Oh, my wanton wife,' he said, coming down over her, his hands in her hair, his mouth on hers. Time ceased to have meaning, moments flowed fast as water one second, slowed to a snail's pace the next. His hands moved, stroked, teased, soothed, probed, pressed until Lina was gasping, aching, reaching for him and then, when she thought she would die of needing, he was there, surging into her, filling her slowly so that she could shift beneath him, adjust to the feel of him, caress him with muscles she was finding by instinct.

'Oh, my love,' Quinn murmured, his eyes dark as shadows in the mill pool. 'Come with me now.' And he moved, taking her, teaching her, driving her until the bliss she had known would be there caught her up, dizzying, all consuming and then, when she was limp with pleasure, dropped her down into darkness and safety and Quinn's embrace.

'Come with me,' he said again, 'and we will make love in countries you have never heard of, beside seas with no name and rivers with no beginning and no end.'

'I will come,' Lina told him, her lips pressed to

the sweat-sleeked, beautiful muscles. 'And we will travel together always, my love and all our dreams will come true.'

* * * * *

HISTORICAL

Large Print

INNOCENT COURTESAN TO ADVENTURER'S BRIDE
Louise Allen

Wrongly accused of theft, innocent Celina Shelley is cast
out of the brothel she calls home and flees to Quinn Ashley,
Lord Dreycott. Lina dresses like a nun, looks like an angel,
but flirts like a professional – the last thing Quinn expects
is to discover she's a virgin! With this revelation, will he
wed her before he beds her?

DISGRACE AND DESIRE
Sarah Mallory

With all of London falling at her feet, wagers abound over
who will capture the flirtatious Lady Eloise and her fortune.
Dashing Major Jack Clifton has vowed to watch over his late
comrade's wife, but her beauty and behaviour intrigue him.
The lady is not what she seems, and Jack must discover
her secret if he is to protect her…

THE VIKING'S CAPTIVE PRINCESS
Michelle Styles

Dangerous warrior Ivar Gunnarson is a man of deeds,
not words. With little time for the ideals of love, Ivar seizes
what he wants – and Princess Thyre is no exception! But
to become king of Thyre's heart, mysterious and
enchanting as she is, will entail a battle Ivar has
never engaged in before…

 MILLS & BOON

HISTORICAL

Large Print

COURTING MISS VALLOIS
Gail Whitiker

Miss Sophie Vallois has enthralled London Society, yet the French beauty is a mere farmer's daughter! Only Robert Silverton knows her secret, and he has other reasons to stay away. However, Sophie is so enticing that Robert soon finds that, instead of keeping her at arm's length, he wants the delectable Miss Vallois well and truly *in* his arms!

REPROBATE LORD, RUNAWAY LADY
Isabelle Goddard

Amelie Silverdale is fleeing her betrothal to a vicious, degenerate man, while Gareth Denville knows that the scandal that drove him from London is about to erupt again. In Amelie, Gareth recognises a kindred spirit also in need of escape. On the run together the attraction builds, but what will happen when their old lives catch up with them?

THE BRIDE WORE SCANDAL
Helen Dickson

From the moment Christina Atherton saw notorious Lord Rockley she couldn't control her blushes. In return, dark and seductive Lord Rockley found Christina oh, so beguiling… When Christina discovered that she was expecting, Lord Rockley knew he must make Christina his bride…before scandal ruined them both!

MILLS & BOON

HISTORICAL

Large Print

LADY ARABELLA'S SCANDALOUS MARRIAGE
Carole Mortimer

Sinister whispers may surround Darius Wynter, but one thing's for sure—marriage to the infamous Duke means that Arabella will soon discover the exquisite pleasures of the marriage bed…

DANGEROUS LORD, SEDUCTIVE MISS
Mary Brendan

Heiress Deborah Cleveland jilted an earl for her true love—then he disappeared! Now Lord Buckland has returned, as sinfully attractive as ever. Can Deborah resist the dark magnetism of the lawless lord?

BOUND TO THE BARBARIAN
Carol Townend

To settle a debt, Katerina must convince commanding warrior Ashfirth Saxon that *she* is her royal mistress. But the days—*and nights*—of deceit take their toll. How long before she is willingly bedded by this proud barbarian?

BOUGHT: THE PENNILESS LADY
Deborah Hale

Her new husband may be handsome—but his heart is black. Desperate to safeguard the future of her precious nephew, penniless Lady Artemis Dearing will do anything—even marry the man whose brother ruined her darling sister!

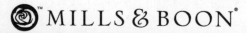 MILLS & BOON®